SECRETS OF PEACE

SECRETS OF PEACE BOOK ONE

T. A. Hernandez

Sanita Street
Publishing

SECRETS OF PEACE

Copyright © 2016 by T. A. Hernandez

The Sanita Street Publishing name, imprint, and logo are trademarks of Sanita Street Publishing

This is a work of fiction. Names, characters, places, and incidents are a product of the author's imagination or are used fictitiously. Any resemblance to actual people, living or dead, or to businesses, companies, events, institutions, or locales is completely coincidental.

Cover design by T. A. Hernandez

ISBN-13: 978-0692743201

CHAPTER 1

EVERY STEP ZIRA TOOK ACROSS the moonlit floor sounded to her like a hammer slamming against a concrete wall.

She took a breath and let it out slow through parted lips. *It's just the adrenaline,* she reassured herself. Even if anyone else in the house had been awake—and they weren't—they couldn't possibly have heard her. She took a few more deep breaths to slow her heart, which was beating so fast it threatened to force its way out of her chest, then turned her attention back to the door at the end of the hall. She closed the distance in a few quick steps and twisted the knob.

She could see the shadowed outline of her target in the bed at the center of the room. Arion Dreyfus, as successful a businessman as it was possible to be these days. Most of his wealth could be attributed to the illicit drug trafficking operation he ran down the entire Pacific coast—an operation which flourished due to his uncompromising brutality. He looked harmless enough sleeping peacefully in front of her now, but Zira's mission file had contained photographs of his most recent executions. Her upper lip curled as she remembered the violence. She padded across the floor with the carefully controlled movements of a wildcat and stared down at her prey.

Dreyfus was not alone. Zira didn't recognize the woman curled up next to him, and her file had said nothing about a wife or girlfriend. A one-night stand, then, or an escort of some sort. She probably didn't even know about the horrors committed by the man sleeping beside her. Or maybe she did. Either way, Dreyfus wasn't the sort of man you said 'no' to if you wanted to keep your head firmly attached to your neck.

Zira considered her options. The Project made allowances for situations where leaving a witness might compromise the mission; she would be within her rights to execute the woman along with Dreyfus. And it would be so much easier.

She frowned. No. Whoever she was, the woman was innocent. Or at least innocent enough that she shouldn't have to pay for Dreyfus' crimes.

Zira slid a suppressed pistol out of the holster at her hip and held it just an inch above the man's chest. She flicked the safety off with her thumb, took a breath, and held it in as she put two rounds into the drug dealer's heart.

The woman jolted at the sound, but by the time she understood what she'd heard and looked in the right direction, Zira was gone. A shrill scream followed her as she walked out the front door and vanished into the night like a ghost.

■ ■ ■

The following afternoon, Zira's plane landed at the South Central Regional Airport in Amarillo. She collected her bags and left in the same black sedan she'd arrived in several days before. The compound wasn't far from the airport, but the road was monotonous, cutting across miles of barren, monochrome terrain. Zira selected the destination from the car's autopilot system and leaned her seat back for a quick nap.

The car stopped thirty minutes later when it reached the perimeter of the PEACE Project's property. "Caution," said the robotic voice of the autopilot system. "Restricted area. Please reset destination."

Zira rubbed sleep out of her eyes. A familiar red sign warning against unauthorized visitation stood at the beginning of a dirt road, which veered away at a diagonal into the flat landscape beyond. The walls of the compound rose up on the otherwise empty horizon a few miles away. "Override restriction," she said. "Unit E-2, Zira."

"Authorization confirmed. Continuing to final destination." The car pulled onto the dirt road, and Zira watched the walls grow larger as she approached. The dirt turned to asphalt at the parking lot, and the car maneuvered itself into a spot at the end of a row devoted to unit E-2's black vehicles. "You have arrived," it announced before shutting itself off. Zira removed the key and took her bags, then walked towards the compound's front gate.

The tall concrete wall cast a long shadow over her. It reached towards the sky five stories high and extended for more than a mile on all four sides. The wall enclosed the entire area that made up the compound, though the Project owned much of the surrounding land as well. The only way inside the compound was through the single gate on the east side, which had a complex security lock and a guard on-duty at all times. Zira approached that gate now, passing a large granite sign that read "PEACE Project Headquarters, est. 2095."

She pushed a button on the panel to the side of the gate and waited as two red beams of light shot out and scanned her entire body. The beams crossed over each other several times before Zira realized she'd forgotten something. In the same moment, the guard's voice came through the speakers below the panel. "Your armband?"

"Just a minute," Zira said, rummaging through her bag to find it. She was so used to wearing it at all times that when she removed it outside the compound, she often forgot to put it back on when she returned. She slipped the simple black band into place over her upper left arm and waited patiently while the red beams scanned her again. They turned green upon finishing, then disappeared.

"Thank you," said the guard. There was a soft mechanical whirring as the gate slid into the wall, leaving an opening wide enough for two vehicles to pass through. Zira walked in and the gate closed behind her. She headed towards the apartments along the northern wall to drop her things off at home. Her stomach rumbled; she hadn't eaten anything since breakfast. Food first, then a shower. Her written mission report to Chairman Ryku could wait for a few more hours.

A girl with long brown hair and a radiant smile detached herself from a group of friends and called to Zira as she rounded the corner of an apartment building. The red band around her upper arm designated her a member of unit C. "Zira—wait."

Zira raised a hand to greet her best friend. "Hey, Aubreigh."

"You going to dinner? We can head over there together."

"Sure. Let me drop off my stuff first."

Aubreigh fell into stride beside her. She was average height, which still put her several inches taller than

Zira. She eyed the bags Zira carried with a curious spark in her eyes. "Where were you?"

Zira kept her voice flat and her response vague. "Mid Pacific Region." She already knew where this line of questioning was going. They'd been through a hundred different versions of it since Zira had been placed in unit E-2 when she was eleven.

"You going to tell me what you were doing this time?"

Zira rolled her eyes. "Right. You'd love that."

Aubreigh shrugged and grinned. "It was worth a try."

"Of course it was." They stopped in front of Zira's apartment door and she pressed her thumb to the print scanner to unlock it. Trying to figure out what Zira did as a member of unit E-2 seemed to be a game to Aubreigh. Zira couldn't blame her for that; if their roles had been reversed, she'd be just as curious. That didn't stop her from wishing Aubreigh would drop the subject, though. Each time her friend asked, Zira felt a little guiltier about not being able to tell her anything.

She set her bags just beyond the threshold and locked the door again. "Aren't you going to unpack?" Aubreigh asked. "I'll help you, if you want."

Zira cocked an eyebrow, wondering what Aubreigh's reaction might be if she saw the contents of her luggage. Bloodied gloves, a long knife, ammunition, the pistol she'd used to kill a man in his sleep—not the sorts of things a nice girl like Aubreigh would appreciate. If she ever learned the truth about what Zira really was, it could destroy their friendship forever. She was much too selfish to jeopardize that, even if it meant keeping secrets from the most important person in her life. "You'd do anything to get a clue, wouldn't you?"

Aubreigh put a hand over her heart and gave Zira an exaggerated scowl. "Now that *hurts,*" she said. "I was just trying to be nice."

Zira shook her head and shifted the conversation to a more comfortable topic as they walked to the cafeteria in the center of the compound. They'd almost made it there when a strong voice called to her from behind. "Zira, stop."

Both girls turned, and Zira easily picked out the speaker among the other people who walked about the compound. The young man approached them with long, brisk strides. "He's huge," Aubreigh whispered. Her voice had a slight tremor that sounded like a mixture of fear and awe.

Zira nodded. She'd had the exact same reaction the first time she'd seen Jared. His hardened expression would have been unnerving on any man, but Jared's size and obvious strength only made him that much more intimidating. He was well over six feet tall, with a broad, muscular build and deep brown skin. He carried himself with strength and confidence and had the reputation of being unit E-2's best operative.

Zira held her head a little higher as he approached, surprised and a little flattered that he even knew her name. "Chairman Ryku wants to see both of us," he said.

"Now?" She couldn't imagine what this might be about.

"Now." Having delivered his message, Jared turned and walked back in the direction of the chairman's office.

Zira sighed. Dinner would have to wait a while longer. She muttered a quick goodbye to Aubreigh and scrambled to catch up with Jared. "Do you know what this is about?"

His face was deadpan. "I'm sure he has a lot to say to you after your screw-up last night, but I have no idea why he's dragging me into it."

Zira's steps faltered for an instant. She ran through all of the previous night's events in her head but couldn't see whatever screw-up Jared was talking about. She'd done everything exactly like she'd learned in her training; this had to be some sort of misunderstanding. The knot in her stomach tightened, but she didn't dare ask Jared anything else. If she *had* made a mistake, she wanted to hear about it from Ryku himself.

They reached the small building that served as the chairman's office and living quarters, and Jared rapped on the door. Ryku swung it open wide a few seconds later. A middle-aged man with short black hair and dark eyes, the chairman's default scowl held the power to quiet a room in an instant. Zira studied his face, trying not to stare at the thick scar that ran in a jagged line from his brow to his cheekbone. His stern expression did nothing to ease her anxiety.

Ryku led them down the hallway a few feet and through the first door on the left. The office was simple, but elegant. Two black couches faced each other on a simple carmine rug in the center of the room, and a long window framed the sleek desk near the back wall. Ryku gestured for Zira and Jared to sit down on one couch while he took the one across from them. "You're probably both wondering why you're here," he said. His tone was even, but there was something sharp in his eyes as he looked between the two of them. "I'll get right to the point. Zira, did you get a chance to watch the news before you flew back this afternoon?"

"No, sir."

"It seems there was a problem with your assignment. You killed someone in front of a witness."

Zira crossed one leg over the other and folded her arms, feeling inclined to justify her actions even though she knew it would be useless. "I was gone before she even saw me."

"Regardless, the story was all over the news before unit E-1 had a chance to pull it."

"The things we do make the news all the time." The words hadn't even finished coming out before she realized how childish the excuse sounded.

"Not like this," Ryku said. "Not when it's avoidable."

"So I should have killed her."

"Why? She was innocent. We don't kill innocent people if we don't have to."

"Exactly." Her tone was more antagonistic than she had intended, but Ryku's reprimands were unfair. He had authorized her to kill Dreyfus and she'd been forced to make a decision in the moment. If he didn't trust her to make those decisions, what was the point of even sending her on assignments in the first place? Still, a bad attitude wasn't going to help anything. She sighed and tried for a little more humility. "Tell me what I should do next time."

"There might not be a 'next time' for you if you do something like that again," Ryku said. "Unit E-1 is going to have a hard time convincing the woman and local law enforcement to drop this, and I'm even more concerned about your future decisions. Mistakes like this at the wrong time or place could jeopardize the entire Project."

Zira nodded and tried to conceal her annoyance at having to ask her question again. "What was I supposed to do?"

"You were supposed to wait for the most opportune moment to strike. You've been taught that throughout all your training. If the circumstances weren't right, you should have backed out to wait for a better time. Did you even know she was there, or did you just rush in without a plan?"

Zira's mouth started to open in protest, but she stopped herself. He was right, though she hated to admit she'd made such an obvious mistake. Her shoulders slumped and she averted her eyes. Even though she couldn't see his face anymore, she could sense Ryku's disapproval burning into her. "I'm sorry, Chairman."

"Was I wrong to promote you from training when I did? You were so young. Perhaps I should have waited."

Most people in unit E-2 weren't promoted from training until they were at least eighteen or nineteen, but Zira had been a few months shy of her eighteenth birthday. It had caused a bit of a stir, but completing training early wasn't unheard of, and everyone trusted Ryku's judgment enough not to dispute the decision.

"No," Zira insisted, meeting his gaze with fierce confidence. "You weren't wrong."

Ryku regarded her through narrowed eyes, then sighed. His voice took on a gentler tone. "I know how much you wanted to prove yourself to everyone who said you weren't good enough to make it. I gave you that victory because I knew you could handle it. But if you're going to waste the opportunity on such irresponsible mistakes, I can't help you."

"I know, sir. I won't let you down again."

"No, you won't. You've been on your own until now because I hadn't yet found a good partner for you. That's changed." He motioned to Jared.

Jared snapped out of a bored daze and stared at the chairman with almost comic disbelief. He started to say something, but Ryku cut him off. "You've been doing solo work for almost two years now. That's long enough. There are plenty of missions that require your skills, but even you need someone to watch your back."

"With respect, Chairman—" Jared said.

"The decision is final." Ryku's tone left no room for argument. Jared sat back, his hands clasped tight as he glared at the floor. The chairman turned back to Zira. "I'm giving you a new assignment, and I expect you to fully cooperate with Jared. Follow his lead and learn from his experience. He will report back to me on your performance. If everything goes well, we can put your recent lapse in judgment behind us. If he sees any problems, there will be further consequences. Termination of your status as an operative is not out of the question. Do you have any objections?"

Of course I have objections! This was degrading and unnecessary. Most E-2 operatives worked in pairs as their assignments frequently required or benefitted from teamwork. She'd always known it was only a matter of time before she was partnered with someone. This, however, felt more like a punishment. Jared had been explicitly instructed to supervise her work, and her future in the unit depended on his assessment of her performance. She'd completed her training more than three months ago and had already proven her ability to carry out assignments. She didn't need anyone holding her hand.

She couldn't say all of that to Ryku, though, and instead settled for resigned acquiescence. "If that's what you think is best, sir."

Ryku turned to Jared, who gave a brusque nod that said he still didn't approve of the idea.

The chairman stood and walked to the desk, then pulled out a large envelope and handed it to Jared. "Here's the assignment. I want to see both of you again when it's finished. You're dismissed."

Jared stormed out of the room, and Zira followed like a dog slinking away with her tail between her legs. Once outside, he wasted no time sharing his feelings. "This is ridiculous. I don't need some useless amateur screwing up my missions."

"If I were useless, Ryku never would have picked me for this unit in the first place," Zira retorted.

"Right. You've done a great job proving your skills so far."

"I have, actually. It was one little mistake. You can't honestly tell me *you've* never made one."

Jared glared at her but said nothing. Zira rolled her eyes. He was so quick to judge when he hardly knew her, but whether she liked it or not, she needed his approval if she wanted to keep her job as an E-2 operative. They were partners now, and if everything went well, they'd be working together for a very long time. That could be an ongoing problem if his opinion of her didn't change. She gritted her teeth and tried to strike up a more civil conversation as they walked. "Where are we going?"

"I'm going to my apartment to look over this assignment." His voice was still hostile. "If you want to come, fine, but I don't need any stupid ideas. If you have something to say, make sure it's useful."

Zira held back a biting response and followed him up a flight of stairs to his apartment. They stepped inside and she took a few moments to look around. The residence was similar to her own, with the standard Project-issued couch and low table in the front room. A concrete half-wall divided the living area from the bedroom and bathroom in the back. Jared's personal furnishings were minimal and unremarkable, but the place was immaculate, giving Zira the impression that he was as meticulous and attentive in all aspects of his life as he must have been in his job.

Jared sat on the couch. He opened the file and spread its contents on the table in front of him. Without looking at Zira, he said, "Are you going to stand there all day, or did you want to come and look over this with me?"

Zira guessed that was the nicest invitation she would get from him. She sat down and glanced over the papers he'd laid out, looking for the photos that were almost always enclosed with a file. Jared got to them first and went through them one by one. When he finished, he passed them to Zira.

The pudgy white man in the photos was in his fifties and dressed in a smart, gray suit. Zira looked at his reference sheet for more information. His name— Marcus Collins—was listed at the top of the page, followed by some basic physical descriptors and employment information. An attached note from unit C read that Collins appeared to have recently and illegally vacated the residence assigned to him, and it was unknown where he currently lived. He taught chemistry at a university in the South Pacific Region and, in his spare time, built and sold high-tech explosive devices to criminals in foreign countries.

Zira set the photos down and looked through the rest of the file's contents. There were a few maps marked with places Collins was known to frequent, some blueprints of various buildings at his university, a list of his known clients, and a detailed schedule of his activities over the past few weeks. Another stack of papers contained notes the informant had written while observing him. Zira picked these up and skimmed over them.

"Is there anything in there about where Collins lives now?" Jared asked.

Zira read the last few lines. "Just this. The informant tried to follow him home one afternoon, but it seemed like Collins recognized her from the university where she'd been watching him and knew he was being followed. She had to back off after that to avoid making him more suspicious." She flipped back to the first page and looked over the notes more thoroughly. Something else caught her eye, and she leaned over to show Jared. "He's currently working with the Red Flag Brotherhood."

Jared's eyes narrowed as he took the pages from her. The Red Flag Brotherhood was a terrorist group based in the Republic of Asia. They opposed the alliance of nations that had led to the formation of their country in the years just before the devastating global war of the late twenty-first century. Most of their attacks were directed at their own government, but they caused trouble in America from time to time and were considered a major threat. Still, that didn't fully explain the taut expression on Jared's face or the way every muscle in his body seemed to have tensed. "He's building a bomb for them," he said.

"Do you think they're going to use it here?"

"It's a possibility."

"So we just need to eliminate Collins before he can finish it." It was a fairly straightforward mission, which was something of a relief. Zira didn't intend to make any mistakes, but the less opportunity there was for Jared to find fault with her tactics, the better.

"We should try to gather some intel on the Brotherhood while we're at it," he said. "They haven't been active in America for two years. Why now? I think we should find out what they're up to."

Zira bristled at the suggestion. "Are you sure that's a good idea? The Brotherhood isn't our priority."

"Collins is making a bomb for them," Jared said. "A bomb that they'll use to kill and injure hundreds of people."

Zira tapped the client list from the file. "All of his sales have been to people outside the country. The bomb probably wouldn't even be used here."

"And that makes it okay?"

"Of course not, but it's not our job to worry about the rest of the world."

"At least you've got your priorities straight," Jared muttered. Zira couldn't tell whether it was supposed to be a compliment or an insult. "I still think they could be planning an attack somewhere in America. If Collins is out of the picture, they'll just find someone else to build their bomb. We should at least take a look into it."

"That sounds like something unit E-1 should handle."

"Maybe, but we're already assigned to this. There's no point wasting their time opening a whole new investigation. Besides, they have a bad habit of screwing things up with all of their stupid rules and procedures."

"Fine. What do you want to do, then?"

"There's this diner he goes to once or twice a week to meet with someone. The informant says they talk and sometimes exchange money—cash." He pointed to the note on Collins' schedule so Zira could read it herself. "Sounds like some kind of illegal business dealing to me, probably something to do with the bomb he's making for the Brotherhood."

Zira couldn't disagree with his logic, though she still didn't like the idea of shifting focus from Collins to the Brotherhood. As long as they still got their primary target, though, she supposed there wasn't any harm in at least trying to find out what the terrorist group was up to. "So you want to just show up at this diner and find out who Collins is meeting with and why."

"Yes. We should also figure out where he lives, and this is as good a place to start as any. We'll stake out the diner and wait for both of them to show up. When they do, we'll slip him a tracking and recording device so we can find out what they're talking about and where he goes afterwards."

"You make it sound so simple."

Jared raised an eyebrow and gave her a sidelong glance. "How good are you at playing a sweet, innocent little girl?"

Zira smirked. With her round blue eyes, white-blonde hair, and tiny frame, she was the picture of harmlessness. She'd learned to use that to her advantage, whether it was to get information, gain access to a target, or just get her way. "Better than you," she said.

Jared laughed. He had a nice smile, she noted. If he didn't go around scowling all the time, he might not intimidate people so much. "Good," he said. "You might be more useful than I thought."

This time Zira knew he meant it as a compliment, and they managed to plan the rest of the mission without so much as a snide remark between them. Zira had expected him to allow her only minimal involvement, so she was pleasantly surprised when his ideas developed to fully include her. She looked forward to the opportunity to prove herself to him, and not just because her career hinged on this assignment or because they would be working together for the foreseeable future. She could learn a lot from him, and she wanted his approval just for the sake of it. There were few people she respected enough to care what they thought of her, but Jared, apparently, was one of them.

An hour later, his apartment door snapped shut behind her. Zira hurried to the cafeteria to get some food before the kitchen shut down for the night. Aubreigh sat down across from her as she was finishing a rather disappointing bowl of vegetable soup. "What happened?" she asked.

"Ryku just wanted to talk to me about my assignment."

She'd meant for it to sound casual, but Aubreigh seemed to sense her frustration. "You all right?"

Zira sighed. "Yeah. I just made a stupid mistake. He wasn't too happy about it."

"Is Chairman Ryku ever really happy about anything?"

"Good point." Zira licked the back of her spoon and set it in the empty bowl in front of her. "He finally gave me a partner."

"That's exciting. Who is it?"

"Jared."

"The big guy?"

She nodded and stood up from the table to return her bowl to the kitchen. Aubreigh followed. "We didn't get off to a great start," Zira said. "He called me a useless amateur."

"I can think of at least ten things you've been called that were a lot worse than that."

Zira's mouth quirked up in a wry smile. "That's true."

Aubreigh pushed the door open and they walked out into the fading evening light. "Try not to let it bother you. I know you don't like working with other people, but you knew this was coming sooner or later, right?"

"Yeah. I just didn't expect it to be him. He's the best in our unit, and he clearly wasn't happy about being paired with me."

"He'll get over it," Aubreigh reassured her. "Once you two get to know each other better, I'm sure it will work out. Maybe just try not to be so confrontational."

Zira frowned. "I'm not confrontational."

"Yeah, right. You realize who you're talking to? I know you too well." Zira couldn't dispute that.

There was a soft beep and the screen of the CyberLink around Aubreigh's wrist lit up. The devices had replaced cell phones and other past technology and, as mandated by law, everyone old enough to attend school wore one. They served as a means of communication and connection to the Net and allowed the Project to monitor the whereabouts of all citizens. Aubreigh raised her arm to read the message and sighed. "I wish I could be around for moral support," she said, "but it looks like my team is scheduled to leave on a new assignment tomorrow morning. We won't be back for a couple weeks."

"Where are you going?" Zira asked.

"Just to inspect the distribution office in the South Atlantic Region. We've been getting a few complaints." She launched into one of her speeches about the importance of making sure every citizen had the resources they needed, which was one of unit C's main responsibilities.

Sometimes, like now, Zira envied Aubreigh for being able to talk so freely about her unit's work. Unit C was one of the more prominent units of the PEACE Project, and everyone in America had at least a basic understanding of their roles and responsibilities. They had no secrets to hide. Zira still remembered their mission statement from her elementary training, where she and her peers had been taught the fundamentals of the Project before being separated into different units. Unit C—Control. *We uphold peace by controlling the distribution of limited resources in order to discourage conflict and provide greater equality and stability for all.*

In the promotional videos for the Project that sometimes played over the Net, people wearing the red armbands of unit C were always shown offering a helping hand or providing someone with food, medicine, or shelter. Project members with the blue, green, and yellow armbands of units P, E-1, and A—Protect, Enforce, and Advance, respectively—also appeared prominently in such advertisements. Once or twice, she even remembered seeing someone with the white band of a compound auxiliary staff member in the background. These other units and support staff were the heroes of the PEACE Project, the men and women who provided stability, unity, and harmony to a nation nearly destroyed by war.

Zira had never seen anyone with a black armband in the videos.

No one wanted or needed to know about the secret, bloody things that happened in the night behind closed doors. Zira preferred it that way; she'd never thought of herself as much of a hero. Probably more the opposite, actually. Still, she thought it might be nice, sometimes, to be able to confide in someone about the true nature of her work. Perhaps that would be an additional benefit to having a partner; at least she wouldn't have to keep any secrets from Jared.

CHAPTER 2

AFTER ZIRA LEFT, JARED SAT back down on the couch and began gathering the pages strewn across his table. Not for the first time, he wondered why Chairman Ryku had chosen to give him a partner now after two highly productive years of solo work. Had it always been his plan to pair them together, or had Zira forced the issue with her carelessness the night before? The Red Flag Brotherhood's involvement in this assignment could have prompted the chairman's decision as well; Ryku might have given Jared a partner with the intention that Zira keep him in line just as he was expected to do with her. She simply didn't know it yet, and Jared had no intention of telling her unless it became necessary. He hadn't had time to decide how much he could trust her in their few hours of conversation, and he certainly wasn't about to tell her anything that personal—not yet, anyway.

He closed the file, set it on the table, and let out a long sigh. Zira seemed smart, at least. A bit impulsive, but that could be corrected with a little guidance. On the other hand, she was green—very green. He'd heard about her early promotion from training a few months ago but never expected it to affect him directly. While he trusted Ryku's judgment, he wasn't thrilled about working with someone so new and untested. His last partner, Rowan, had been older than him and more experienced. He hadn't ever worried about whether or not Rowan had his back or if he'd perform competently when they got in a jam. He just *knew*.

Zira was an unknown, and that made her a potential liability. He was being judgmental and maybe that was unfair, but both of their lives were on the line here. They did dangerous work, especially when the likes of the Red Flag Brotherhood might be involved. He couldn't afford to take chances on unfamiliar variables. Luckily, they still had two weeks to prepare for the assignment before their scheduled flight. They could both use that time to get used to working together, which would give Jared a chance to learn as much as possible about his new partner's strengths and vulnerabilities.

He knew that Zira frequented the E-2 training facility and the shooting range in her spare time. He'd seen her in both places on multiple occasions, even when she was still a recruit. In fact, she had probably spent more time practicing her skills than any other recruit from her age group, which helped explain why she'd been promoted from training early. She was a hard worker then, and dedicated. Good. That was one of the most important parts of this job, and if she at least had that, he could work with the rest.

He found Zira the next morning sitting alone at the end of one of the long, concrete tables in the cafeteria. "Mind if I sit here?" he asked, motioning to the empty place across from her. Her eyes widened in mild surprise at the request, but she nodded. "I was thinking we could go to the training facility after this," he suggested. "Maybe spar a little bit or run some simulations, then go to the shooting range after."

Zira glanced at him over her bowl of oatmeal with a flat expression. "You want to make sure I'm not just some useless amateur."

He sighed. "I shouldn't have said that. Sorry."

She shook her head and went back to stirring her breakfast. "Don't be. I think it's a great idea. I need to make sure you're not completely useless, too."

Her head was bowed at an angle where her bangs shielded most of her face, but Jared thought he saw the faintest hint of a smile on her lips. He suppressed a grin of his own. Most people in the compound who didn't know him well treated him with a sort of careful deference due to his size and reputation; Zira's unabashed teasing was a refreshing change.

They finished their meal in silence and walked to the training facility together, which stood in the northwest corner of the compound next to Chairman Ryku's office. The ground floor was a wide, open space with foam mats on one side and various exercise machines, weights, and additional training equipment on the other. The second floor housed an armory and four simulation rooms that could be programmed to run an endless variety of scenarios in a virtual environment. Zira and Jared went to one of the mats at the edge of the room and began sparring.

Considering their size difference, Zira performed better than Jared had expected. She'd clearly learned to use her agility to make up for what she lacked in size and brute strength, though the strikes she did manage to land proved that she was stronger than she looked as well. She never came even respectably close to beating him, but she managed to hold her own. She wasn't too proud to ask for advice and tried to implement whatever suggestions he made, which Jared took as a promising sign for their new partnership.

After a particularly long and brutal round of sparring, he pulled Zira to her feet for what must have been the hundredth time that morning. Strands of hair clung to her flushed, damp face, and both of them were breathing hard. She hadn't said anything to him these last few rounds, and now her lips were pressed together in a firm line. "Are you hurt?" he asked.

"I'm just sick of being knocked down today. Can we go shoot something now, please?"

"Sure."

They went upstairs to the armory and checked out a few weapons and ammunition, then drove one of E-2's cars out to the Project's shooting range, which was really just a few square miles of empty land to the west of the compound. An impressive system of holographic targets that could be connected to any CyberLink had been set up at various distances, heights, and angles. They could read all kinds of information from the bullets fired through them and would then send that data back to the CL, allowing the user to see where they were making mistakes and how they might adjust.

Zira's mood seemed to improve as soon as they arrived. She started loading bullets into a magazine, and her expression softened as she stared out across the dry, open plain. "I love this place," she said. "I used to spend entire days out here."

Jared nodded. "I remember seeing you here sometimes." He set up the target interface on his CyberLink as Zira slid her magazine into a semi-automatic rifle and chambered a round. As soon as the targets popped up, she sent bullets flying through them in rapid succession. Jared looked at the data on his CL. She'd hit almost dead center with every single shot. He showed her the numbers. "Apparently, all the practice paid off."

She said nothing and traded the rifle for a handgun, this time firing on the closer targets. Again, she didn't miss a single one. Jared raised his eyebrows. "I've got to admit, that was impressive."

Zira turned to him and shrugged. "I'll never be as strong as you or probably anyone else in our unit, but this—" She gestured to the targets behind her. "This, I can do."

Jared took his own turn with the rifle. He hit every target, though not with quite the same precision as Zira had, and it took him a few seconds longer to finish them all. Now it was her turn to give him advice, which he paid close attention to and applied with some success. They spent most of the afternoon there. After returning to the compound and taking the guns back to the training facility, they agreed to meet again the next morning.

This routine continued each day for the next two weeks. Sometimes they used the simulation rooms as well. Jared began to see a moderate improvement in Zira's hand-to-hand combat skills, and according to the feedback from the target system at the shooting range, his accuracy with various firearms also improved slightly. He wasn't sure how well the numbers would hold up in an actual firefight, but the extra practice couldn't hurt anything.

They were cleaning their weapons at the shooting range one day in the middle of that second week. The sun was a burning orange circle poised just above the horizon. Zira sat on the hood of the car, her jaw slack as she pushed a blackened cloth through the barrel of a rifle. Jared leaned against the car on the other side. Neither of them had spoken for a long time, but the silence wasn't uncomfortable. He'd learned early on that Zira wasn't a very talkative person; even if they'd known each other better, Jared didn't think he would have gotten much more conversation out of her. That was fine by him. After all the time he'd spent working alone, he didn't think he could have handled a partner who jabbered all the time.

Zira stopped what she was doing and turned to him. "Why haven't you had a partner for two years?" she asked. The way she blurted it out made him think that it was something she'd been wanting to ask for a while now.

His throat became gummy and tight. He focused his attention on the handgun he was reassembling and took a moment to collect his thoughts. He couldn't blame her for asking, but he still wasn't ready to talk about that just yet. "Pass," he said.

"Pass?"

"I just don't know you well enough to answer that."

Zira's eyebrows drew together and she glanced down at the car beneath her. "Oh. Sorry."

"No, it's fine. I get why you'd want to know. It's just— it's a bad memory."

They both went back to their work, but now the silence felt stiff and heavy. Jared tried to break the tension with a different line of conversation. "How many assignments will this make for you?"

"Four," said Zira. "Honestly, I was getting so used to doing things on my own that I didn't think Ryku would ever give me a partner."

Jared raised an eyebrow. "Wishful thinking?"

She hopped off the hood of the car and shrugged. "Maybe a little. I'm not much of a people person."

"That's a shock," Jared muttered.

Zira rolled her eyes at him as she carried her weapons to the trunk of the car. "Watch it with sarcasm," she said. "My best friend thinks I'm confrontational. I'd hate to prove her right."

"Nothing wrong with a little confrontation," said Jared. He loaded his own weapons into the trunk and slammed it shut. "Just try to save it for Collins."

They got in the car and it drove them back towards the compound. "Do you think we're ready?" Zira asked. Jared thought he caught a hint of worry in her voice. "We only have a couple more days."

"We're ready," he said. He'd had his doubts about this in the beginning, but his interactions with Zira over these past days had gone a long way to put them to rest. She still had a lot to learn, but that was natural and would come with time and experience. She was far more capable than he'd originally given her credit for. "We make a good team."

Zira gave him a small smile. "Yeah," she said. "I think we do."

CHAPTER 3

WHEN THE MORNING OF THE assignment arrived, Zira found Jared waiting for her at the compound gate. "All set?" he asked.

She nodded. "Let's go."

Jared slung his backpack over one shoulder and Zira did the same with her own. It was heavy. Buried beneath the clothes and other basic necessities were two handguns, a disassembled rifle, and suppressors and ammunition for all three weapons. Jared was sure to have a similar arsenal in his own bag.

They checked out with the guard at the front gate and went to a small, black car at the far end of the parking lot. Jared gave the override command to the autopilot before it could tell them they were in a restricted area. He input the airport's address, put on some music, and leaned back in his seat as the car pulled away from the compound.

Zira watched the walls disappear through the window. Up until a few months ago, she'd never been away from home for more than a few hours at a time. In fact, the idea of spending the night so far from the compound still unsettled her a bit. She was eager to see more of the outside world, but she'd be lying to herself if she didn't admit she was a little apprehensive, too.

Everything in the compound was safe and predictable; out here, there was no telling what she might run into.

Jared interrupted her thoughts. "Nervous?"

"No," she lied.

He smirked as if he didn't entirely believe her. "Good."

They didn't say anything else to each other all the way to the airport. Once there, security bots scanned their CyberLinks to check their credentials and allowed them to pass without checking their bags. They boarded and found their seats, and aside from the elderly man who snored in Zira's ear for the duration of the flight, they arrived in Seattle without incident.

From the airport, Zira and Jared took a bus to the hotel they'd be staying at until their mission was complete. Seattle was the first city Zira had seen that had been impacted so severely by the war. Even though the conflict had ended almost three decades ago, the signs of its devastation surrounded her. The rubble of once-proud skyscrapers littered the sides of the streets, and many of the buildings still standing were in shambles. Twice, she saw the corpses of old combat robots, stripped of every useful component and left slumped in the street to corrode with everything else. The city's inhabitants were like rats, crawling in and out of the wreckage with grim determination. Still, it wasn't all gray and somber. The people had repaired what they could, creating a unique patchwork of architecture from pieces of fallen structures. Here and there, splashes of color brightened the bleak environment. Flowers grew along a patch of sidewalk, a mural decorated one long wall lining the street, and a little girl in a pink coat and blue rain boots skipped through a puddle.

They got off the bus and walked a few blocks to a hotel that might have been one of the best in the city before the war. Using false names, they checked in to two separate rooms. Zira dropped her bag off in her room, made sure the door was locked, and met Jared back in the lobby. "Do you have it?" he asked, referring to the tracking and recording device they planned to plant on Collins.

Zira patted her pocket. "Of course."

They walked back outside and around to the back of the hotel where a few vehicles were parked. Jared stopped next to the most pathetic-looking van Zira had ever seen. It was old, the kind of pre-war automobile that had a steering wheel and manual controls instead of an autopilot system. White paint peeled from the hood in large patches, revealing the gray body underneath. At first, Zira couldn't believe this was what they'd be using to carry out their surveillance on Collins, but when Jared began digging in his pockets for the keys, she knew. "This is it?"

"It's perfect," said Jared. "Nobody will look twice. They'll assume it's just another abandoned vehicle from before the war."

"It's a heap of junk."

"Be nice," said Jared. "This isn't junk—it's a *classic.*" He kept his tone even, and Zira was unsure whether or not he was joking until he glanced at her with one eyebrow raised.

She rolled her eyes but couldn't help smiling back at him. "Let's go."

They got inside and Jared put the key in the ignition. The van emitted a grinding metallic screech as he tried to start it. "You sure this even runs?" Zira asked.

"No."

He tried the engine again with no success, but on the third attempt, it wheezed to life. They drove to the diner listed in Collins' file. Few people in America's cities owned cars, so most of the other working vehicles on the road were public transportation, buses and taxis which could be used by anyone who fulfilled their required work or educational duties and presented a valid ID. It was midday and most people were still working, so traffic was minimal; they reached the diner in just a few minutes. Jared parked the van across the street, keeping it partially hidden behind the remaining half of a ruined movie theater.

The diner's large glass windows allowed them a clear view of its interior. One waitress wiped tables while another chatted up the lone customer sitting at the counter. It was not Collins. Zira sighed and settled back in her seat. She'd known they would have to wait for Collins to show up, possibly for several days, but a part of her had hoped he might just happen to be here already when they arrived. This was the part of the plan she liked least—waiting, watching, sitting on her hands and doing absolutely nothing.

In the driver's seat, Jared seemed unperturbed by the prospect of spending hours or even days waiting. He sat stone still with his head turned, gaze fixed on the diner. Zira tried to follow his example. She scanned the surrounding streets, searching for Collins. Time dragged on and her mind drifted. Her eyelids began to droop. She closed them for a second, then snapped awake again to see that the customer inside the diner had left, though she couldn't remember watching him go.

She yawned and stretched her arms and legs out in front of her. "I can't do this all day."

"Do what?" Jared asked, still staring across the street.

"Just sit here, not doing anything, not saying anything. Aren't you bored?"

"We need to focus."

"We can have a conversation and still focus."

After what felt like a very long silence, Jared said, "Okay. What do you want to talk about?"

"I don't know. Anything." She thought for a moment, recalling the conversation they'd had just a few days earlier. "You never told me how many assignments you've been on."

"Forty-nine."

Zira let out a low whistle. It was more than she'd expected, especially since he didn't seem that much older than she was. "How old are you?"

"Twenty. But I've been doing this since I was sixteen."

"Why did you get promoted so early?"

He looked over at her and shrugged. "Partly because Chairman Ryku thought I was ready. Partly just because the unit needed more active operatives at the time. Either way, I *wasn't* ready. No one is—not that young. I'm lucky I didn't get myself killed."

Eighteen wasn't that much older than sixteen, but when Zira thought about herself at that age, she couldn't imagine being asked to complete an assignment with any semblance of competence. The fact that Jared had managed to accomplish so much was impressive, if a bit lamentable. He'd been forced to grow up too soon. So had she, and just about everyone else in the Project, but it seemed especially true for Jared.

"How did you do it?" Zira asked.

"Do what?"

"Stay alive. Become so good at what you do." She shrugged. "I just think I could learn something."

"I work hard," said Jared. "And I always think before I act."

"That's it?"

"That's it. Were you expecting some kind of big secret or special technique?"

"No, I guess not."

The streets began to fill as more and more people finished their daily work duties and went home for the evening. Some of them entered the diner, exchanging their ration coupons for a hot meal. The waitresses hurried from table to table, taking orders and delivering food. As they watched for any sign of their target, Zira and Jared continued to talk, trading stories about past assignments and their days as recruits. Collins never showed, and when night fell over the city and the diner's lights went out, they called it quits and drove back to the hotel.

Collins didn't appear at the diner the next day, nor the day after. Zira and Jared filled the time as best as they could with conversation, food, and music from the van's old radio, but the hours still dragged on. Zira was beginning to regret having agreed to this plan and thought they might have been better off trying to track Collins down at the university. As Jared parked the van for the fourth day of their stake-out, she thought about how she might be able to make that suggestion to him without it coming across as a complaint. She was still mulling it over when a man with a black umbrella walked into the diner. He unzipped his jacket and collapsed the umbrella, turning to the window as he did so, and Zira caught a glimpse of his face.

"It's him," she said, hardly able to believe she was finally seeing their target in the flesh.

"You're up." Jared handed her a small earpiece that was linked to her CL so he could communicate with her privately as needed. Zira put the earpiece in, slipped her arms inside her jacket, and got out of the car. Heavy raindrops pelted her back as she ran across the street. She checked her pocket to make sure the device was still there. It was no bigger than her thumbnail and as thick as a coin, so she was careful not to accidently drop it when she removed her hand. She pushed the door of the diner open and nodded to the waitress who smiled at her.

Collins had taken a corner booth next to the window. Zira chose a place at the counter and the waitress came to take her order. She selected a muffin and a cup of orange juice from the menu and tried to determine what might be the best way to slip the device to Collins without arousing his suspicion.

Her CL beeped and lit up. Jared. She answered the call. "Yes?"

"There's a man coming your way." Jared's words came through the earpiece in a rush. "Asian. Average height, dark hair, mid-fifties. Give him the device instead."

Zira glanced out the window to her right. She thought she could see the man Jared was talking about, though it was hard to see anything clearly through the rain. Why was he changing their plan all of the sudden? Collins was their target, not this random stranger. "That's not what we talked about before," she said, keeping her tone as pleasant as possible in case Collins was paying attention to her conversation.

"Just do it, Zira!"

The line went dead. Zira resisted the urge to turn around and glare at the van through the window. "All right," she said, continuing the conversation in order to keep up appearances. "I'll be right there." She called to the waitress in the kitchen. "I'm sorry, but can I have that to go, please?"

"Sure, honey." Moments later, she brought out a paper sack and cup. Zira took them, paid, and turned to leave. The Asian man was reaching for the door. Zira held her food in one hand and stuffed the other in her pocket. Her fingers found the device, and she pinched it tight between her thumb and forefinger.

The man opened the door and entered. Pretending to look at something on her CL, Zira bumped into him hard on her way past. He stumbled a step back and she slipped the device into the pocket of his jacket. "I'm *so* sorry," she said in a voice as sweet as syrup. She put on her most apologetic smile. "I wasn't paying attention. Are you all right?"

The man's expression shifted from annoyance to understanding. "That's okay, dear. No harm done."

It was the *dear* that assured Zira she didn't need to worry about the man becoming suspicious. She smiled at him again and walked back to the van.

"Did you do it?" Jared asked once she was inside.

"Yes," Zira snapped. "You want to tell me what that was all about now?"

"That guy is one of the Red Flag Brotherhood's top-ranking members."

"How do you know that?"

Jared ignored her question. "Tracking him could give us a better idea of what the Brotherhood is up to."

"He's not our target." Zira's patience was fraying rapidly. "And what about Collins? We still don't know where he really lives."

Inside the diner, Collins and the Asian man seemed to have already concluded their business. Both of them stood up to leave.

Jared shrugged his jacket on and pulled the hood over his head. "I'll follow Collins. You go back to the hotel and start pulling the recordings from that device." He got out of the car and shut the door without giving Zira a chance to protest. She watched him walk into the rain, confused, irritated, and once again wondering if this partnership was going to be an abysmal failure after all.

CHAPTER 4

JARED REMAINED A SAFE DISTANCE behind Collins as he followed his black umbrella through Seattle's streets. The man didn't seem concerned about being tailed; he walked at an easy pace and never looked back. One minute into the pursuit, Jared was soaked and found himself wishing he had his own umbrella.

This was stupid. He shouldn't have asked Zira to change the plan at the last minute, slipping the device to the Brotherhood member, Li Huang, instead of Collins. There was no guarantee that Collins was even going home now. He could get in a cab and be gone in an instant, and they'd be right back where they started at the beginning of this mission. For his own sake, he hoped that wouldn't happen; Zira would kill him.

If he was honest with himself, Jared knew he'd decided to change the plan more out of selfishness than because he actually thought it was a good idea. It was a split-second decision, and even as he'd called Zira, he knew it was wrong. But just seeing Li's face again had been enough to raise goosebumps all over Jared's skin. Rage steamed and festered inside him as memories of his captivity in a Brotherhood outpost rushed to the surface. He tried to shut them out, focusing on his target's back to avoid thinking about the smirk on Li's face as he'd come to interrogate Jared day after day.

Collins caught a bus several blocks away from the diner. Jared ran to catch up and made it on board just before the doors closed. Collins didn't seem to notice anything unusual, and Jared took a seat in the back corner where he could keep an eye on his target.

He should tell Zira. He hadn't before because he hadn't known how much the Brotherhood would actually be involved in their assignment. If they weren't directly involved before, they were now; Jared had seen to that when he'd told Zira to bug Li instead of Collins. He had to give her an explanation; it was only fair that she knew what she was getting into. Still, his insides twisted at the thought of talking about it. She'd have questions, and then there would be that unavoidable pity in her eyes whenever she looked at him. Or worse, admiration—like he was some sort of hero for enduring what he had and coming back to do his job the same as before. There was nothing heroic about those memories, though, and nothing noble about the way he'd just changed the parameters of their mission without thinking through it clearly. Wasn't that what he'd told her just a few days ago, that he always thought things through before acting? Most of the time that was true. Today, it was nothing but a load of crap.

He could worry about that later. Right now, he just needed to do his job. He shoved the memories back down where they'd been buried before and focused all his attention on Collins. The man got off the bus with half a dozen other people at a stop in front of a unit C distribution center. Jared waited until the new passengers boarded, then slipped out the back door and found Collins' black umbrella. He let the man get a fair distance ahead of him again. They walked a few more blocks to a small neighborhood with old townhouses lining the street end to end. When Collins unlocked the door to one of them and walked inside, Jared smiled to himself. Maybe Zira wouldn't kill him after all.

■ ■ ■

Once he got back to the hotel, Jared took a hot shower to get rid of the chill in his bones before knocking on Zira's door. "I hope you found out where he lives," she grumbled, standing aside to let him in. "Otherwise, we just wasted four days in that stupid van for nothing."

"I found his house," Jared said. "Is the bug working?"

"Yeah, but I waited for you so we could listen to it together. Because that's what good partners do. You know, communication."

He ignored the jab—he probably deserved it—and walked over to the small table where she'd moved the room's hologram projector. Using a PEACE Project access code, he set up a secure connection between his CL and the projector to pull up the readings from the device Zira had planted on Li. She sat on the bed and he took a place beside her, then played the audio recording from the beginning.

"Hello, Marcus," said Li Huang. His voice still had the ability to send ice across Jared's skin.

"Mr. Li," Collins replied.

The waitress came to take their order, attempting to make small-talk before Li abruptly dismissed her. When she was gone, the two men resumed their conversation in murmured voices. "You said it would be ready by now," said Li. "My boss is getting impatient."

"I told you there would be delays. I had to disassemble the whole thing and start from scratch because of the changes Mr. Feng requested. The cloaking parameters—"

"Will it get past the sensors?" Li asked.

"Absolutely. But I need a little more time. I'm waiting on a shipment from Nevarez Industrial Supply, but until it gets here, my hands are tied."

The waitress came back with their coffee and Collins paid her. "So be it," Li said when she was gone again. "However, Mr. Feng has insisted that you complete your work before you receive the rest of your payment."

"That's not what we agreed. Some of the parts have been expensive, and I have to pay for all of that up-front myself."

"That's not our problem."

"I've done everything you wanted, no questions asked. I should be compensated."

"And you will be," Li said. There was a dangerous edge to his voice that Jared was all too familiar with. He could picture the threat in the man's eyes as he looked at Collins. "No more delays, Marcus. Mr. Feng's patience won't last forever."

The conversation ended, and there was the sound of the door opening and shutting as both men left the diner and went their separate ways. Then there was only the patter of the rain.

Jared fast-forwarded the recording. More rain, then silence. Li was indoors somewhere, likely alone. The quiet was interrupted by voices again. The timestamp at the bottom showed 1:32 P.M.—just half an hour ago.

Li was talking to someone over his CyberLink—someone who's voice instantly froze Jared's blood. They conversed in Mandarin Chinese. Jared was about to ask Zira to pull up a translator on her CL, but she was a step ahead of him; the translation was already scrolling by on the projection above her wrist.

Hello, Mr. Feng.

What did you find out from our friend?

It's not finished yet.

What's his excuse this time?

The changes you requested are causing some delays.

Did you tell him about the new payment arrangements?

Yes. He wasn't happy.

Does he realize that I am not happy with the current situation?

I told him.

Good. If he hasn't made any more progress by next week, bring him in. It might be time I talked to him myself.

Yes, sir. I'll keep you updated.

The conversation ended. They listened for a few more minutes, but there was nothing. Zira turned to Jared. "Any idea who this Feng guy is?"

Jared gnawed at his lip, trying to figure out the best way to tell her. There was really no good way to go about it. "Feng Kai is the leader of the Red Flag Brotherhood." He busied himself with severing the connection between his CL and the projector in order to avoid looking at her. He didn't want to see her reaction when she put the pieces together. "He's also responsible for the death of my last partner."

"That's how you knew Li was with the Brotherhood," she said. She didn't sound angry—not yet, anyway. "That's why you had me plant the device on him instead.

And your last partner—that's why you haven't had one for two years."

Jared nodded. He sighed, ran a hand over the top of his head, and turned to face her. "I should have told you. I just didn't want to talk about it."

"Because you don't know me well enough?" Now she sounded angry. "That's not fair. You dragged me into this without giving me any idea what it really was."

"I told you I thought it was worth looking into the Brotherhood's plans, and I meant that. That's all I wanted to do—just look into things. I figured we'd pass some information on to Ryku and that would be the end of it. But then Li showed up. I couldn't just let him walk away."

The memories engulfed him like quicksand. Karyn, Titus, and Rowan—the three other operatives who'd gone on that assignment with him almost two years ago. His friends, his partner, all killed by members of the Red Flag Brotherhood. They only needed one to answer questions, they'd said. Jared had been the youngest; they'd thought he would be the easiest to break. He was locked in a cage like an animal, starved and beaten and interrogated about his mission for hours on end. Feng gave the orders and watched Li carry them out. Both men chatted and joked while Jared watched his own blood drip onto the floor.

How could he have let Li just walk away after all that?

He leaned forward and rested his elbows on his knees. Zira turned towards him, waiting for an explanation. "About two years ago," he began, "a group of us were sent to the Republic of Asia to take out the Brotherhood's leadership. There were more of them than we anticipated and things went bad. They killed the other three operatives I was with, including my partner, Rowan. I was captured."

He paused and attempted to distance himself from the memories, focusing on the impartial facts about what had happened. "Americans generally aren't allowed in the RA in the first place, so the Project denied any knowledge of the incident. The RA government refused to get involved because they didn't want to associate themselves with the Brotherhood. Negotiating my release was impossible."

"You were left to fend for yourself," Zira said.

"I was there for two weeks." He didn't go into the details of what had happened during that time. She already knew more than he wanted her to, and talking about it wasn't going to improve anything. "I was sure I'd die there. Then Ryku showed up with a whole team of operatives. They took out most of the Brotherhood's key players and brought me home, but no one ever found Feng and Li. I never expected to run into them again here."

Jared waited for the questions he knew Zira must have, but she didn't ask them. She didn't say anything for a long time, and when she did, the hostility had left her voice. "I get it now. I still don't like it, but I understand."

"I'm sorry. I know I compromised our mission and that's unacceptable. You should call the shots from now on. Whatever you want to do, I'm with you."

Zira stood and walked to the window, considering this for a few moments. "We should eliminate all of them."

"All of them?" Jared wanted to make sure he understood her. He'd expected her to insist that they focus on Collins and forget about the Brotherhood altogether. That's what he would have done, if their positions were reversed.

"Li, Collins, Feng," said Zira. "All of them. You were right about the Brotherhood. If Collins is dead, they'll just find someone else to make their bomb."

"How do we pull that off?" Jared had a few ideas of his own, but he wanted to know what she was thinking. That, and he didn't entirely trust his own judgment right now given his history with Li and Feng.

"We make sure Collins doesn't finish that bomb. Feng will be mad that he missed the deadline again. Li will pick Collins up to go talk to Feng, and we'll follow them to wherever it is they're all meeting."

Jared nodded; it was a solid plan. "We'll need to get approval from Ryku." He doubted the chairman would have an issue with the change; Li and Feng had been on his list of targets ever since they'd eluded capture in the RA two years ago. Still, with Ryku, it was always wiser to ask for permission before stepping too far outside the given mission parameters.

"He likes you a lot better than he likes me," said Zira. "You ask him."

"I'll call him tomorrow morning." He stood and walked to the door, then turned back to look at her. He couldn't meet her gaze for long; there was something in her cool blue eyes that seemed to see straight through him. "Thank you," he said.

"Don't thank me. I'm still pissed at you for not telling me any of this up front."

"I know. But still, thanks." He walked out and shut the door behind him before she could say anything else.

CHAPTER 5

AFTER JARED LEFT, ZIRA SAT by the window, watching the rain fall and thinking about what he'd told her. Had she made the right decision? In giving her control of the assignment, he'd given her an easy way out of this mess with the Brotherhood, but instead, she'd chosen to plunge into something that might be more than she could handle. And for what? Revenge? Jared hadn't said exactly what had happened to him in the Brotherhood's custody, but two weeks was a long time, and Zira was not so naïve as to believe they hadn't made him suffer every minute he was there. They'd killed his friends and held him captive, and if anyone deserved vengeance, he did. But that was his problem, not hers. Getting herself mixed up in this might be the most foolish thing she'd done as an E-2 operative so far.

This wasn't just about Jared's revenge, though, and she knew that wasn't solely what it was about for him, either. They both understood that the Brotherhood was a real threat. Eliminating Collins would slow them down, but it wouldn't prevent them from conducting some kind of attack later on. Maybe killing Li and Feng wouldn't do much good either in the grand scheme of things, but it was a start. They were as much a threat to peace as Collins was, if not more so, and it was her job to eliminate threats.

Early the next morning, Zira and Jared met in the lobby to eat breakfast before splitting up for the day. Chairman Ryku had agreed to their plan, so now they needed to intercept the shipment Collins was waiting on. They'd looked up Nevarez Industrial Supply and found out it was a legitimate company; whatever components Collins had ordered from them likely weren't dangerous on their own, and making arrangements to receive them in secret probably would have roused unnecessary suspicion. The package would therefore most likely be delivered by regular post to either the university where Collins taught or the unregistered townhouse he lived in. Jared took a bus to the university, and Zira drove the van to Collins' house.

Surveillance was even more boring here than it had been at the diner. With no one to keep her company, the hours dragged by mercilessly. Collins returned home for the evening just after five o' clock. Zira waited until six to drive away; postal delivery usually stopped at five, and if the package hadn't arrived by now, it wouldn't until tomorrow. Or the day after. Or the day after that. Just thinking about spending another four days cooped up in the van irritated her.

Thankfully, it only ended up being one more day. Zira was sitting in the van humming along with the radio the following afternoon when the delivery bot wheeled down the street. She looked around; there was no one outside, so unless Collins had particularly nosy neighbors, she shouldn't have any trouble intercepting the package. She got out of the van and hurried to Collins' house, standing at the end of the sidewalk as if she'd just walked out to meet the delivery bot. It stopped in front of her. "I have a package for Marcus Collins." The electronic voice emitted from a set of speakers just under its blocky head. "Please confirm identity."

Zira pulled up her PEACE Project ID and credentials on her CyberLink and held her wrist under the robot's scanner. It took longer than normal, and for a moment, Zira worried that the bot wasn't going to accept the override. She had a pistol under her jacket just in case, but she hoped to avoid shooting the thing.

The bot chirped, and the metal box that made up most of its body slid open. "Accepted. Please remove your package."

Zira took the top package from the stack inside and the door slid shut. The robot continued on its way, and Zira headed back to the car with the box tucked under her arm. She sent a quick message to Jared. *I got it. Meet me back at the hotel.*

■ ■ ■

Zira watched Jared turn the box over in his hands as they sat in his hotel room. They were waiting for a call back from the unit A tech girl who was setting up a system to reroute Collins' outgoing calls and messages. "Will you stop doing that?" Zira said. "What if you break something?"

The contents needed to remain intact and untouched, so they hadn't opened the box and didn't know exactly what was inside. Chairman Ryku wanted unit E-1 to inspect the package when they got back to the compound. If Collins was able to acquire the materials to build a bomb so easily, it was worth looking into how he'd done it.

Jared sighed, but to Zira's relief, he put the box down anyway.

His CL lit up. He answered the call and projected the girl's face as a hologram. "We got that all set up for you," she said. "All of Mr. Collins outgoing messages and calls will now be redirected to your CL. You can decide whether or not you want to let them through, disconnect, or answer them yourself."

"And he won't be able to detect any of that?" Jared asked.

"No. For him, everything will still show up as normal. If you answer a call, he'll be able to hear your voice and see your face if you choose, like any other normal call. If you reply to a message he's sent, the real recipient's name and information will show up in place of yours."

"Perfect. Thank you, Amelia." Jared disconnected the call and turned to Zira. "Well that was easy."

"And now we just wait for Collins to call someone about his package," said Zira. This part of the plan had been Jared's idea. When Collins realized that his package hadn't shown up when it was supposed to, he was sure to try and contact someone about it. The last thing they needed was for some helpful representative of Nevarez Industrial Supply to tell Collins that he had, in fact, approved delivery for the shipment and offer to send him a replacement. As an added bonus, Jared could also prevent Collins from contacting Li to convince him to extend his deadline. Not that that was likely, but it was still reassuring to have such contingencies in place.

Now that they'd set Collins up, Jared and Zira had little else to do but wait. Neither of them were keen on the idea of just sitting around the hotel doing nothing, so they took to wandering the city and jogging every morning together. More and more, Zira became aware of how she'd misjudged him at first. Jared was serious about his work, but outside of that, he was easy to talk to and had a quick sense of humor. Since they were both in the same unit, Zira didn't have to keep her guard up for fear of revealing information she shouldn't. It was liberating to finally be able to talk to someone about the things that had become such a big part of her life.

Collins did attempt to contact someone about his package. First he sent a message, which Jared replied to in the politest and most unhelpful manner possible. He told Collins the package was on its way and would be delivered "soon." The man's response was considerably less civil, and Jared didn't bother answering.

While Zira and Jared were on one of their morning runs, Collins finally tried to call customer service. Jared took a few seconds to catch his breath before answering. "Hello, thank you for calling the Nevarez Industrial Supply Support Center. How may I help you?"

"I ordered a package from you two weeks ago and it still isn't here," said Collins. He sounded flustered. "Can you tell me where it is?"

"One moment sir. Can you just verify some information for me?" He proceeded to ask for Collins' name, address, and order number, then pretended to look it up in his system. "Sir, our records are showing that the order is en route and should be arriving soon."

"That's what the last guy told me. Listen, this package is very important. Can you at least tell me where it is now?"

"Of course, sir. According to our system, the package appears to have left the South Atlantic Region this morning."

"Why did it go all the way over there?"

"I don't know, sir."

"I want a refund," said Collins. "It was supposed to be here three days ago. I needed it for a job, and these delays are putting me behind schedule."

"I'm sorry, sir, but we can't issue a refund until you have received the shipment and returned it to us."

Collins screamed curses at Jared, then disconnected. "Such a nice man," Jared said as they walked back towards the hotel.

"You were way too good at that," said Zira.

"I guess I know where I can find work if I ever decide to quit this job," he joked. They both knew quitting the PEACE Project was not an option. Once you were in— and most of them had been in since infancy—you were there for life, one way or another.

Jared's CL lit up again, showing that Collins was now trying to contact Li. Jared disconnected him. Collins tried a second, third, and fourth time before giving up.

"Don't you think that will make him suspicious?" Zira asked as Jared disconnected the final call.

Jared shrugged. "Maybe. More likely, he'll think it's some kind of threat. Either way, I doubt he's stupid enough to do anything about it. If I were him, I'd tread lightly around Li and Feng right now."

"So now what?"

"Now, we hit the streets in that beautiful van again," said Jared. "It's only a matter of time before Li comes for Collins, and we need to be there when he does."

Zira groaned. "When we're finished with all of this, I'd love to set that van on fire and watch it burn."

■ ■ ■

True to Feng's orders, Li gave Collins exactly one week to make progress on the bomb before coming to get him. Jared and Zira were parked around the corner from Collins' house when the black SUV pulled up. "This is it," Jared said as Li and another man got out of the vehicle. "Run the plates."

"Already on it," said Zira. She entered the license number into the Project's database. The vehicle it was linked to appeared to match the one sitting in front of Collins' house now. "Got it," she said, pulling up the autopilot navigation system for the SUV. "The location matches, too. We're all set."

They watched Li and the other man return to the car with the bomb-maker in tow. Collins looked terrified as he tried to tell the men something, but they paid him no mind. All three of them got in the SUV and it pulled away from the house.

Zira watched the holographic map above her wrist. The red dot in the center moved with Li's car, leaving a thin line behind it. They waited a few more minutes, then Jared started the van and began to follow the same route as their targets. Zira gave him directions along the way. They drove for twenty minutes before the red dot on Zira's map stopped. "Just a little farther," she said. They were in an old, deserted area on the outskirts of the city, without a single person in sight. The buildings were boarded up and abandoned, the road broken and pockmarked from lack of maintenance. Zira pointed out the windshield. "There—that abandoned trailer park up ahead."

Jared pulled the van into a nearby alley and cut the engine. The sudden silence that fell in the absence of the vehicle's clattering seemed heavy and strange. Jared's face took on its familiar, hard scowl. Zira could only imagine what he might be thinking or feeling right now, but she didn't know what to say, so she slipped into the back of the van without a word and began unpacking the bag they'd brought along.

She found her jacket and slipped it on, then tossed Jared his. Bulletproof material lined everything but the sleeves, making them much heavier than they looked. In the bottom of the bag, she found two suppressed handguns, a pair of rifles, and several knives. She picked out her own weapons and handed the bag up to Jared with the rest.

Zira's heart started pounding. Her hands shook as she checked the mags in both the rifle and the handgun. Jared looked back at her. "You okay?"

She nodded. She could manage her nerves once they got moving; it was always the few minutes leading up to the action that rattled her most.

"There are at least four of them," Jared said as they exited the van. "Maybe more. We'll have to act fast. Suppressors or not, they're going to hear that first shot and come looking for us. You ever been in a real firefight before?"

Zira's throat felt dry. "No. Just simulations."

"That's okay. You've been training for this for years, remember? Just let that training take over." He put a hand on her shoulder and leveled his gaze at her. "I've got your back."

"Let's just get this over with."

He smiled. "That's what I'm talking about. Come on. Eyes on me."

They crouched low as they moved down the street, hugging the walls of buildings and sticking to shadows wherever they could. They reached the nearest mobile home, and Jared opened the door and motioned Zira inside. The floor was littered with dirt and debris, and Zira took care not to step on anything that would make too much noise as she crossed to the window. Jared moved the ratty curtain aside and they peered out. "There's Li's car," he said. "The other one is probably Feng's."

The man they'd seen with Li at Collins' house stood outside one of the trailers, armed with an assault rifle. "You think they're in there?" she asked Jared.

"Got to be."

Movement caught her eye and she turned her head. "I've got another man patrolling the area over here. He's armed, too."

They watched for a few more minutes, but only saw the same two men. "I think that's all there is," Jared said. "There might be one or two more inside with Li, Feng, and Collins. You okay with that?"

Zira nodded.

"You get the guy guarding the door. I'll get the other one. Fire as soon as you hear my shot."

She nodded again and they slipped back outside. She shifted her rifle against her shoulder, raising it in front of her as she hurried to the next trailer. Peeking around the corner, she surveyed her options. There was a spot about thirty yards ahead with decent cover that would give her a good angle. She looked at her target; his back was turned. Zira darted to the spot she'd picked out, pressed herself against the side of the trailer, and took aim.

The muffled sound of Jared's gunshot cracked twice. Without thinking, Zira pulled the trigger. The man went down with a new hole in his head, but Zira followed it up with another round just to be safe.

The door of the trailer burst open and another man ran out. Zira didn't recognize him and was so startled by his sudden appearance that her first shot only grazed his shoulder. He fired back at her. Zira ducked behind the trailer, took a breath, and tried again. This time, she hit her mark.

Collins came through the door in a panic and tried to run between two trailers, but dropped just before he reached them. Jared stepped out over his body and made his way to Li and Feng, who still cowered in the relative safety of their shelter. Zira swung her rifle to her back and pulled out her handgun as she ran to the trailer.

Shots rang out in rapid bursts. She took the stairs in a single leap. Inside, Jared crouched behind an upturned couch. Someone peered out from a room down the hall. Jared shot him twice. Li's head jerked back as he fell to the ground.

Jared jumped over the couch and bolted down the hall. "Wait!" Zira called after him. By her count, there was at least one more enemy still in the trailer, and rushing headlong into the unknown was a reckless move. She sprinted after him.

Jared burst into the room at the end of the hall. He jumped back an instant later as Feng came at him with a knife. It was a clumsy attempt, probably due to the fact that he'd been shot in the other arm and bled heavily. Jared grabbed his wrist and slammed him against the wall, then wrenched the knife from his grasp. It clattered to the floor and Jared kicked it away. He loomed over Feng, every muscle of his face twisted in rage as he stared down at the Brotherhood leader. "Sit down," he barked.

Feng complied, and Jared crouched down in front of him. The anger dissipated from his face, leaving an expression that was as impassive as still water. Zira felt like an intruder as she stood in the doorway and watched. This was something deeply personal and important to Jared—something she shouldn't be seeing—but there was no escaping it now.

Shock and recognition flickered across Feng's face as he met Jared's gaze. "I remember you," he said. The corners of his mouth turned up in a cruel smile. "You've come a long way for your revenge."

Jared's voice took on an eerie chill as he answered Feng. "This is bigger than revenge."

"I doubt that. It doesn't matter why you came or who sent you. Deep down, this is all about the way we killed your friends and chained you up in that cell."

If Jared was at all bothered by any memories Feng's words dragged up, he didn't show it. "I'm finally ready to answer all those questions you kept asking me two years ago."

"I thought you said you'd never tell."

Jared shrugged. "It doesn't matter now. You're dying. I think you should know why." He stood up, towering over Feng. "My name is Jared. I'm a member of the PEACE Project. Two years ago, my team and I were sent to kill you and the rest of your organization. We failed. Today, I'm fixing that mistake."

"I didn't realize the PEACE Project employed mercenaries," said Feng.

Jared crossed his arms. "Sometimes killing people like you is the only option. Every breath you take is a threat to the peace and safety of this country."

"You think you can stop that threat just by killing me? My organization is stronger now than it ever was before."

"We'll see," Jared said. "As far as I can tell, your predecessor was twice the leader you are. Once you're gone, I don't think it'll be long before everything else starts unraveling."

Feng spat at Jared's feet and glared up at him. Jared brought his gun back up to Feng's head and fired twice. Zira watched, unblinking, as blood sprayed across the floor and onto Jared's arm.

He turned away from the crumpled figure on the floor and walked past Zira. "What about the bodies?" she asked.

"Let their friends find them," said Jared. "Come on. I'm sick of this place."

CHAPTER 6

ZIRA PRETENDED NOT TO NOTICE the way Jared's hands shook so much he couldn't even get the key into the ignition. He dropped it on the floor and slammed his hand against the steering wheel, cursing. Zira focused on the branches of a tree outside, but she could see him in her peripherals, hunched over with his head bowed as he rubbed his hands over his coarse, black hair.

"I'm sorry," Zira said. "About your team and...what he did to you."

"I don't need your pity," Jared growled.

"I know. I don't pity you."

He sighed and sat up. "Yeah, well, it's over now."

"Are you relieved? That they're dead?"

Jared met her gaze, and Zira was caught off guard by how much pain she saw in his eyes. She hadn't noticed it before, or maybe he'd just done a good job of hiding it until now. "I wouldn't say that I'm relieved. But I do feel better somehow—safer—knowing they're gone." He took Zira's hand, an unexpected gesture that made her flinch. "Thank you."

"For what?"

"I've been dreading this since we first saw Li in that diner. It was easier knowing I wasn't going into it alone."

"Anyone could have done that."

"Maybe. But it was *you* who put me at ease all week and gave me something else to think about."

"I didn't—"

Jared shook his head and gave her a small smile. "It's just a 'thank you,' Zira. You don't need to get defensive about it."

"All right," she muttered. "You're welcome."

They left the trailer park and drove the van to a scrap yard, then took a bus back to the hotel to gather their belongings. An automated taxi took them to the airport and they boarded the first flight back to Amarillo. Doubts and questions raced through Zira's mind as she watched the clouds outside her window. She replayed the past few days in her head, trying to determine if she'd done everything right. She knew what her mistakes might cost her, and she wasn't ready or willing to face those consequences. Judging from the way the past week had gone, she thought she'd earned Jared's approval. He was so hard to read sometimes, though, and Zira didn't dare make any assumptions.

When the plane landed, she retrieved her bag from the overhead compartment and went to meet Jared at the car. "All set?" he asked as she slid into the seat beside him.

She nodded. "Yeah, let's go."

The car began driving them home. "Nervous?" Jared asked. It was the same question he'd asked her as they'd left the compound together, though perhaps with a bit more understanding between them now.

Zira raised her eyebrows at him. How could she *not* be nervous?

He shrugged. "You did good. If it makes you feel any better, I plan to give Ryku a good report."

Some of Zira's tension began to dissipate, but she bristled when she realized that Jared might have his own reasons for wanting to give Ryku a good report. "You're not just saying that because of all the stuff back at the trailer park, are you? I helped you deal with Feng and Li, so you feel obligated to do me a favor or something? I don't want you telling Ryku anything unless it's true. I don't need *your* pity, either."

"What? No—that's not—" He sighed. "You still don't trust me."

"I trust you," she said, and frowned at how easily the words had come out. There were few people she truly trusted, and in just a few weeks, he had become one of them. She stared at her feet. "It's just—ever since I was placed in this unit, I've been fighting to prove I deserve the spot. People look at me and all they see is a small, weak little girl. I hate that."

"That's not what I see."

"Maybe not now, but you *did*. Right?"

"Small, yes. But almost everyone looks small to me."

Zira shook her head, but smiled. "I guess that's true."

"I never thought you were weak. I shouldn't have been so hard on you when we were first assigned to work together. It wasn't your fault; I just didn't like the idea. My last partner was killed right in front of me. I didn't want to work with anyone else after that. Ever."

Zira regretted that they'd gotten off to such a bad start. It seemed they had both misunderstood each other, but Zira couldn't deny that she'd enjoyed working with him since then. She'd learned a lot from his experience, but it was more than that. In all the time they'd spent together these past few weeks, they'd become friends.

"Look, I'm going to tell Ryku the truth when we get back," Jared said. "And the truth is that you're a great operative. He'd be making a mistake if he got rid of you."

It was one of the highest compliments Zira had ever received. "Thank you."

Even though it was late when they got back to the compound, Jared suggested they go straight to Chairman Ryku's office. Anxious to get the whole thing over with, she agreed. He went in alone while Zira waited in the hall for what seemed like hours. When the chairman finally opened the door and beckoned her inside, Zira's first thought was that he seemed angry. Then again, Ryku wasn't the sort of man who put too much stock in smiles and reassuring words.

Jared was standing next to Ryku's desk and nodded to Zira as she sat rigid on the couch. She nodded back, unable to relax until she heard the verdict from Ryku himself. The chairman stared at her for a long time, almost as if he enjoyed making her squirm. Just as Zira was about to demand that he get on with it, he said, "Jared seems very impressed by your work. With his recommendation, I am allowing you to continue your work as a member of this unit."

The tension in Zira's muscles released. "I appreciate the opportunity, sir. I won't make you regret it."

"I hope you'll remember this lesson. Always be aware of your actions. Mistakes cost lives, and we don't need more blood on our hands than necessary. Is that clear?"

"I understand. Thank you, Chairman."

Ryku turned his back and gave them a wave over his shoulder to dismiss them. As soon as they were outside, Zira let a broad grin break across her face.

"I told you it was going to be fine," said Jared.

"Thank you," she said again.

He shrugged. "You earned it."

They walked towards the apartments together. "Did you give him Collins' package?" Zira asked.

"Yeah. He's going to pass it along to unit E-1 to look into. At the very least, they'll be keeping close tabs on the rest of the Brotherhood."

"Good."

"I have a favor to ask," Jared said. "What are you doing this week?"

"Nothing. Why?"

"I'm supposed to work with a group of recruits at the shooting range. I was wondering if you'd help out. You're a better shot; you can probably teach them more than I can."

"Sure," Zira agreed. They had reached her apartment and she unlocked the door.

"Great," said Jared. "I'll see you tomorrow morning then."

Zira nodded. "Goodnight."

■ ■ ■

Aubreigh still hadn't returned from her job in the South Atlantic Region, so Zira sat alone in the cafeteria for breakfast the next morning. As she took a bite of her powdered eggs, she glanced around the room and noticed something unusual. Almost a third of the people in the cafeteria wore the green armbands of unit E-1, a strange phenomenon considering there were typically just a few dozen of them stationed in the compound at any given time. Unlike the other units, most of E-1's members lived outside the compound and worked at various regional law enforcement offices across the country. She had no idea what so many of them might be doing here now.

"Mind if I join you?" said someone behind her. Zira turned and found Jared standing there. She nodded and he took the seat next to her.

"Do you know why there are so many E-1s here?" she asked him.

"They're doing an internal investigation."

Zira frowned. By her recollection, unit E-1 had done an internal investigation not even two years ago. "I thought they only did one every four or five years."

Jared shrugged. "I hear there's been some tension about the rationing system lately, especially in the North Pacific Region. They're probably here to look into that. It's mostly a formality, keeps everyone happy. People out there still have a hard time trusting the government after everything that happened before the war. If they know we're being monitored just like they are, they feel safer."

Having lived in the compound since before she could even remember, it was sometimes hard for Zira to imagine what things were like for those on the outside. She thought she understood this, though. Before the war, democracy had all but collapsed under the rule of the rich and powerful few, and many believed it was their greed and corruption that had caused the war in the first place. The use of nuclear weapons and robot soldiers had led to the destruction of entire cities. Radiation had left much of the land uninhabitable, and almost one third of the world's population had been wiped out before a truce was reached between the war's key players. Afterwards, the PEACE Project had been established as America's governing body with the main objective of preventing such a thing from happening again, but that hadn't even been three decades ago. The scars of the conflict were barely starting to heal, and Zira understood why some people might still mistrust their leaders.

"What about us?" She lowered her voice. "If people knew what we do—they wouldn't understand."

Jared shrugged. "I like to think they would. Sometimes the best way to protect someone is to just get rid of the threat. That's all we're doing."

"If it were that easy, we wouldn't have to sneak around or worry about covering our tracks."

"Maybe," said Jared. "Either way, revealing our mission files would be a threat to national security. Ryku always gives them some harmless informant files instead. The public is satisfied, and as far as they know, we're just an intelligence organization."

"Probably better that way," Zira said.

"Probably, but some of the E-1s think we're sweeping things under the rug."

Zira glared at the nearest person with a green band, a young woman sitting at the table in front of them. They could think whatever they wanted; at the end of the day, it was always the E-2 operatives who were called on to do what was necessary to keep everyone alive and safe. Suddenly annoyed by the sea of E-1s surrounding them, Zira drummed her fingers against the table. "You ready to go?" she asked Jared.

"Yeah, we'd better. It's almost time to meet the kids at the range."

The five recruits Jared had been charged with training were already at the shooting range when he and Zira arrived. They had some unexpected company as well. A small group from unit A, identifiable by the yellow bands around their left arms, appeared to be testing some sort of non-lethal weapon with the assistance of one of their robots. Members of unit A dedicated themselves to researching and developing advanced sciences and technologies that would prevent or protect from future conflicts. Two E-1s stood nearby, watching and jotting down notes on their CLs. Zira assumed that the weapon unit A was testing had been developed for their law enforcement needs.

Turning her attention back to the task at hand, she demonstrated the proper grip for holding a pistol to a girl who couldn't have been more than fourteen while Jared pulled up a ballistics chart on his CL for another. As she was moving on to work with someone else, Zira turned to see one of the E-1s staring at her. He was older than her, probably in his mid-twenties, with thick black hair and tawny skin. His dark eyes flickered back to the unit A robot as soon as she looked at him, but that wasn't the last time Zira noticed him watching her. She could feel his gaze on her back through the rest of the training session and caught him glancing away several times. She thought about approaching him to ask what he thought was so interesting about her, but the group finished their testing and drove away before she got the chance. By the time Jared decided to let the recruits go, Zira wondered if she'd just been overreacting about the whole thing.

She might have forgotten about the incident if the same man hadn't shown up at their training session the next afternoon, this time alone. Jared gave him an acknowledging nod as he passed by, but didn't seem too happy to see him there. "You know him?" Zira asked as they set up the range and organized their group.

"We've talked a few times. His name's Seth."

"What's he doing here?"

"I'm sure it's just part of their investigation. They like to observe and make sure we're not doing anything too dangerous around the kids." He gave one of the younger boys a joking smile as he said this and handed him an enormous rifle. The boy grinned back, shaking his head.

"I wish he'd go observe something else," Zira said, but she tried to forget about Seth as she showed the recruits how to sight in their scopes.

About an hour into the training session, Zira heard an unfamiliar voice call her name. She whirled around to see Seth waving to her. "Can I have a word with you?"

Still skeptical of him and unsure if talking to him one-on-one was a good idea, Zira glanced back at Jared for direction. He was busy resetting targets and hadn't noticed anything. With a reluctant sigh, Zira told the recruit she'd been working with to keep practicing long-range shots and went to Seth. "What do you want?" she said with as much civility as she could muster.

"My name is Seth. As you may know, my unit is conducting a routine investigation into the activities of the rest of the PEACE Project."

Zira nodded, wondering whose job it was to investigate unit E-1. She decided it was in her best interest not to get smart-mouthed with him, though, and didn't ask.

"I just have a few questions for you," he said.

"Fine."

"I saw you here yesterday with this same group. At first I thought you were one of the recruits, but then I noticed *that*." He gestured to the band around Zira's upper left arm, which was solid black. Recruits who hadn't graduated training yet had a white stripe running all the way around the middle of their bands, regardless of which unit they were in.

"I finished training three months ago," Zira said.

"I'm sorry if this sounds rude," said Seth, "but you're—small. You just look so young. I was surprised, so I decided to dig into your background a little more. It seems you graduated your training program early."

"Yes."

Seth raised his eyebrows. "Impressive. I've heard the training program for your unit is rigorous, both physically and mentally. You must be quite talented. Ryku obviously sees you as a valuable asset to this Project."

"Yeah, I guess so." Zira held in a proud smirk.

"However, since then, it seems you've accomplished very little," Seth said. He abandoned any pretense of courtesy as his voice took on an obnoxiously superior tone.

The change caught Zira off guard, and she struggled to find a good response. Seth stared down his long nose at her like she was a bloodstain on his perfectly ironed shirt. "You've done *nothing*, in fact. It makes me wonder what the point was of accelerating you through training."

Zira crossed her arms. "I wasn't *accelerated* through training. I worked hard and did everything I was expected to, just like anyone else. And I've done plenty since then."

Seth gave her a small, pompous smile that only increased Zira's desire to punch him in the face. "I see. But according to your file, you've been completely inactive all this time. Perhaps you'd care to explain what exactly it is you've be doing for your unit. Or maybe you could tell me why I'm not able to find any of that information."

Realizing her mistake, Zira clenched her fists and locked her jaw. She'd just told Seth exactly what he wanted to hear. While she hadn't directly revealed anything she shouldn't have, she hadn't done a good job of concealing things either. Chairman Ryku was always going on about how important it was to keep the details of their missions secret, even from other units in the Project. Zira's insides churned at the thought of enduring another one of his lectures; she'd only just recovered from her last lapse in judgment.

And yet, Seth must know their work was classified. So why was he taking such an interest in her specifically? He'd asked about what she'd been doing since graduating from training, so perhaps he had a hunch about one of her recent assignments. Or maybe he just thought she'd be an easy target since she was still a new operative. She pursed her lips; he wasn't going to get any more information from her. "If you have any questions about my file, you'll have to ask Chairman Ryku."

Seth waved a hand. "Ryku will give me the same run-around he does every time we come to him with questions. I'm asking you."

"And I'm telling you I have nothing else to say. I've got work to do." She spun on her heel and marched back to Jared and the recruits.

"Right," Seth called after her. His voice was so loud that everyone was sure to hear it even over the gunshots. "We'll continue this later then? Excellent."

It was all Zira could do to smile at the recruit she'd been working with, trying to portray an image of calm and composure.

Jared wasn't fooled by the act. He came to stand beside her as she watched bullets rip through targets and bury themselves in the sand. "Is there a problem?" he asked.

She shook her head, more out of frustration than to answer his question. "Ryku is going to kick me out of the unit for sure this time."

"What happened?"

Not wanting to discuss the issue in front of the recruits, Zira simply said, "Later," and went back to work.

It seemed Jared didn't want to wait until later, though. He called the training session to a halt well before dusk when they were scheduled to finish. The recruits seemed excited to be done early until Jared told them they would be jogging the five miles back to the compound. "No complaints," he said as a few of the younger ones let out dismayed groans. "It's a good opportunity to work on your endurance. Get going." They set off as a group while Jared and Zira shut down the target system and loaded the weapons and ammo back into the pickup they'd come in.

The truck set off at a cautious pace across the rough trail and Jared turned to Zira. "So?"

Zira described her conversation with Seth. To her relief, Jared's face didn't convey any sort of disappointment or annoyance with her as she spoke. She'd almost been more afraid of his disapproval than she was of Ryku's. "I know I should have just told him to go to the chairman right away," Zira said. "It just got to me, him telling me that I don't do anything important."

"Because you still feel like you have to prove yourself to everyone."

He'd articulated her feelings better than she could herself. "Yeah, I guess so."

"The good news is that you're not the first person to say something stupid in an E-1 investigation. And it really wasn't *that* stupid."

"You think?"

"I'd be surprised if Ryku even hears about this at all. Seth is—well, let's just say that I don't even think his friends like him very much. He's the kind of person who has to have all the answers, whether it's good for him or not. He's done this sort of thing before. He'll go straight to his chairman with whatever it is you said to him and make a big fuss over it. She'll tell him she'll look into it just to make him shut up, and it won't go any farther than that."

"Oh."

"The bad news is that he's probably not going to leave you alone for the next few weeks."

"But you said Chairman Ava wouldn't take him seriously," said Zira.

"She won't, but that's not going to stop him. He's very dedicated to his job. Just keep your head down and try not to add any fuel to his fire. He's harmless. In a few weeks, E-1 will finish their investigation, and Seth will leave with the rest of them."

Zira nodded and stared out the windshield in front of her, contemplating Jared's advice as the walls of the compound loomed closer. He was right, of course, but Zira had never been particularly good at backing down once someone confronted or challenged her. It was going to be difficult to keep her head down if Seth kept looking for...well, whatever it was he thought he was looking for.

Zira looked over at Jared in the seat beside her. The golden light of the sunset pouring in through the window cast a warm glow on his dark skin and illuminated his eyes so that they seemed almost amber at the edges. Something stirred in the pit of Zira's stomach, a soaring feeling that was both alarming and exhilarating at once.

Jared caught her watching him and smiled. Zira turned away, trying to ignore the warmth spreading over her cheeks. "Something else bothering you?" he asked.

"Nothing," she said flatly.

The truck parked itself in near the gate and Zira got out and began to unload the guns. They carried them back to the E-2 training facility and locked them up in the proper storage room. "Same time tomorrow?" Jared asked.

Still preoccupied about her conversation with Seth, Zira hesitated a moment before answering. "Er—yeah, that sounds good."

"Unless you don't want to," Jared said, and his expression fell just a little. "I can work with them on my own if you'd rather not go."

"No," Zira said quickly. "I'll be there. I like working with you—them. I mean, it's been good to help with their training." Flustered, she turned to the door. Why was she stumbling over her words like this? "I'll see you tomorrow."

Jared bid her goodbye, and Zira hurried outside and made her way to the cafeteria for dinner. She spotted Aubreigh at a table and went to sit next to her.

"I was hoping I'd see you here," said Aubreigh. "How was your assignment? Did everything go okay with your new partner?"

"Better than I thought it would, actually. Jared's not so bad."

"See? I told you it would work out if you just gave each other a chance."

Zira sighed in mock exasperation. "Yes, you were right, as usual. How were things in the South Atlantic Region?"

"Good. Their distribution center was an absolute mess; that's partly why all the E-1s are here. The rest of my team is still down there trying to sort things out."

"So why did you come back early?"

Aubreigh glanced around and leaned across the table to whisper to Zira. "I'm not supposed to say anything because it's not official yet, but they're transferring me to population control."

"Oh, wow," said Zira. She wasn't exactly sure why Aubreigh seemed so pleased about it, but it must have been a step up from her previous duties. "Congratulations."

"Thanks. I think it will be a good change." She got a message on her CL, glanced at it, and hurried to finish the last few bites of her dinner. "I've got to go—some mandatory training meeting for the new job. I'll see you later."

She ran off, leaving Zira to finish the rest of her meal alone in what seemed to be a sea of unwelcome green armbands.

CHAPTER 7

THE NEXT FEW WEEKS PASSED without incident as Jared and Zira finished working with the recruits. Zira introduced Jared and Aubreigh, and the three of them ate meals together regularly now. Aubreigh seemed especially busy with her new job in unit A, but she still made plenty of time to talk to Zira, taking particular interest when Jared came up in conversation. She broached the topic directly one day as they sat outside enjoying the midmorning sun. "What's going on with you and Jared anyway?"

"Nothing. We're friends."

A sly twinkle appeared in Aubreigh's eyes. "You've been spending a lot of time with him. Every time I see you two together, I can tell he likes you."

"No he doesn't," Zira insisted, but she couldn't help the smile that tugged at her lips.

"Ah, see?" Aubreigh pointed to Zira's face. "You get that look every time you talk about him."

"You're imagining things." Zira turned her head and pretended to be fascinated by the ladybug crawling across their bench.

"Fine," Aubreigh said. "You might not realize it yet, but you like him. I've known you too long; I can read you like a book."

This time, Zira didn't even bother denying it. She liked Jared as a friend, and considering how short her list of friends was, that was saying something. But maybe it was more than that. She had to admit to herself that she'd been pleased when Aubreigh suggested Jared might have feelings for her.

"When you finally figure out that I'm right," Aubreigh said, "you should talk to him. Don't start avoiding him like you did with the last guy we thought you liked."

"*You* thought I liked," Zira corrected her. "And I stopped talking to him because he was a jerk."

"Well, Jared doesn't seem like a jerk. You two are cute together—"

"You've barely even seen us together."

"—and if you mess this up for yourself, so help me, I will kill you."

Zira raised her eyebrows. "It's like that, then?"

"Yes, it is. Seriously though, just think about it. I've never seen you like this before. You're happy. Not that you weren't before, but this is different. I like it."

Zira nodded. "Yeah, all right."

To her credit, she did put a lot of thought into what Aubreigh had said. There were a few times when she even believed there might be some truth to it. On occasion, she thought she caught Jared looking at her with something more than friendly affection in his eyes. But that was the problem; they were friends. No matter what else Zira might have felt for him, she valued his friendship above all else. Even just talking about something more than that might change the rapport between them, and she didn't want to jeopardize that. She decided not to do or say anything. Not yet, at least. Not until she had a better idea of what she was actually feeling.

Seth did not approach Zira again until the final day of the internal investigation. The E-1s were packing up and leaving in droves, but Seth had apparently chosen to stay behind until the last possible moment. He approached their table at lunch that day, and Aubreigh greeted him like he was an old friend. "Hey Seth! Have a seat—here." She scooted to one side to make room for him. "Guys, this is Seth. We worked together a little bit in the South Atlantic Region."

"We've met," said Zira.

Aubreigh's eyes darted between Seth, Zira, and Jared. The smile fell from her face as she sensed the tension between them. "Actually," said Seth, turning to Zira, "I was hoping to catch you before I left. Could you spare a few moments to answer some more questions?"

"I'm eating," Zira said. "Can it wait?"

"It won't take long."

Jared looked like he was about to say something, but Zira put a hand on his arm and stood up from the table. "I'll be right back," she said, then followed Seth to a more secluded area in the cafeteria.

"Sorry to interrupt your meal," Seth said, raising his arm to examine something on his CyberLink. His fingers darted across the screen in a sort of calculated dance. "This will only take a few minutes."

Zira folded her arms. "No problem."

Seth brought up a holographic display over his CL and held it out to Zira. Her stomach dropped when she recognized the face of Arion Dreyfus, the successful businessman and drug lord she'd assassinated over a month ago. How Seth had managed to find out about it— and how he'd managed to connect her with Dreyfus— Zira had no idea. She tried to conceal just how much it unnerved her as she stared at the three-dimensional projection of Dreyfus' face hovering there above his arm.

Seth looked at her with an intent expression, eyes narrowed and flitting across her face as if waiting for some sign that she knew what this was. She wasn't going to give him the satisfaction. She raised an eyebrow—a question.

"You know who he is," Seth said.

Still unsure of just how much Seth thought he knew, Zira decided it was best not to play dumb. "Arion Dreyfus, former CEO of Dreyfus Pharmaceuticals."

"Former," Seth emphasized. "He was killed several weeks ago."

"I know." Dreyfus' death had been on the news, if only for a short time, so it would have been pointless to pretend she was surprised by his passing.

Seth's eyes narrowed even further. "He also ran a pretty big drug smuggling operation."

"Really?" Zira said. "Well then why hadn't your people caught him and put him in a labor camp where he belonged?" She knew she shouldn't provoke him, but she couldn't resist the jab. It was often E-1's worst unresolved cases that Ryku drew on when giving assignments; E-2 operatives did the dirty work when the E-1s hit a dead end.

Seth lifted his chin and clenched a fist. "We tried— we just couldn't find the evidence. If the jury hadn't been so afraid of him…" He straightened, seeming to regain composure as he set his mouth in a long, thin line. He tapped the screen of his CL again. Dreyfus' face was replaced with footage from a security camera at the airport in Amarillo. Zira recognized herself striding across the camera's view. "That's you," Seth said.

"Obviously."

"You got on a plane to Los Angeles."

"And?"

"Dreyfus was murdered at his home just outside LA."

Zira said nothing, her expression deadpan as she waited for Seth to continue. Let him come out and say what he was thinking; she wasn't going to incriminate herself.

"What were you doing there?"

"I was on an assignment."

"Right. And what was the nature of your assignment?"

"I told you before. If you have questions about my file or my assignments, you'll have to talk to Ryku."

The holographic interface vanished as Seth lowered his arm. "I think you had something to do with Dreyfus' death," he said.

"What, just because we were in the same city at the same time? It's a big city, and that's a big conclusion to jump to."

Seth pursed his lips. "So young and new, but you're already just like the rest of them. You think you can bypass the law because you're only taking out the trash. And to hell with anyone who tries to tell you you're wrong."

Before Zira could respond, Seth turned and walked away.

Zira returned to her table and sat down beside Jared. Though she did her best to maintain an expression of neutrality, Aubreigh—of course—sensed that something was wrong. "You okay?" she asked.

"Fine." Zira's voice was a little harsher than she'd intended, but she was irritated at Aubreigh for having welcomed the enemy with open arms, even if it had been unintentional. She pointedly avoided looking at her friend's hurt expression and speared her wilted green beans with her fork. "That guy is way too clever for his own good."

"Meaning what?" Jared said.

Zira glanced between the two of them. As much as she wanted to tell Jared what Seth had shown her, she couldn't discuss it now. Not in front of Aubreigh. "He just knows things he shouldn't."

Across the table, Aubreigh frowned. "Isn't that the whole point of this investigation? They're supposed to find out what the other units are hiding. Maybe if E-2 wasn't so secretive—"

Zira rolled her eyes. It always came back to the same argument. "We've been over this."

"Yes, but your unit makes it *really* hard for the rest of us to trust you when you won't tell us anything about what you're doing. We're all in this together, right? We all want the same thing. So why all the secrets?"

"It's a necessary part of our work."

Aubreigh let out a cold, humorless chuckle. "Well that's convenient, isn't it? You're hiding something, but it's *necessary,* so I guess that makes it okay?"

"Yeah, it does," Zira said.

"That's a really shady excuse, you know that?"

No matter how many times they'd had this conversation, Aubreigh still didn't get it. "You don't know what you're talking about."

"No, I don't. Because my *best friend* won't tell me anything that really matters."

The words cut Zira deeper than she'd expected. "I can't—you know that! And I think it's ridiculous of you to keep bringing it up."

"Yeah?" Aubreigh seized her tray and stood up. "Well I think it's ridiculous that we've been friends this long when you won't even talk to me."

Zira dug her fingers into her knees under the table as she watched Aubreigh storm off, then noticed Jared sitting beside her as if he'd just appeared. He was arranging the silverware on his empty tray and looking supremely uncomfortable. Zira shook her head and pushed her own tray aside, no longer hungry. "Sorry about that," she said. "She's always been curious about what I do."

Jared nodded. "She probably knows more than you think she does. Most of them do. Or they guess, at least. Aubreigh's smart. I'm sure she's put some of the pieces together by now."

"So why make such a big deal out of it if she already knows?" Zira asked, but even as Jared shrugged in response, she thought she knew the answer. Aubreigh wanted to hear it from Zira herself. They'd known each other since before they were old enough to remember and had been inseparable until the Project placed them in different units. Since then, the different colored bands around their arms had put a small rift between them, but they were still best friends. Aubreigh likely took Zira's refusal to confide in her as a personal insult.

When they were done eating, Jared and Zira walked outside together. It was their last day working with the recruits and they were headed to the shooting range. As they carried weapons from the training center to the truck, Zira told him about Dreyfus and Seth's suspicion that Zira had something to do with his death.

"Like I told you before," Jared said, "you shouldn't worry about it too much."

"But why is he looking into Dreyfus specifically?"

Jared shrugged. "I don't know, but I don't think anything's going to come of it. He's just making guesses. Seriously, Zira—stop worrying about Seth. He'll be gone by the end of the day anyway."

That, at least, was something to look forward to.

■ ■ ■

Once they'd returned from the shooting range, Zira accompanied Jared back to his apartment. Ryku had sent out new assignments today and she wanted to see if they'd received one. Jared unlocked the door and swung it wide. An unmarked folder lay on the floor. Zira snatched it up before he could and threw herself on his couch. He sat down beside her, so close that their arms brushed as Zira opened the file. Warmth fluttered across her skin where they'd touched.

She pulled an unusually thick stack of papers from the file. The top ones were photos, and she spread them out on the table in front of them. There were nine portraits of nine different people, the kind local law enforcement often took to put in their criminal databases. There were also several pictures that showed a large building from multiple angles and what appeared to be the same people going in and out. "Are they all targets?" Zira asked, glancing through the rest of the papers in her hands.

Jared leaned over so he could read the pages, too. "It looks that way," he said. "They're radicals."

She'd learned about the people the Project called radicals during her training. Their specific motives varied individually, but they all seemed to believe that the PEACE Project was too controlling or otherwise unjust. In the worst cases, they started riots and attempted to take up arms against the Project; thankfully, units P and E-1 always managed to shut them down before they got out of hand. Most of them simply attempted to get off the Project's grid, either defecting to other countries or just hiding out somewhere in America beyond the Project's reach. The nine radicals in their mission file appeared to be doing just that, having taken refuge in an abandoned factory that was dangerously close to a nuclear fallout zone.

"Why not just have E-1 arrest them and send them to a labor camp or something?" she asked.

"They already have. Look here." Jared pulled out one of the papers in Zira's hands. "Six of these people have been arrested for protesting before and managed to escape the labor camps. They're also smuggling weapons out of that old factory, so they're either planning some kind of uprising or trading the weapons to criminals. Either way, we can't allow it."

"So they're armed," Zira said. "And there are nine of them. This isn't going to be easy."

"They're also untrained and inexperienced. We'll be fine. I've still got your back."

They looked through the remainder of the file, discussed their options, and carefully studied the layout of the factory. Outside, dusk turned to night as the hours passed by. They'd missed dinner, which had ended hours ago, and Jared got up to get them something to drink.

Zira stretched out on the couch, looking at the photos of their targets one by one. Her eyelids drooped and the faces began to blur together. She should go home soon. She should have gone home a long time ago, but the couch was so comfortable. Just a few more minutes. Then she'd say goodnight to Jared, go home, and go to bed. She continued to flip through the photos.

Moments later, she drifted off to sleep.

CHAPTER 8

JARED WATCHED THE SLEEPING GIRL on his couch with a smile as he tied his shoelaces. She looked so peaceful there in the morning sunlight, just as she had last night. He hadn't wanted to wake her and had instead lifted her feet onto the couch and draped a blanket over her shoulders before retiring to his own bed. Now, he shook her shoulder gently. "Zira, wake up."

Her eyes fluttered open and her eyebrows drew together in confusion for a moment as she glanced around at her surroundings. Finally, her gaze settled on his face. "Sorry," she said. "I didn't mean to fall asleep here."

"It's all right. I didn't want to wake you. You looked comfortable."

She yawned, sat up, and stretched her arms. "I was. Your couch is fantastic."

"It's the same as yours."

"Yeah, but this one is better."

He chuckled. "Let's go eat. I'm starving."

"Sure. Just let me use your bathroom real quick."

She came out looking less disheveled than before and they walked outside. "Did we ever figure out when we want to leave?" Zira asked.

She was talking about the assignment. "We can leave

whenever you want," Jared said. "We're driving, so there's no flight schedule to worry about."

"I think I just want a couple days to practice with the grenades," said Zira. "I've never had to use them before."

They'd decided that infiltrating the building from two separate entry points would be their best option, but they were still outnumbered, even if their opponents were untrained. Each of them planned to carry a few stun and smoke grenades to give them an extra advantage over the radicals. "Sure," he said. "We can run some simulations after breakfast, if you want."

Aubreigh sat with another group of friends in the cafeteria that morning, though if Zira noticed—and Jared was sure she did—she pretended not to care. After that, they spent most of the day running hologram simulations in the E-2 training facility. They did the same thing the day after, and the following night, Zira said she felt like she was ready. They decided to leave the next morning.

After loading all of their equipment into the car, they started driving. Their destination was a remote ghost town called Medvale on the eastern side of the South Central Region, another forgotten victim of the war. When both sides started using robots to do the fighting, things had gotten ugly for civilians. Bots were supposed to be able to distinguish soldiers from ordinary citizens, but they'd never been particularly good at it. Most of Medvale's population had been employed at a nearby computer parts factory that had been converted to manufacture weapons for the military during the war. The RA had sent in the bots to destroy the factory, but they'd taken out the rest of the town in the process. Now, it was just another ruin, as bleak as the landscape that surrounded it.

It was late in the afternoon when they arrived, and they wanted to wait until dark to fly a drone over the factory for surveillance. The information from their mission file was less than a week old and showed two months' worth of fairly consistent behavior, but Jared still thought it would be a good idea to get a quick look at the area before moving in. Surveilling the place themselves, however, would only give the radicals an unnecessary opportunity to find out he and Zira were there, and with so many armed hostiles inside, they needed to catch their targets off guard. They didn't dare go near the building until it was time to strike, so the drone was a good solution. Get in, do the job as efficiently as possible, and get out. That was their objective here.

They found a creaky old house with a garage that had been left open and parked the car inside. "We should try to get some rest while we wait," Jared suggested. There were still several hours until dark.

"You go ahead," said Zira. "I'll keep an eye on things and wake you up when it's time."

Jared agreed and leaned back in his seat. The car was cramped, especially for a person his size, but he'd learned to be comfortable just about anywhere and fell asleep in minutes. When he woke up, night had fallen. He looked around for Zira and saw her out the rear window, sitting on the trunk of the car with the drone controller in her hands. Jared glanced at his CL for the time. 8:47 P.M. He rubbed his face and got out of the car.

"You didn't wake me up," he said, jumping up on the trunk to sit beside Zira. He tried to find the drone in the night sky, but couldn't see it anywhere.

"I was going to. Just wanted to set this thing up first." She studied the video on the controller for a few more seconds, then brought the drone down to rest on the ground in front of them. She passed him the controller. "You want to do the honors?"

"Sure." He lifted the drone into the air again and sent it towards the factory. A shadowed landscape flew by beneath the drone as it passed over crumbling houses and old, rusted cars.

Zira scooted closer to him to see the video feed better. "You ever been on an assignment with this many targets?" she asked.

"Just when we were in the RA going after Feng and the rest of the Brotherhood."

"Oh." She glanced up at him. "Sorry—I didn't mean to bring it up."

"No, it's fine. I was nervous, even though we had better odds there. There were four of us and only ten of them."

Zira huffed. "Nice of Ryku to give us a little reinforcement here, huh?"

Jared smiled. "That's all right. I like it better with just the two of us."

He wasn't sure if she knew he was talking about more than just the assignment. She didn't say anything in response, and in the dark it was hard to read her expression. There was more he wanted to say, but now was not the time. Later, perhaps, when this was all over and she wasn't so distracted. He tried to project confidence and give her whatever reassurance he could, but this was a dangerous situation, and they both needed to stay focused.

Once the drone reached the factory, Jared took it around the perimeter a few times, then moved in closer to get a better look. There was nothing out of the ordinary. Two armed men guarded the front and back entrances, but that information had been in their mission file. He flew the drone around a few more times, just to be sure they weren't missing anything, then set its autopilot to return it to their position.

"You ready to go?" he asked Zira.

She nodded. They slid off the car, opened the trunk, and suited up for the operation. They'd borrowed some body armor from the unit P officer's armory, which was heavier and offered more protection than their standard, more lightweight garb. Each of them carried an assault rifle, a handgun, stun grenades, smoke grenades, and an assortment of knives tucked into various parts of their gear. Overkill, perhaps, but it was better to be safe than dead.

Each of them wore an earpiece as well, which was connected to their CLs and would allow them to communicate with each other throughout the mission. Jared switched his on and tested it. "Can you hear me?" he whispered.

"Yeah. You?" Zira's voice echoed in his ear.

"Got it. Let's move."

The factory was three miles north of where they were parked, and they set off at a steady jog through the derelict town. They split up about two hundred yards from the front entrance. "Don't shoot until you have to," said Jared. They needed stealth and surprise on their side for as long as possible. "See you when it's over."

Zira nodded and waved over her shoulder as she made her way to the door at the back of the building. Jared continued until he reached a sign bearing the factory's name and crouched behind it. He raised his rifle and looked through the scope. A man with a shotgun walked from one corner of the building to the next, crossing in front of the main entrance. His shoulders slumped and his feet shuffled from boredom, fatigue, or both.

Jared waited until the man's back was turned, then ran. By the time the man tensed at the sound of footsteps behind him, it was too late. Jared locked one arm around his neck and squeezed. The man thrashed, but Jared was significantly bigger and stronger. He lifted his arm, drew a knife across the man's throat, and laid the body on the ground. "One down," he said to Zira.

"Same here," came her reply. "I'm going in now."

Jared moved to the door and pushed it open. There were a few dim lights along the base of the wall, but they didn't offer as much visibility as the moon and stars had. He slipped in and shut the door, then waited a few minutes for his eyes to adjust to the dark. The factory was silent, and Jared could hear his own footfalls as he moved down the hall. He checked a few offices as he passed, but there was no one inside.

A burst of gunshots rang out from somewhere deeper inside the building and echoed in his ear. "Zira?" he hissed.

"Sorry—one of them jumped me over here, caught me off guard."

"It's fine. Keep your eyes open. The rest of them are probably on their way to check out the noise."

He heard muffled voices ahead and flattened himself against the wall. The voices came closer. He chanced a quick glance around the corner. One of the radicals spotted him, yelled to her companion, and began shooting.

Jared drew himself back behind cover and tossed a stun grenade. He took advantage of his targets' disorientation to take them both down, then proceeded down the hall.

"How you doing over there Zira?" he asked.

There was no response. He looked at his CyberLink, which showed that his communication line with her was still open and active. He tried again. "Zira, how are things looking where you're at?"

Still no answer. The factory had gone dead quiet again. "Zira, answer me."

Someone screamed—a woman's voice. The sound was abruptly cut off by another brief exchange of gunfire.

Something in Jared's chest constricted. His feet flew over the floor in long strides as he headed to the area she should be in. "Zira!" He didn't care who heard him now as long as he found her. "Zira!" Stepping over two more bodies, he entered a large room filled with boxes and conveyer belts.

He'd almost reached the door on the other side when it opened. He raised his gun, ready to shoot the hostile the instant he saw their face. But it wasn't one of their targets.

Jared's lungs filled with a rush of air and his heart settled into a normal rhythm as Zira stepped through the doorway. She had a hand pressed over one eye and there was blood oozing into her hair, but she was alive. "We got them all, didn't we?" she asked.

Jared tried to tamp down some of the residual panic in his voice. "I think so. How many for you?"

"Four."

He tensed and began to raise his gun again. "I only got three."

She seemed unconcerned and motioned to the two bodies he'd stepped over earlier. "Yeah, but those two came around the corner and shot each other before they even knew what they were aiming at."

Jared shook his head; this was exactly why people had no business handling guns unless they had the proper training. "That's all of them then. Why didn't you answer me when I called?"

"I was trying to hide from a couple of them back there," said Zira. "It wasn't exactly a good time to chat."

"Sorry. Just...you were unresponsive. I thought something might have happened to you."

She tilted her head to one side and frowned. "I can take care of myself."

"I know." He wanted to embrace her and tell her how relieved he'd been to see that she was okay, but he doubted she would appreciate the gesture right now. He pointed to her injury. "We should go clean that up."

"What about them?"

"We'll come back and bury them later."

She nodded, and he led her back outside the same way he'd come in.

CHAPTER 9

As THEY WALKED TOGETHER UNDER the dim starlight, Zira thought about what Jared had said inside the factory. He hadn't meant to be condescending when he'd said he thought she was in trouble—she knew that. He'd been genuinely concerned, and she shouldn't have taken offense. *Defensive* was her automatic response to unfamiliar situations, and she was so unaccustomed to anyone besides Aubreigh truly caring about her that it caught her off guard when Jared had been so alarmed.

She glanced over at him now, tall and straight as he walked beside her. A familiar tingling sensation twirled in her stomach—the one that sometimes told her to reach out and take Jared's hand while also terrifying her enough that she didn't dare do so. They hadn't said anything to each other since leaving the factory. Not that the silence was uncomfortable, by any means. That was one of the things she liked about being with him; there was never any pressure to force a discussion. Their conversations were relaxed and effortless, but so were their silences.

They reached the house where they'd parked the car. Jared popped the trunk and rummaged around for a first aid kit and some water while Zira opened the car door and sat with her legs hanging out the side. He knelt on the ground in front of her and opened a bottle of water. "Let's see," he said.

Zira removed her hand, sticky with blood, and let him look at the deep gash above her eye. He wet a cloth from the first aid kit and began to dab away some of the mess. She winced. "That's cold."

"Sorry." He kept working. "How did this happen, anyway?"

"I got in a little scuffle with one of the guys in there. I won, but he smashed his rifle into my face."

"You're going to have a black eye."

Zira shrugged. "Won't be the first."

His brows knit together in concentration as he studied the cut under the light from the car's interior. This close, Zira could see every angle and curve of his face. Strong jaw, full lips, eyes like a warm autumn day. He took some ointment from the first aid kit and put a drop on his finger. His palm was rough and calloused, but his touch was gentle as it moved across her face. He finished applying the ointment and used a few strips of tape to hold the edges of the cut together. "There," he said. "Good as new."

She smiled at him. "Thanks." The word came out in a whisper as she tried to still the fluttering in her stomach.

He looked at her for a few seconds, then took her hand casually, as if he'd done it a hundred times before. Zira's heart missed a beat as he pulled her up. Her feet seemed to move of their own accord, taking another step towards him so that their bodies were mere centimeters apart.

Their fingers intertwined. Zira let out a shaky breath and tilted her head to look up at him. With his free hand, Jared brushed the hair away from her eyes, then bent and pressed his lips against hers.

The kiss was soft and almost timid at first, but became more fervent when she didn't shy away from him. Zira hadn't realized until now how much she'd longed for this moment, and when Jared pulled back, it was almost too soon. She wanted to kiss him again, but her head was spinning so much already she wasn't sure that would be wise.

Then again, she reasoned, recklessness was more her nature than good sense. She reached a hand to Jared's face, drawing him close once more, and kissed him again. A euphoric, dizzy sort of feeling filled her, lingering even after their lips parted. They wrapped their arms around each other and Zira leaned her head against his chest, content to let the world keep turning around them for just a little longer.

■ ■ ■

They slept in the car the rest of the night, and in the morning, went back to the factory to bury their targets' bodies and clear out whatever weapons were inside. They found a dozen guns in addition to the ones the radicals had been carrying, three old military bots in various stages of repair, and two blocky pre-war computers that somehow seemed to still be functional. They loaded all of this into the trunk of the car to bring back to the compound and began the long drive home that afternoon.

As they drove, Zira thought about what had happened the previous night. She was starting to regret the kiss. Not so much the kiss itself, but what it meant. They hadn't talked about it, but things had clearly changed between them. She looked down at Jared's hand on her knee and her own hand on top of his as he told a funny story about his childhood. This was what she had wanted, but it terrified her. She didn't know what came next and hated to think of what might happen if things ended badly between them. By the time they got back to the compound, she felt so conflicted about the whole thing that she turned her cheek when Jared tried to kiss her goodnight and bolted into her apartment at the first opportunity.

The next morning, she went to see the only person she knew who could help. As she walked to Aubreigh's apartment, she spotted two of the people she least wanted to run into right now—or anytime, for that matter. She didn't know much about the young man except that his name was Lucas, but his partner, Cecilia, was an old enemy. She quickened her pace and kept her head down, hoping they wouldn't pay her any attention.

"Oh look," said Cecilia as Zira approached. She made a face as if she'd just smelled something awful. "It's the little runt."

Zira cursed under her breath and kept walking. When both of them had still been young enough to be in elementary training together, Cecilia had often bullied Zira and convinced other children to join in. Since then, she'd always done her best to avoid the older girl. She tried to sidestep the pair, but Cecilia stepped in front of her. "Excuse me," said Zira.

"Hold on a minute," said Cecilia. "It's been a while. How's life treating you?"

"Fine." Zira had learned a long time ago that it was best to participate in the conversation as minimally as possible; Cecilia would lose interest eventually.

"Fine? You get partnered with the best operative in our unit, and all you have to say is *fine?*"

"What did you have to do to pull that off?" Lucas asked with a lewd wink. Zira shot him a glare.

Cecilia shrugged. "It makes sense, I guess. Ryku puts the strongest, most skilled operative with the smallest and weakest to even things out a little bit. It's just such a shame you have to drag Jared down with you. Do you even do any of the work, or do you just stand back and watch while he takes out all of your targets?

"You got any new lines?" said Zira. "I think everyone knows I'm small already."

Cecilia tossed her long, black hair over her shoulder and gave Zira a cold smile. "You just tell Jared to come talk to me when he gets tired of picking up your slack. I've got a few good ideas on how he could get rid of you."

Zira didn't let herself rise to the bait. Cecilia had been saying the same things for years now; it was nothing Zira didn't know about herself already. Yes, she was small, and yes, her partnership with Jared was perhaps a little unbalanced. But she'd worked hard to earn her place in this unit, and she deserved to wear that black band around her arm just as much as Cecilia. She stepped past the two of them and ignored their snickers behind her as she walked away.

A few minutes later, she knocked on Aubreigh's door. There was no answer. "Come on, Aubreigh." She knocked again. "I know you're still mad at me, but I need your help."

The door swung open. Aubreigh stood in the entrance, half-ready for the day in a ruffled blouse and pajama pants. She'd piled her long brown hair on top of her head in a messy knot and clutched a toothbrush in one hand. If it weren't for the fierce expression on her face, Zira might have laughed. Aubreigh took great pride in her appearance and always looked so put-together, so it was unusual to see her in this disheveled state.

"Well?" Aubreigh said. The fact that she didn't even comment on the cut and ugly bruise over Zira's eye was a testament to how angry she still was. Or at least, how angry she was trying to be; Zira had never known Aubreigh to remain upset about anything for very long.

"I need to talk to you." Without waiting for an invitation, Zira ducked under Aubreigh's arm and walked into the apartment.

"Just come right on in then," she grumbled as she turned around and shut the door behind them. "If this is about our argument the other day—"

"It's not."

"Then what?"

"It's about Jared."

The anger retreated from Aubreigh's eyes a little. She crossed her arms, waiting for Zira to continue.

Zira turned her attention to a colorful poster above Aubreigh's couch. "We kissed."

She could just make out her friend's face in her peripherals. Aubreigh was trying hard to contain some sort of joyous outburst. She settled for raising herself up on her toes instead of leaping into the air and beamed at Zira as if she'd just been handed a basket of puppies. "I knew it," she said. "I knew you two were perfect for each other."

Zira resisted the urge to roll her eyes. "I'm glad you're excited about it."

"Oh, please. Don't tell me *you're* not."

Zira shrugged and shook her head. "I don't know what to think."

"But you like him."

"I do. But we were friends, and now—I don't know. I don't know what happens next."

"What do you want to happen next?"

Zira sighed. "I just don't want to mess this up."

"So talk to him."

"And say what?"

"Just tell him how you feel. And don't look at me like that. The only way this works is if you talk to each other." She pulled a pair of pants from where they'd been hanging over a chair and walked into the bathroom to finish brushing her teeth. As if anticipating Zira's next question, she shouted an afterthought through the door. "And I can't tell you exactly what to say, so don't ask. You'll have to figure it out yourself."

Zira slumped onto the couch. Aubreigh was right, as she always was about these things, but the idea of discussing this with Jared made Zira want to lock herself in her apartment and never face the light of day again. How was she supposed to talk about her feelings when she couldn't even sort them out herself?

Aubreigh emerged from the bathroom fully dressed, looking much more herself with her hair and makeup done. She sat on the couch next to Zira. "Now that we've sorted that out, are we going to talk about our argument, or are we just going to pretend it never happened?"

"Is that an option?" Zira asked, hopeful.

"No. You owe me an apology."

"And you owe me one."

"Fine. We're both sorry. But seriously, Zira, I wish you would just talk to me."

"I can't."

"I know. And I also know that whatever it is you do in E-2, it's dangerous. Violent, even."

"Violent?" Zira crossed her arms. Aubreigh was uncomfortably close to the truth.

"You show up here with your face looking like *that* right after an assignment, and you want to argue with me that your job isn't violent? I'm not stupid, Zira. Everyone knows the E-2s spend more time at the shooting range than the rest of us combined. You're not law enforcement, and you're not working with unit P to protect us from some hostile foreign invasion or something. Everything you guys do is a big secret. I'm just guessing, but I think you're all spies or assassins or something. And please don't tell me how crazy that sounds, because I know it does. But I'm right, aren't I?"

A weight dropped into the pit of Zira's stomach. "You're not completely wrong."

Aubreigh studied her face for a few moments. "Look, whatever it is, I don't care. I'm just worried about you. You've changed since you got back from your first assignment."

"Of course I have," Zira said. "So did you. So does anyone in the Project. That first assignment is what makes you a real part of all this, isn't it? It changes all of us."

"You know that's not what I'm talking about."

Zira looked away. Yes, she did know, but she didn't even want to think about her first assignment. Her target had been involved in human trafficking, and although she'd known he deserved to die, killing him had taken a toll on her. That night, she had crossed a line somewhere between innocent girl and cold-blooded killer. A person couldn't go back from something like that. Since then, she'd become even more withdrawn from those around her, putting on a cool facade to mask how difficult it had been to come to terms with her new identity.

"If you already guessed what it is I do," Zira said, "why did you get so upset the other day?"

"Because of what you said about Seth and his investigation. I know you don't like him and it seemed unfair that he focused all of his attention on you. But it's good that they investigate everything, isn't it?"

"It's a waste of time. We're all just doing our jobs; that should be good enough for everyone."

"Yes, but what if it's not?"

"Meaning what?"

Aubreigh began playing with the hem of her shirt, an old habit she fell into when she was nervous or uncomfortable. "Lately, I've been wondering if some of the things we're doing here are wrong."

"Wrong how?"

"Maybe we take things too far. Overstep our boundaries."

"What are you talking about?"

"The training I've had to do for my new job in population control has been...very eye-opening." Aubreigh's brows drew together. "Look, you can't say anything about this. Not to Jared, not to anyone. I'm not supposed to talk about it."

"Then maybe you shouldn't be telling me."

"No. I need to."

Zira balked a little at the idea of learning things she had no business knowing, but curiosity and concern for her friend outweighed her misgivings. "Fine. What is it?"

"For starters, they lied to us about where we came from."

Zira frowned as she considered the implications of this. Almost everyone in the Project had been brought to the compound as infants, taken from families who didn't want them or couldn't care for them. At least, that's what they had always been told. There were exceptions among the older members who had joined the Project when it was first organized, but for a majority of the people who worked here, this life was the only one they had ever known. If all of that was a lie, as Aubreigh was suggesting, then what was the truth?

"Most of us came from loving families who would have kept us if they could," Aubreigh continued. "We weren't abandoned or unwanted. They took us from our parents as infants because we were third children."

"There are no third children," Zira said. "Doesn't your unit make sure of that? You have mandatory birth control, abortions if necessary."

"Not everyone follows the rules. Accidents happen, people refuse to get an abortion, and sometimes third children are born. Like you, like me, like everyone who was brought here after the Project was founded. Instead of just killing us, they adopted us out to people who couldn't have kids or brought us here to put us to good use. Who else would agree to spend their entire lives inside these walls?" There was a bitter note to her voice that Zira had seldom heard before. "They get us when we're young and teach us that this is our family and our purpose in life. That's why the Project works. That's why we're all so dedicated to it. Even if they told us the truth, there's nothing else out there for us."

"That doesn't change anything," Zira said. "It's not like we can go back to our old families now. And we have a good life here. We'd be a lot worse off if we had stayed in a family where there weren't enough resources to go around."

"But what about those families? Can you imagine it? You have a baby, and then some stranger comes to your door to take her from you." Her mouth curved down in a grimace. "That's what they expect me to do now. That's my job."

"Those people broke the law. They have to face the consequences."

"Is that how you justify doing *your* job?" Aubreigh snapped.

"I don't have to justify my job. Not to you, not to Seth, or to anyone else."

Aubreigh's anger shattered in an instant, and she turned away in an attempt to hide the tears welling up in her eyes. Zira cursed under her breath. The reveal about third-children was hardly surprising and seemed to be a natural consequence for families who decided to have an extra child. There had to be something else going on or Aubreigh wouldn't be this upset. "What's really wrong?"

"I'm sorry." Aubreigh wiped her cheek with her palm. "I just don't know how they expect us to—" She dissolved in a new round of tears and buried her face in her hands.

Zira wrapped an arm around her friend's shoulder and gave her an awkward squeeze. They sat like that for what felt like forever, Zira trying to comfort Aubreigh as best as she knew how until the crying subsided.

"Sorry," Aubreigh said again when she had composed herself enough to speak. "It's just—sometimes, a woman ends up with a fourth child." Her voice had dropped to a whisper, as if she was afraid to even speak her next words. "When that happens, we're supposed to—to euthanize the baby."

Now Zira understood what Aubreigh had meant when she'd suggested that the Project sometimes overstepped its boundaries. Her chest felt hollow, but she kept her face calm, knowing that a stronger reaction would only make Aubreigh feel worse than she already did. "That never happens though, right?" she said. "I doubt you'll ever be put in that situation. I mean, third children are almost never even conceived, and if they are, you guys make sure the mother gets an abortion. Fourth children must be even more rare; there probably haven't been any for a really long time."

"It's happened a handful of times." Aubreigh wiped the moisture away from her eyes and seemed just a little less despondent. "But you're probably right. The chances that I'll ever have to deal with that are slim. Knowing that it's even in our policies, though—I guess I just understand why the E-1s do their investigations."

"They don't know, do they?"

Aubreigh shook her head. "It's a closely guarded secret. I didn't even know until I got assigned to population control. Zira, you *can't* tell anyone."

"I know," Zira reassured her. "I won't. Promise."

■ ■ ■

Later that afternoon, Zira worked up the nerve to go to Jared's apartment. He looked somewhat surprised to see her when he answered the door. "I was starting to think you were avoiding me."

"Maybe just a little," she admitted. "Can we talk?"

"Sure. Want to take a walk?"

Zira nodded and he stepped outside. She took his hand as they walked, drawing resolve and comfort from the feel of his fingers entwined in hers. She still wasn't sure that any of this was a good idea, and maybe she'd regret it later, but it just felt so easy and right in the moment. She had worried that the kiss would change their friendship, and it had, but it seemed to have added something rather than taking anything away.

They walked in silence for a full five minutes before Jared said anything. "You're making me nervous. What's going on?"

Zira chewed her lip, not quite knowing where to begin. "I like you," she said at last.

She could hear the smile in his voice. "I know. I like you, too. That's why I kissed you."

He was altogether too pleased with himself, and Zira sighed in exasperation. "No, this is bad. We were friends. I liked that. And now we're—" She stopped herself there as warmth rushed from her fingertips to her face. She'd always made it a point to avoid discussing her feelings so openly and cringed a little at every word now coming out of her mouth.

"Zira," Jared said gently, "we're still friends."

"No. We're—more than friends, now."

"Why can't we be both?"

"Both—what?"

Jared shrugged. "Why can't we be friends and something more?"

"Because it makes everything so complicated. And you're a really great friend." One of the best she'd ever had, actually. She looked up at him. "I don't want to ruin that."

Jared let go of her hand and put his arm around her shoulder. "I know. I'm scared of that, too. If I wasn't, I would have kissed you weeks ago. But I can't just pretend I don't have feelings for you."

Zira felt her resistance fading. That was the heart of the matter, wasn't it? She had those same feelings for him, too, and denying them wasn't going to make them go away. She'd tried that already.

"Look," Jared said, "I get that you have doubts and questions or whatever. That's good, actually. It means you've thought about this. Whatever you need from me, just let me know. I'm here. I'm not going anywhere unless you want me to."

Zira searched his eyes and saw only honesty and sincerity. She nodded and leaned her head against his arm. "Okay. But let's just take things slow, please. I don't want to put any stupid labels on whatever this is. Not yet. Aubreigh's already way too excited about all of this."

Jared chuckled. "Sure. Whatever you're comfortable with. But we are going to have to tell Chairman Ryku and fill out the paperwork with unit C."

Zira groaned. She'd forgotten about that part. Sexual and romantic relationships were allowed between members of the Project under a full disclosure policy, which meant the parties involved were required to tell their chairman and document the relationship with unit C. The relationship was then evaluated to ensure that it wouldn't create a conflict with their professional work or the Project's interests. Zira already saw a potential issue with the fact that she and Jared were partners and suspected chairman Ryku might disapprove. She sighed. "Let's get it over with, then."

They filled out the required documents in unit C's main office the next day, where Aubreigh spotted them holding hands. She talked to them for a few minutes and, as Zira had predicted, seemed barely able to contain her delight. Thankfully, she managed to keep the tone and volume of her voice at a socially-acceptable level. Zira exchanged a knowing glance with Jared, but he seemed more amused than annoyed by Aubreigh's excitement.

Chairman Ryku was much less enthusiastic. He stood with crossed arms and a flat expression as they explained the situation to him. Or rather, Jared explained while Zira stared at a scuff on her boot and wished she was somewhere else. "I won't say I'm not disappointed," Ryku said when Jared had finished. "Still, I appreciate your candor. I'm going to have to assign both of you to different partners, but that will take time. For now, you'll each be running solo missions."

It was no worse than Zira had expected, but her shoulders slumped a little at Ryku's words. She'd learned a lot from Jared in just two missions and enjoyed working with him. In some ways, it seemed a shame to throw that away just so they could have a more personal relationship.

Jared must have sensed her disappointment. "You all right?" he asked as they walked back outside.

"Everything's just changing so fast."

"I know. I'm sorry about all that."

"It's not your fault." It wasn't just the uncomfortable discussion about their relationship and all that had come after that had her preoccupied. She was still thinking about her conversation with Aubreigh the previous day. She had told Aubreigh that it didn't matter where they came from, and that was true enough. But combined with the revelation that fourth children were euthanized and the fact that unit E-1's investigations might be more warranted than she'd originally thought, it was a lot to take in all at once. Her clear, black-and-white views on the Project and its objectives had blurred, and she wasn't sure yet whether that change was for better or worse.

CHAPTER 10

TO JARED'S GREAT RELIEF, WHATEVER skittishness he had sensed in Zira about the whole affair of committing their relationship to paper seemed to fade over the next few days. It helped that Aubreigh gave them her full support. Despite Zira's outward indifference about what other people thought, he knew how much she valued her friend's opinion. Jared pulled Aubreigh aside to thank her privately one afternoon after lunch. "I didn't really do anything," she replied.

"I know she was scared. She never would have given me a chance if you hadn't talked to her."

Aubreigh shrugged. "She doesn't like to get too close to people, but she trusts you. Don't screw it up."

He had no intention to. The interim between their previous assignment and whatever solo work Ryku could find left him and Zira plenty of time to spend with each other. They trained in the mornings and sometimes helped the E-2 instructors with various recruit classes. At sunset, they often took long walks around the compound and talked for hours into the night as they stared up at the stars. Once, they drove out to some long-forgotten public art site just outside of Amarillo and painted their names on the antique cars standing there. Whatever they did, they were together, and Jared couldn't remember a time he'd ever felt so happy and at ease in another person's company.

Zira got a solo assignment first, three weeks after Ryku had split them up as partners. She was looking through the file one morning when Jared stopped by her apartment. She let him in, then made room on the couch so he could sit beside her. "It's another group of radicals," she explained. "Smaller—looks like just three people. The ones we took down at the factory were communicating with this group using those old computers we found."

"When do you leave?"

"I've got a flight to Anchorage in three days."

"All the way up north? Try not to freeze to death."

Zira smiled. "If that's the worst thing I have to worry about, I'll be fine."

She had better be. He wouldn't be there to watch her back this time. Not that he thought he needed to; she was a good operative and plenty capable of handling herself. Still, sometimes it didn't matter how skilled or careful an operative was. He'd had friends who were just as good as she was, and one tiny misstep had cost them their lives. It had nearly cost Jared his. He just wanted her to be safe, though in this line of work, he knew that might be asking for the impossible.

The assignment would be a lengthy one; Zira couldn't get a flight out of Anchorage for at least two weeks, if not longer. Jared wanted to do something special with her before she left, so he made arrangements for them to go hiking in the canyon just past Amarillo. That morning, he knocked on her door with two backpacks in hand. "Wake up and get dressed," he said when she opened it. "We've got things to do."

She cocked an eyebrow at the backpacks. "Oh really? And where exactly are we going?"

"It's a surprise."

Zira rolled her eyes and muttered something about surprises under her breath, but the half-concealed smile on her face told him she was pleased. "Give me a few minutes," she said and disappeared into her bedroom to change. When she emerged, she seemed to have taken her cue from his own comfortable, hiking-appropriate attire. She wore lightweight cargo pants, sturdy boots, and a loose-fitting tank top. She also clutched a jacket in one hand.

"Ready?" he asked.

She nodded and took the smaller of the two backpacks he held, slinging it over her shoulder.

"Oh sure, leave me with the heavy one," he teased.

"This *was* your idea."

He laughed and opened the door for her. They chatted on the drive to the canyon, and when they arrived, Zira's eyes gleamed with excitement. "I've heard about this place," she said, admiring their surroundings as they got out of the car. "I always wanted to come here. It's amazing."

"Wait until you see the view from above." They picked out a secluded trail through the earthy red rock and started walking. Lizards scurried over the sand, and once, a roadrunner darted across their path. Zira took it all in with the awe and wonder of a child, stopping to admire the wildflowers or stare up at a hawk circling above. Jared couldn't help smiling as he watched her.

When they reached the height of the trail, they ventured off the path a short distance to a shady spot where they could look down at the canyon below. The dark green of the trees stood out in stark contrast against the red, orange, and tan layers in the rocks. Neither of them said anything for a long time, sipping out of their water bottles and taking in the view. "It's beautiful," Zira said almost reverently. "Thank you for bringing me here."

Jared nodded and began unpacking his bag, which contained a blanket and food for a picnic. He'd gotten up before the sun rose to get it all ready, but he didn't tell her that. She was worth it. He spread the blanket on a slab of rock and they sat down to eat. When they were finished, he lay down with one arm behind his neck and Zira scooted closer to him, resting her head on his chest. Jared ran a thumb across the soft, pale skin on her shoulder and inhaled a deep, contented breath.

They lay like that for what felt like hours, but it couldn't last forever. "You're leaving tomorrow, then?" he asked.

"Yeah," Zira said. "My flight leaves early in the morning."

"Just be careful, okay? Please."

"I will. Stop worrying."

Jared watched the clouds drift by overhead for a few minutes, then glanced down at Zira. Her eyes were closed, but he knew she was still awake. "I have something for you." He sat up and pulled a small box out of his backpack.

Her head tilted to the side and her eyes narrowed, but it was hard to tell whether she was simply taken aback by the gesture or getting ready to put her guard up. "Why?" she asked.

Jared shrugged. "Why not?"

Zira took the box and pulled off the top. A black pocketknife lay inside, and around its handle, Jared had wrapped a necklace. Zira unwound the thin chain and held it up so the pendant dangled in front of her, a translucent, blue stone surrounded by a silver ring. She gave Jared a questioning look.

"I bought the necklace first," he explained. It had reminded him of her—the color of her eyes. "But anyone can buy a girl jewelry, and I knew you'd probably think it was stupid, so I got the knife, too."

Zira laughed and fastened the chain around her neck, then examined the knife. She pulled out the blade and turned it in her hands. "Well, I do like this better," she said. "But the necklace is nice, too—even if it is a little cliché. Thank you."

She leaned forward to kiss him, and the thought struck him then that he loved her.

The idea felt comfortable, relieving, and a part of him wanted to shout it out loud for all the world to hear. But he doubted Zira was ready to hear it yet, especially after her insistence that they take things slow and not assume any labels. She wasn't the kind of girl who formed attachments easily, and saying the words would only complicate things if she didn't feel the same way.

So instead of saying it, Jared pulled her closer and wrapped his arms around her. He kissed her deeply, trying to say with silent lips what his voice could not. *I love you, Zira.*

CHAPTER 11

AFTER AN EIGHT HOUR FLIGHT and accounting for the time difference, Zira arrived in Anchorage just past noon. She collected her bags and reluctantly walked outside; the late October air was frigid here compared to the warm southern climate she'd just come from. She stuffed her hands deep inside the pockets of her coat and stood on an icy sidewalk to wait for the man who was supposed to pick her up.

The man was an informant, and though Zira hadn't been given his name, meeting him would be a rare opportunity. Operatives almost never interacted with the men and women in the outside world who gathered the intel for their assignments. Their true identities were a closely guarded secret, but it was widely known among the members of E-2 that some of them were former operatives themselves, either too old or injured to carry out the physical demands of that work anymore. They were still able to assist their unit in other capacities, however. They gathered information about potential threats and passed it on to Chairman Ryku. In some cases—like this one—an informant might transport an operative through unfamiliar territory or provide weapons and other materials they might need.

After a few minutes, a middle-aged man with a dark ponytail and weathered, russet-brown skin approached her. "Zira?"

She nodded and they scanned each other's CLs for identity confirmation. "Come with me please," he said.

As she followed him across the street, Zira noticed that he walked with a slight limp and held his left arm at an awkward angle. She wondered if he'd been crippled while serving the Project and hoped she would never share a similar fate, incapable of carrying out her own assignments and forced to become little more than a courier. Informants were a necessary and vital part of unit E-2's work, but no one wanted to be relegated to such a position. The compound was home, and even the thought of being forced outside its walls left a bitter taste in the back of Zira's throat.

The man stopped in front of a white car and opened the back door, motioning for Zira to get in. He got in the front and punched a location into the navigation system. Once they were on the main road, he turned back to her. "I'm taking you to an old vacation lodge not far from where the radical group is hiding. Everything you need should be there, but we'll go over it together when we arrive. Under no circumstances are you to leave the lodge grounds except to do surveillance and complete your assignment. There's a small town nearby, and the people there tend to be overly curious about newcomers and strangers. They can't know you're here."

Zira nodded. "I understand."

He scowled and looked out the window, muttering under his breath. "Sending a little girl all the way out here on such a dangerous mission—I hope Ryku knows what he's doing."

Zira smirked, but said nothing. Let him think what he wanted to. She'd learned to take advantage of the way people underestimated her.

They drove for an hour through a landscape of ice, snow, and trees until they finally reached the lodge Zira would be staying at. A large log-style cabin stood nestled among frosted pine trees. The snow had drifted in perfect slopes at the base of the cabin. As the car rolled to a stop, Zira spotted a moose wandering lazily back into the woods. It was a beautiful scene. She could understand why people might have liked to take vacations here before the war had ruined any opportunity there might be for such frivolities.

Zira took her bags and followed the informant to the cabin. It wasn't much warmer inside than it had been standing in the snow. "No electricity, no heat," the man said as he led her to a spacious kitchen, where a week's worth of food sat on the table. "Your room has a fireplace. You can get wood from the shed out back. There's some more food in the fridge—should be enough to last while you're here."

They went up some stairs to a long hall lined with doors. The informant opened the nearest one, which had a fireplace as promised. A mattress took up most of the floor space and a tall safe stood in the far corner. The informant showed her the code to unlock it and they went through its contents together. There was a long knife much like the one Zira usually carried on assignments, several smaller knives and daggers for her to choose from, a semi-automatic rifle, and a few pistols of various calibers. There were also suppressors, extra magazines, ammunition, and a small drone similar to the one she and Jared had used on their last assignment. It was more than she could ever see herself using, but she was glad to have so many options.

She nodded her approval and the man closed the safe. "Do you need anything else?" he asked.

"No, everything looks fine. Thank you."

He started towards the door. "I'll be back for you in two weeks. If you're not here, I'll return a week later. After that, you'll have to find your own way back to the compound. I'll remove anything you've left here and dispose of it."

"I'll be here," Zira assured him.

He gave her a curt nod and limped back to his car. She watched him go through the window, and as the car disappeared around a bend, it struck Zira that she had never been so completely alone and far from home in her entire life.

■ ■ ■

Zira's assignment file on the radicals had been dismally empty, so she planned on spending at least a week doing surveillance. She might not learn anything new, but she wasn't about to let herself botch another assignment. If she'd learned anything from Jared in their short time as partners, it was to do her research, play it safe, and consider every option before taking action.

The trio of radicals was holed up in an old resort similar to the one Zira was in now just a few miles through the trees. It was comprised of several smaller cabins rather than just one big lodge, surrounded by an equally stunning landscape of tall trees and pure white snow against a mountain backdrop. According to Zira's map, a road ran right through the resort, though it hadn't been used in so long that she couldn't even see it under the snow. It wound down through the hills to a small town called Grayridge, then joined a major highway back to Anchorage about twenty miles out. Zira worked out how to follow the road to that highway in case she needed to get back to the compound on her own, though she doubted that would be necessary.

For the next several days, she familiarized herself with the area so she'd be able to navigate with confidence when the time came to carry out the assignment. The hills where the resort sat were rugged and heavily wooded, providing excellent cover but also making it a little difficult to move quickly and quietly. Once she felt sufficiently comfortable with the surrounding area, it was time to move in and survey the cabin itself and the occupants within. Using the drone and the scope of the sniper rifle from the weapons safe, she watched from a secluded hiding place beyond the tree line.

There wasn't much to see. The windows had all been boarded up, and the radicals never went outside unless it was to gather more wood for their fire. Whatever food they needed, they must have stockpiled inside already. They kept three old snowmobiles under some fallen branches just inside the tree line, though Zira never observed them using the vehicles. Each day, she saw all three of the individuals from her file as they took turns gathering and chopping more wood. There was a burly man with a thick brown beard and pale skin. There was also a stocky brunette woman who looked so similar to the man that Zira wouldn't have been surprised if they were siblings. The third radical was a younger woman with olive skin and curly black hair. They all took turns carrying the same bolt-action hunting rifle whenever they went outside.

Zira watched the cabin for days, but nothing out of the ordinary happened. She never went beyond the shelter of the tree line to avoid leaving visible footprints, and if the group suspected they were being watched or were concerned that they might be attacked, they showed no sign of it. A few days before the informant was scheduled to pick her up, Zira decided to make her move.

As soon as night fell, she donned her usual set of black clothes and bulletproof jacket, then picked a few items out of the safe. She took a set of lock-picking tools, the long knife, and two handguns with suppressors and extra magazines. At the last minute, she slipped both the necklace and pocketknife Jared had given her inside her jacket. She could justify carrying the pocketknife for its usefulness, but she was bringing the necklace along for pure sentimentality and mentally kicked herself for it. She hated to admit how much she'd missed Jared since coming here. If they were still partners, he'd be here offering her some last-minute encouragement before the mission. She missed Aubreigh, too. She missed everyone. She wasn't particularly fond of people in general and relished some time on her own, but being so totally isolated in this cold, deserted landscape with just her own thoughts to keep her company had gotten old after the first week. It was almost over though, and soon enough she'd be back at home, laughing with Jared and fending off Aubreigh's incessant questions about the new developments in her romantic life.

Zira walked to the cabin after midnight, camouflaged by the darkness. The sky was overcast, but what little light there was reflected off the snow and offered adequate visibility once her eyes adjusted.

She hid in the same shadowed trees she'd used to watch the cabin over the last week, looking for signs of movement. All was still except for the steady stream of smoke that floated from the chimney. She made her way to the cabin's front door, leaving deep gouges in the snow behind her. It didn't matter; in just a few more minutes, no one would be around to notice. More snow and wind would erase the tracks from existence soon enough.

She tried the door with a gentle hand. Locked, as expected. It was an old building though, and the lock was one of the basic pre-war kind that would be simple enough to pick. Zira knelt in front of the door and got to work.

She slid the pick and tension wrench into place and began feeling for the pins. One at a time, she lifted them carefully. As the last one gave under the pressure, Zira twisted the knob and darted inside. She shut the door behind her before a draft of cold air could follow.

The light from the low fire against the wall cast a warm, orange glow around the cabin. Zira raised her pistol and glanced around the room quickly. Three piles of blankets lay in front of the fireplace. She thought she could see the tops of two of her targets' heads underneath two of the piles. The last target, she assumed, was buried beneath the third heap.

She approached the blankets at a slow, deliberate pace, testing the weight of each step to ensure the wood floor wouldn't creak under her. Reaching the nearest one, she bent to get a closer look. She squinted, sure she wasn't seeing the person correctly. Short-cropped hair. *Blond* hair.

None of her targets had blond hair.

In the same instant that she realized there might be another person in the cabin, she heard a creak behind her. She whirled around and fired two shots at the shadowy figure taking cover behind a wall. In her panic, her aim went wide. The bearded man shot back. His bullet ripped through Zira's right leg, and she cried out as searing pain radiated throughout the entire limb.

The man was on her before she could fire another shot. He threw her on the floor and ripped the gun from her grasp. Zira fought to take it back, but the man flipped her over and pinned her arms above her head. He yanked her other gun from its holster around her leg and slammed it into the side of her skull. Zira's vision shattered in a thousand painful colors.

More voices joined the chaos, but the man's drowned them all out as he screamed at Zira. "Who are you?"

He didn't give her a chance to answer before he struck her again, this time in the side. She gasped for air. "Get off of her!" someone else shouted. A different man. The blond man. The man who wasn't even supposed to be here. He tackled the bearded one to the floor. "She's just a kid."

Zira rolled onto her back and looked around. If she could just find her gun—

Ah, there it was, staring her right in the face as the curly-haired woman aimed it at her head. "Alma, don't!" said the blond man, scrambling back over to Zira.

"Just making sure she doesn't try anything stupid," said Alma.

Zira heard a whimper and turned toward the source of the noise. Two young children, a boy and a girl, stood in the doorway. Her third target, the brunette woman, stood behind them. Their wide eyes and gaping mouths were frozen in surprised terror. Zira's file had said nothing about children, either. This was all wrong.

"Liza—get the kids out of here," said the blond man. The woman, snapping to her senses, quickly ushered the children away.

Zira closed her eyes and squirmed, overwhelmed by the pain in her leg. She had been so careful. There should have only been three people in the cabin. This was all a big mistake, but how could she have known?

The blond man turned to Alma. "Get that thing off her wrist, then go get the first aid kit." Alma complied, using Zira's own knife to cut through the thick plastic of her CyberLink. A quick glance around the room revealed that none of them seemed to be wearing one.

"What the hell do you think you're doing, Tripp?" asked the bearded man.

"Trying to keep her from bleeding out." He clasped his hands over the hole in Zira's leg in an attempt to stop the steady flow of blood that seeped through her pants and pooled on the floor beneath her. The bone shifted under the pressure, and Zira bit back a scream.

"She was going to kill all of us!"

"She was just following orders. She doesn't know any better."

"Nate?" Liza came back into the room and stood beside the bearded man. Zira was sure they were siblings now; even with her vision blurring at the edges, she could see that they shared the same aquiline nose and deep-set eyes. "What happened?"

"This murdering Project coward slunk in here to kill all of us in our sleep, and now Tripp wants to save her worthless life."

"I could use a hand here," said Tripp.

Alma knelt down beside him and opened a big plastic box. "Got it."

"Get me as much gauze as you can. And bandages."

"Are you two insane?" Liza's voice was shrill. "She was going to hurt my kids!"

If she'd had the strength to do so, Zira might have rolled her eyes. She would never harm an innocent child. If she'd known there were children inside, she wouldn't even be here right now. She would have contacted Ryku to ask him how he wanted her to proceed; he probably hadn't known about the children, either. This entire assignment had been doomed to fail before she even got here.

"Look at her," said Tripp. "She's barely more than a kid herself. We kill her and we're just as bad as them."

"Well we can't keep her alive," said Nate. "They'll come looking for her."

"They'll come looking for her either way," said Alma. "And us. They knew we were here—that's why *she* came. We can't stay."

Zira couldn't see her leg; she was having a hard enough time staying conscious as it was and didn't dare look. All she saw were Tripp's bloody hands flying back and forth to take gauze pads from Alma as fast as she could unwrap them. "We need to get her to Mei," Tripp said. "We all need to get to Mei's. We can hide out there until we have a chance to get to a new safe house."

Nate cursed. "You want to drag Mei into this?"

"No, but we don't have a choice."

"We should leave her. We go to Mei's, but we leave her here. Let her bleed out and die for all I care."

"What if she doesn't die?" Liza hissed. "She'll tell the Project what happened and where we went."

"She's not dying," Tripp said. He looked into Zira's eyes as he said it, like it was supposed to be some kind of reassurance. She wasn't comforted. She was wounded and surrounded by strangers. Two of them wouldn't hesitate to shoot her if Tripp wasn't around to stop them, and she had no idea what his motives were for doing that. She'd failed her assignment and had no way to contact anyone at the compound. Her chances of even making it back there at all seemed to be shrinking by the second. She felt as far from reassured as a person could possibly get.

"We could blow the place up," Alma said. "We still have some of those explosives from the old Medvale factory."

Tripp considered this as he wrapped a thick bandage around Zira's leg. He nodded. "Let's do it. If we're lucky, the Project will assume we died in the explosion. If we throw her CL in, they might think she's dead, too. We'll take her to Mei's and hold her there until we can move somewhere else. By the time she makes contact with the compound, we'll be long gone."

"What about Mei?" Alma asked. "If they find out she's been helping us, they'll kill her."

"She can come with us when we leave," said Tripp.

"You know she'll never leave Grayridge."

"She'll have to. Look, I know this wasn't part of the plan, but we're going to have to make the best of it."

"You can start by killing the girl then," said Nate.

Tripp stood and turned to face him. "If anyone touches the girl, I'll turn them in to the Project myself. Let's go; we're wasting time."

"I'll get the snowmobiles," Alma said. She put on a coat and ran outside.

Tripp looked down at Zira. "Mei's a doctor. She'll help you."

Zira was too weak to protest. Her vision became increasingly fuzzy around the edges and her whole body felt cold and shaky. She wasn't sure how much time passed before she heard the growl of a snowmobile's engine outside. "Help me carry her," Tripp said to Nate. He grumbled, but did as he was asked. As they lifted Zira, her vision darkened. The next thing she knew, she was sitting behind Tripp on the snowmobile with a quilt draped over her back. Alma wound a rope around both of them, binding her to Tripp. It was a good idea; right now, Zira had little faith in her ability to remain upright on the seat.

They started moving. Zira's eyes took in the journey in patches as she fought to keep them open. Glimpses of trees and endless snow. Snatches of Tripp's voice shouting at her over the rush of cold air in her face. A bump in the road that would have sent her flying if not for the rope securing her to Tripp.

They stopped in front of a modest-sized house and Tripp began tugging at the rope. A light turned on inside and a huddled figure ran out to meet them. Zira closed her eyes; she just wanted to sleep.

"What are you doing here?" A woman's voice. Concerned. Tired. Old.

"I need you to help her." Tripp lifted Zira and carried her towards the house. "Nate shot her."

"Who is she?"

"An assassin from the PEACE Project."

"And you want me to help her?"

"Mei, look at her. She's just a kid."

Someone brushed the hair away from Zira's face. There was a sharp intake of breath, a clicking of the tongue. "She needs to go to the hospital. She's in shock, and I can't treat a gunshot wound here."

"If you take her to the hospital, they'll put her in the system and the Project will know she's there. They'll come for her and find us."

"Maybe not. Doctor Gregor still owes me. Come on. Get her in the car. I'll take care of it."

"I have to ask you for another favor. We can't stay at the lodge anymore. We're blowing the place up to throw them off track, but I was hoping we could stay here for a week or two. Just until we can find something else."

"Of course. Make yourselves at home. I'll be back as soon as I can with an update."

Tripp slid Zira into the back seat of a car and covered her with the quilt. Her eyes flickered open for a moment, and she saw concern etched in the creases around his hazel eyes.

Then everything was strangled in darkness.

CHAPTER 12

Vibrant light from an overhead bulb stung Zira's eyes the next time she tried to open them. She squinted against its brilliance and shaded her face with one hand. There was something attached to the hand—an IV line. Her eyes followed it to a stand beside her where a bag of clear fluid hung and dripped steadily. She closed her eyes, trying to recall how she got here and why she might need an IV.

The last thing she remembered with clarity was getting shot. Everything after that was a blur. She pushed herself up onto her elbows to get a better look at her surroundings. The room she found herself in was small and home-like, with thick, tan carpet and white walls. A man—Tripp, she remembered—sat in a chair near the closed door. "Welcome back," he said. He shifted the pistol on his knee. *Her* pistol.

Seeing him there reminded her of her failed assignment. A weight pressed against her chest. *I have to get out of here.* The sooner, the better. The radicals were unlikely to let her leave willingly, but she might be able to overpower Tripp and take his gun. She could even use him as a hostage to secure transportation back to the compound. First, though, she needed to assess the damage to her leg. She tugged at the covers of her bed.

"Wait," Tripp said. "Just a second. We should talk about—"

Zira ignored him. With her good leg, she kicked the blankets aside. It was only then that she noticed something was terribly wrong. At first, she couldn't even accept what she was seeing. She blinked. No matter how much she willed it to go away, the image before her persisted.

Tripp came to her bedside. He started talking, but Zira couldn't hear what he was saying. A nauseating lump formed in her throat as she stared at the empty space below her knee where the rest of her right leg should have been. Instead, a bandaged stump lay lifeless on a pillow.

A scream burst loud and distraught from her chest. The door across from her flew open and slammed against the wall. Acting on instinct, Zira vaulted out of bed at the noise. She teetered on one leg, then crashed to the floor. Tripp and the old woman who had come into the room hurried to help her.

"Get away from me!" She attempted to stand on her own.

The woman took a step back while Tripp continued trying to lift Zira off the floor. She shoved him away. "You need to lie down," said the woman. Zira recognized her voice from before—the doctor they'd called Mei.

"What happened to my leg?"

"Calm down. We can talk about it once you're back in bed."

Zira relented and let Tripp help her up. Her whole body shook. She grimaced, dismayed by how much she had to lean on him just to stand. Once she was back in bed, Mei examined the bandages on her leg. Zira studied her face as she worked. She looked to be about seventy, with salt-and-pepper hair tied back in a loose ponytail at the base of her head. Her small, dark eyes were set amidst countless lines and wrinkles.

"You shouldn't strain yourself," Mei chided, then put another pillow under Zira's stump. Everything about her seemed gentle and caring, but given the circumstances, Zira wasn't sure how much she could be trusted. "You must be hungry. I'll get you something to eat."

She left the room and Tripp scooted his chair closer to the bed. He set the gun on a dresser just behind him and rested his elbows on his knees. "I'm sorry about your leg," he said. His voice was soft and genuine.

"What happened?" Zira asked. She had to understand; none of this made sense.

"Nate shot you. You remember that?"

"And then you brought me here because Mei's a doctor."

"Right. But there wasn't anything she could do for you here. She had to take you to the hospital, but she couldn't just leave you there and let them treat you. You would have been registered in their network and the Project would have found you, and then they would have found us. We couldn't allow that; you understand?"

Zira refused to affirm the statement and kept her face flat and cold.

Tripp sighed. "Anyway, Mei used to work at the hospital, so she knows people there. One of the doctors has a third child—a daughter. He somehow managed to keep the girl hidden from the Project, so no one knows about her. Five years ago, Mei did this surgery that saved her life, totally off the books. When she brought you in, she asked Dr. Gregor to return the favor."

"So why amputate my leg?"

"I'm not a doctor, so I'm not sure about all the details. But, the way I understand it, there were just too many complications. First of all, the wound was pretty bad. The bullet shattered your bone. Grayridge is a small town, so the hospital isn't very big and they don't have all the resources you might find somewhere else. To keep things secret, they couldn't bring anyone else into the operation—not even bots. It was just Mei and Dr. Gregor, and neither of them specialize in orthopedics. They did the best they could with what they had."

Hearing Tripp talk about what had happened somehow made it more real, and Zira felt her emotions rise as she realized that the leg was really, truly gone. She remembered the informant she'd met just two weeks ago, the way he limped and the awkward bend of his arm. He'd probably been an operative like her, once. Whatever injury he'd suffered had effectively ended his career. Now, Zira saw herself facing a similar, if not worse, fate. She was broken, and the Project had neither the time nor resources to waste on broken things. Her life as an E-2 operative was over.

Her eyes stung as she struggled to hold back tears. "What now?" She was asking herself as much as him. Her entire world had shattered overnight, and she had no idea what came next.

"We can't let you leave. You understand that, right?"

Zira nodded. She didn't like it, but she understood. They were enemies, and she was a prisoner. She knew she should be grateful that Tripp had stepped in before Nate blew her brains out, but she was having a hard time feeling grateful about anything right now.

"We're going to try to be out of here by the end of next week," said Tripp. "Once we're gone, you won't be a threat to us anymore and you'll be free to go. We're still trying to convince Mei that it's safer if she comes with us, but she's stubborn, and she's lived here for years. She says you can stay as long as you like, provided you don't try to contact the Project. She can help you learn to walk again. They implanted an attachment for a prosthesis when they were doing the surgery, and she thinks she can get a leg that fits in a week or two."

Learn to walk again. Zira felt a pang in her chest as she thought of all the things she would have to learn to do again. Walking was the least of them. Hot, turbid desperation filled her. She was lying in a bed in some unfamiliar place, too broken and crippled to stand on her own. She longed for Jared and Aubreigh to be here now, to hear their voices reassuring her that everything would be all right. But that was stupid and naïve, because nothing was all right, and she couldn't see how anything would ever be all right again. Her leg was gone, and no prosthesis would ever be able to replace it.

She was horribly aware of how pitiful she must look to Tripp as she pulled the covers over her head and cried, but she couldn't hold it in any longer. The sobs shook her body, but she stifled the noises as best as she could and told herself he couldn't hear her. It was the only shred of dignity she still had.

■ ■ ■

Mei shook Zira awake and set a bowl of hot broth and crackers on a tray in front of her. She also gave her some pills. "For your pain."

Zira took them. She wasn't sure how long she'd been sleeping, but Tripp was still sitting in his chair wearing the same clothes as before. It was impossible to determine the passage of time in this room. There were no windows and no clock, and her CyberLink had presumably been blown up in the explosion of the cabin.

"How are you feeling?" Mei asked.

"Okay," Zira said. Physically, that was true. The pain was to be expected and manageable so far, so she wasn't too concerned about that. Mentally and emotionally, she still felt defeated, but dwelling on it wouldn't help anything. She'd allowed herself to succumb to a moment of weakness and had a good, long cry. Now it was time to stop feeling sorry for herself and focus on getting her life back.

Mei nodded. "I'll be back to change your bandages later."

Zira sipped her broth and nibbled on some crackers. She didn't have much of an appetite, but refusing food didn't seem to be a great way to regain her strength. She looked over at Tripp. He smiled at her, an odd, crooked sort of grin that gave his face a child-like appearance even though he must have been at least thirty. It wasn't a mocking smile or even a pitying one, but friendly, like he had a funny story he just couldn't wait to share with her.

"Why didn't you let Nate kill me?" Zira asked. The question had been bothering her ever since he'd stepped in to save her. That she was "just a kid" could hardly excuse the fact that she had tried to kill him and his friends, and eliminating her would have made things a lot easier for all of them.

Tripp shrugged. "You're a kid. You didn't really know what you were doing."

"I'm eighteen."

He grinned. "See, that's exactly the sort of response you'd expect from a kid, like an extra year here or there makes such a big difference."

"That's not why you saved my life."

"Call it nostalgia, then. I have a bit of a soft spot for E-2 operatives." He leaned back in the chair and put his hands behind his head. "See, I used to be a member of the PEACE Project. My best friend was an E-2, like you. You probably know him. Ryku. Goes by the title of 'chairman' these days."

Zira choked on a spoonful of broth and stared at him. She wasn't even sure where to begin. "So, what, you just left the Project?" It was treason, a crime so taboo that those even suspected of harboring anti-Project sentiment were executed without contest.

"It's a little more complicated than that, but yes."

"Why?"

"There were too many secrets. Too many lies. I got sick of looking the other way."

Zira's first instinct was to jump to the Project's defense. She opened her mouth to tell Tripp he was wrong, the Project never lied, and any secrets they might have were kept solely to protect the peace. Then she remembered Aubreigh, crying under Zira's arm because she'd just found out the awful truth about fourth children. She remembered the contempt in Seth's eyes as he accused her of thinking she was above the law. Unit E-2 was built on a framework of secrets and lies, and it seemed the other units had skeletons of their own to bury. All of it was justified, of course, but Tripp would never see it that way. She changed the subject. "And Ryku?"

"You could say we had a falling out. He's been trying to kill me ever since I left." Tripp's voice was as casual as if he were discussing the weather.

Of course Ryku was trying to kill him. Tripp was a traitor and a fugitive, and now he was working with radicals. Radicals who had weapons and had been in contact with a larger, better-armed group. Perhaps they'd been planning something—some kind of joint attack or rebellion. She needed to find out more. They couldn't keep her here forever, and when she got back to the Project, she intended to tell Ryku every scrap of information she could about these people and their plans.

"What unit were you in?"

"A. The Project recruited me in my first year of college."

"And how long have you been out here?"

"Almost fifteen years."

Zira nodded and stared at her soup in an effort to hide her surprise. Ryku was one of the most connected and well-informed men on the planet. The fact that Tripp had managed to evade him for so long was impressive.

As if guessing her thoughts, Tripp shrugged. "I'm careful."

"It doesn't seem very careful to let me live."

He laughed. "You're not making a very good case for yourself, kid."

"I just don't get it. If you've been so careful and avoided Ryku for so long, why would you throw it all away on me? You were in unit A, so you must be smart. You have to know I'll go back and tell Ryku all about this the second I can get out of here. Maybe I'll even kill you all in your sleep."

Tripp seemed more amused by the threat than afraid. "It's a risk I'm willing to take. I know you see us as enemies, but I don't think it's that black and white. Maybe all of this will teach you something, open your eyes to the real world. Maybe you'll go back to the Project and remember that I saved your life, so you won't tell Ryku I was here. Even if you do, it won't matter. I'm very good at disappearing."

Zira glared at him as she finished her food. Open her eyes to the real world—*he* was the blind one. Not just blind, but stupid. He'd had a nice, comfortable life in the Project and he'd thrown it away. It didn't matter how good he was at disappearing; Ryku would find him eventually and he'd be executed for treason, just as he deserved.

Mei came in just then to change her bandages. Tripp helped. It was the first time Zira had seen the leg uncovered before, so she watched intently as Mei unwrapped the stump. It was an ugly sight. The skin had been cut and rearranged to fit around a rod that protruded from the end, leaving a patchwork of crisscrossing stitches. She grimaced.

"Does it hurt?" Tripp asked.

"I'm okay." It did hurt, but the pain had subsided a little thanks to the pills Mei had given her earlier. It wasn't unbearable.

"It will look better once the stitches are removed," said Mei. "There should be very little scarring."

"What about infection?" Zira asked. "Won't germs be able to get in where the rod comes out?"

"As long as the incision heals properly, there is minimal risk of infection. The implant is made of a porous metal, so the surrounding skin and tissue is able to grow into it and create a barrier. Think of it like the antlers on a deer. It works in a similar way."

"When can I start walking again?"

"As soon as the prosthesis I found arrives here. Probably in a week or two. Normally, they're custom made, but that's impossible under the circumstances. I managed to track down an old one from someone who's outgrown it. It won't be a perfect fit, but you'll have to make do. I'm sure the Project can provide you with something more suitable when you go back."

"Will I be able to do everything I used to?"

Mei met Zira's gaze with a sharp look. "You mean run around in the middle of the night and shoot people?"

"Yes," Zira said, her voice cool and even.

Mei clicked her tongue and shook her head. "It's going to take some time. At least a couple months for rehabilitation. Longer, if you want full functionality again. But you're healthy and active. I think you can make a full recovery." The time-line was no worse than Zira had expected, and she was glad to hear that she had a chance of regaining her former mobility.

Mei finished wrapping her leg. The old woman had taken a great risk in helping Zira, presumably for no other reason than because Tripp had asked her to. Her stomach squirmed a little thinking about how Mei had been dragged into this. She clearly disapproved of Zira's activities and, like Tripp and the others, it would have been easier for her to just let Zira die. Her selflessness was more than Zira deserved.

"Thank you," she blurted as Mei walked to the door. The old woman paused, and Zira searched for the words to express her gratitude. "I know you think I'm just a killer, and maybe I am. And I know I made things hard for you—" She turned to Tripp. "For all of you. But you helped me anyway. Thank you."

"I'm a doctor," Mei said. "A killer, a child, a soldier, a priest—it doesn't matter. All life is precious. I did what I had to do."

She left, and Tripp put a hand on Zira's shoulder, causing her to flinch. "See, kid? You're not so bad. Even Mei doesn't think so."

CHAPTER 13

TRIPP AND THE OTHER RADICALS ended up having to stay at Mei's for over two weeks. The small basement was crowded between the six of them, but presumably, they made do. Zira had no way of confirming this since she was confined to her room aside from occasional trips to the bathroom across the hall. Liza, still fearing for her children's safety, had insisted on this. Since Zira could do little more than hobble around on a set of old, wooden crutches, she didn't protest the arrangement.

Alma and Tripp took turns guarding her, but she suspected this was for her own protection as much as it was to prevent her from escaping or finding some way to contact the Project. She didn't see much of Nate and Liza, but when she did, they both still looked like they wanted to kill her. Previously, she might have laughed at the idea. In her present condition, it was a challenge just to put on her own pants. If either of them cornered her in the room alone, she wouldn't have a chance of defending herself. She managed to talk Tripp into letting her keep the pocketknife Jared had given her and took to sleeping with it under her pillow at night. A poor defense, but still better than nothing.

Mei brought news from the outside world as the days went by. A small search party came to explore the area where the radicals had been hiding, but they left empty-handed after a few days. The Project had to have organized the search; no one else had any reason to suspect there might be survivors trapped in the rubble from the explosion. They were looking for Zira. Her heart lifted a little when she first heard, then sank again. They'd given up so soon. No one was coming to rescue her. The longer she went without contacting them, the more likely it was that they'd simply pronounce her dead and that would be the end of it. She wondered what Jared and Aubreigh must think of her disappearance; Aubreigh would be especially worried. Zira wished there was some way she could let them know she was safe, but there were no means of communication in her room, and Mei was diligent about removing her own CyberLink anytime she interacted with Zira.

She did physical therapy with Mei every day. The old woman seemed pleased by the way the residual limb was healing and assured her that she was making good progress. Zira might have been more encouraged by this if not for the phantom pains that started just a few days into her stay at Mei's house. While excruciating at times, the sensation frustrated her more than it hurt. She could look down and see that her leg was missing, but no matter how much she tried to tell her mind that, the pain persisted in the empty space where the limb should have been.

Early one morning after a series of particularly bad aches woke her up, Tripp pulled his chair up close to her bed. "Let's talk."

Zira gritted her teeth and shot him a glare. "Not a great time right now."

"It'll take your mind off things. Come on. You've been tossing and turning all night."

Zira began to massage the leg like Mei had shown her. "Fine. Talk."

"There's something I've been wanting to ask you, but it might be a touchy subject."

"Go ahead," she said. Anything to distract herself from the pain.

"What went wrong when you came to kill us all that night at the cabin? You people don't make mistakes like that—not that big."

"Thanks for the compliment."

"Sorry. But it was a pretty big mistake."

"It was," Zira admitted. "But it wasn't completely my fault. There were only supposed to be three of you."

"Nate, Liza, and Alma, huh?"

Zira nodded. "I watched the cabin for days, but I only saw those three. They were the only ones in my file. I didn't know about you or the kids."

"That was our intention. It was safer to stay inside, so obviously we didn't want the kids going out, just in case. And I've had a target on my back for over a decade. If any of Ryku's informants had seen me, it would have been like flashing a neon sign telling every assassin in the compound to come after us. Tough break for you, though."

She forced out a short laugh as another surge of pain burned through her non-existent lower leg. "Yeah, that's a bit of an understatement."

He set the gun down, safely out of her reach, and gently moved her hands aside. Too miserable to argue, she let him take over massaging the stump and leaned back on her pillows. "Are you going to go back as soon as we leave?" he asked after a few minutes. "You can, you know. We asked Mei to keep you here for a few days, just to give us some time to get away. But let's be honest—she's not as spry as she used to be, and you've gotten pretty quick on those crutches. You could just...well, you know."

Zira gave him a sidelong glance. "Kill her and run off? Do you honestly think I'd do that?"

"I hope not, but I can see how this all looks from your perspective. We shot you, cut off your leg, and then locked you in a basement. You're probably excited to get home and start plotting your revenge." He winked at her and grinned, but she'd learned early on that he often dealt with serious matters by making jokes and maintaining an unflinching sense of optimism.

Zira shook her head. "I'm not really looking forward to going home, actually."

"Why not?"

"Because I failed my assignment." She patted her hand against her thigh. "Because of this. I can't do any of the things I need to. What good am I to my unit now?"

"You heard Mei," said Tripp. "You'll get better."

"Eventually. But Ryku is—well, you probably know how he is. I'm not sure he'll give me a chance to prove I'm still worth keeping around."

"You're getting a prosthetic leg. You'll be back on your feet in no time."

"It's not like I can learn to walk again overnight, and that's just a start. I need to run, jump, climb, fight, and about a hundred other things."

"You don't have to do it overnight," said Tripp. "Just stay here. Stay as long as you want to. You can go back to the Project when you're ready, after you've recovered your skills."

"I can't wait that long. What would I tell Ryku when I do go back?"

"The truth. You were held captive by a bunch of mean, nasty rebels who shot you and then cut off your leg. They let you go, but you didn't want to go back to the compound in that state, so you waited until you were well enough to perform at the same level you could before."

"That's a good story," Zira said, rolling her eyes. It sounded easy enough, but would Ryku accept that explanation? She gnawed on her bottom lip. "What about Mei?"

"Mei said you could stay as long as you want, remember? Between you and me, I think she gets a little bored out here all by herself. You might be doing her a favor."

"You just want me to stay here longer so you have more time to run away and hide before I tell Ryku you were here."

"The thought crossed my mind," said Tripp. "But just because it benefits both of us doesn't mean it's not a good idea."

Zira sighed and tilted her head back. She dreaded facing Ryku after this whole mess, but she also missed home. She missed Aubreigh and Jared, and staying here until she'd regained her former strength meant it could be several months before she saw them again. It seemed cruel to continue allowing them to think she was dead—or worse. Still, if the extra time let her keep her position as an E-2 operative, it might be worth it. "I'll think about it," she said to Tripp.

He sat back in his chair and retrieved the gun from the dresser. "How's the leg?"

"Better," said Zira. A slight tingle still remained, but the pain had subsided significantly. "Thanks."

"Good. Try to get some sleep before Mei comes in to drag you out of bed for therapy."

■ ■ ■

Mei did come in to wake Zira just a few hours later, and Tripp left the room to get some sleep. She carried a long cardboard box under one arm. "Is that my new leg?" Zira asked.

Mei handed her the box, and Zira tore it open with the enthusiasm of a young child opening a gift. The prosthetic leg might have been uniformly white at one time. Now it was a dirty gray, battered and scuffed. Still, it was a leg. Zira ran a finger over the hard, plastic material and smiled. She was going to walk again.

She lifted it out of the box. It seemed to be roughly the same length as the missing portion of her leg would have been. Mei knelt and showed her how to attach it to the implant coming out of her stump. "Make sure it's secure," she said. "As long as it's fitted properly, you can wear it as long as you want. It's waterproof and very durable, but you'll want to be sure you wash it and check for any cracks on a regular basis."

Zira bent her knee back and forth, testing the weight of the prosthesis. Now that it was attached to her leg, it felt heavy, but she suspected that was because she'd grown so accustomed to not having any weight below that knee. She stood with Mei's help and put a hand on the wall for support.

"Just take it slow," Mei said. "You don't want to hurt yourself and interfere with your recovery."

Zira gently shifted part of her weight to the new leg. She took her hand away from the wall and Mei backed away a couple of steps. For the first time in almost three weeks, she was standing on her own. She would have jumped into the air for joy if she could have. "Thank you," she said.

Mei put a hand on her shoulder. "You're quite welcome, Zira."

They worked together for the rest of the morning and into the afternoon. Tripp came in later. He leaned back against the wall and watched Zira take a few clumsy steps across the floor. She had to use one of her crutches to stabilize herself, but she was walking. "Not too bad, huh?" she said to him.

"You're doing great. It's probably a good thing we're leaving tonight. A few more days and you wouldn't have any trouble finishing that assignment of yours."

Zira's concentration broke and the prosthesis slipped out from under her. She managed to catch herself on her hands to lessen the fall, but it still hurt. She glared at Tripp as he hurried to her side. There had been no malice in his voice when he'd made the comment, but it still dug at her. It shouldn't have. It was true, after all, even if he'd meant it as a joke. Of course he still saw her as a killer.

"Help me get her up," said Mei.

Zira held out a hand. "No. I can do it myself." With a little careful maneuvering, she did, then went to the bed and sat down.

"I think that's enough for today," said Mei. "I'm going to go make dinner."

Zira stretched her legs and looked at Tripp. "You're leaving tonight?"

"Yeah. Which means you'll be free to go soon, too."

Zira shook her head. She'd thought about their previous conversation throughout the day, and after testing the new leg and seeing exactly how much work she had ahead of her, she'd decided it might be best to wait a couple of months before returning to the compound. Even something as simple as going up and down stairs seemed an impossible task right now. She couldn't face Ryku like that; he'd already given her so many chances. If she went back now, broken and useless after failing her assignment, she doubted he would give her another one. "Not yet," she said.

Tripp nodded and took his usual position in the chair at the center of the room. The smell of Mei's cooking upstairs began to waft through the entire house. Zira watched as Alma, Nate, and Liza carried plates of food through the hall. There was a lot of it—probably some kind of going away feast for the radicals. That made Zira think of something. "How has Mei been able to feed all of you for so long?" she asked Tripp. Food was allocated through a strict rationing system based on whether or not a person had completed their required work duties. Unit C distributed staples like grain, potatoes, and some meats directly through their distribution centers, and citizens received additional ration coupons which could be redeemed for other items in local stores. Zira couldn't imagine how Mei might have been able to get enough food to feed six extra people.

"We brought her everything we had at the cabin before we blew it up," said Tripp. "It was enough to get us through the winter. Once we leave, she'll be better off than anyone else in Grayridge—unheard of for a retired person with no family, especially considering how terrible the food shortage has been here."

"If there's shortage here, it's the same everywhere else. We'll all have to tighten our belts and make the best of it."

Tripp stretched his legs out in front of him and grinned. "That was really good. I almost believed you. You should think about transferring to E-1's propaganda department."

Zira glared at him.

"You ever go hungry back at the compound?" he asked.

The food was meager and tasteless sometimes, but Zira couldn't honestly say she knew what it was like to be hungry for more than a few hours. "No."

"Exactly."

"Why is there a food shortage here, then?"

"It's not just here; it's this entire region. This is an agricultural valley—one of the few you'll find this far north. The growing season this past year was a particularly bad one, so most of the workers weren't able to fill their quotas. Unit C cut their rations. Some of them will try to hunt and fish to make up the difference, but others won't risk it."

"Hunting is illegal," said Zira. "Citizens aren't allowed to have weapons."

Tripp shrugged. "Break the law, or your family starves. They do what they have to do to survive."

"Unit C wouldn't have cut their rations for no reason. They must have been doing something wrong. Something that caused their crops to fail."

"You can't control the weather, kid." He leveled his gaze at her, and any spark of humor vanished from his face. "Remember what I said about opening your eyes to the real world. This is it."

Alma knocked on the door and pushed it open wider. "Food's ready," she said to Tripp. "I'll watch her if you want to grab a bite."

"Sure," Tripp said. "I'll be right back."

He returned a few minutes later carrying two plates stacked high with steamed carrots, beans, caribou meat, and bread. "You could have stayed out there and eaten with the others," Alma said as he set one plate in front of Zira.

"I'm fine right here." He settled into his chair and took a bite of carrots.

Alma looked between them, muttered something under her breath in Spanish, and left. "She's right," Zira said. "You can go."

"And leave you in here all by yourself?"

"You're really still worried that I'm going to kill all of you?"

Tripp shrugged. "I'm on a winning streak for not being killed by you people. I'd hate to ruin it now. Besides, I'm going to be cooped up somewhere with those guys for weeks after this. We don't need any more quality time together."

When they'd finished eating, Tripp left to help the others clear up and gather the things they needed for their journey. Zira listened to them walk back and forth through the hall and up and down the stairs. Then there was silence. Had they all left already?

A few minutes later, Tripp and Mei knocked on her door. "You're still here," Zira said as they entered.

"Don't look so disappointed. You didn't think I'd leave without saying goodbye, did you?"

"Goodbye," Zira said.

He crossed over to her bed and extended a hand. She shook it. "I'm sorry we had to keep you here. And for your leg."

"I'm sorry I tried to kill you." She wasn't sure why she'd said it, but she meant it. Maybe not for the others, but for Tripp, she meant it. In another time, another place, they might have been friends.

"The compound is a dangerous place. Take care of yourself."

"Yeah. You too."

He walked to the door, stopping to hug Mei on the way out. She patted the side of his arm and smiled at him, and then he was gone. Mei stayed behind. She held Zira's gun in one thin, wrinkled hand. When she noticed Zira staring at it, she said, "He told me to stay here and watch you for a few hours to give them time to get away."

Zira rolled over to face the wall and closed her eyes. Of course he did. He was careful, after all.

CHAPTER 14

JARED STARED AT THE CALENDAR on his wall, counting back the days again. It had been over three weeks since Zira had left on her assignment. She should have been back by now.

He'd watched the news every day and knew as much about what had happened near Grayridge as was being released to the media. It wasn't much. A series of explosions at an abandoned pre-war resort just outside the small town had destroyed at least three cabins, the remains of which were later buried under heavy snowfall. Local search and rescue teams had gone to check for survivors based on an anonymous tip from Chairman Ryku, but they'd found nothing. In order to avoid rousing unnecessary suspicion with the locals, the search was called off after two days.

According to the data pulled from Zira's CyberLink before it went offline, she'd been at the resort when the explosion happened. If that were the case, however, Jared was sure that the search dogs would have at least found a body—if not Zira's, then one of the radicals' she was supposed to have assassinated. The CyberLink reports had to be a mistake somehow. Zira had gotten out. She would find a way to make contact or come back home. It was only a matter of time. At least, that was what Jared had repeatedly told himself over this past week.

With each passing day, he believed it less, and darker possibilities began to fill his mind. The time for waiting was over; somebody needed to do something. He ran to the chairman's office, burst through the door, and stood in front of Ryku's desk with clenched fists. Ryku didn't seem the least bit surprised to see him. If anything, he simply looked tired as he pushed his paperwork aside and waited for Jared to speak. "Sir," Jared began, "I'd like to go to the North Pacific Region to look for Zira."

Ryku shook his head. "I'm sorry, but I can't allow that."

"She should have been back by now. Have you at least heard from the informant who was supposed to get her back to the airport?"

"He hasn't seen or heard anything from her since he dropped her off. She missed both of the days he was scheduled to pick her up."

Something pinched in Jared's chest. "What if she's in trouble?"

"She'll have to get out of it herself."

"They never found any of her targets. What if they have her somewhere?" It was what he feared most and seemed the most likely possibility given the circumstances. The thought of her going through anything like his own experiences as a captive of the Red Flag Brotherhood sent prickles of ice down his back.

Ryku placed both hands on his desk and stood, leveling his gaze at Jared. "You know the protocol. She's already been gone three weeks without contact. Honestly, with the way things stand right now, I think we need to consider the possibility that Zira might be dead."

Jared lifted his jaw. There was no expression on Ryku's face—no remorse, no hurt, no sign of sadness for the possible loss of one of his own people. Jared hated him for it. "You don't know that. You can't make that call."

"Somebody has to. That's part of being the chairman of this unit. You may not understand now, but you will."

"That's it? You're responsible for her."

Ryku clasped his hands in front of him and sighed. "The people up north tend to be sympathetic towards these radical groups, and the situation there has been escalating due to the recent food shortage. Unit P just deployed an entire company to deal with the unrest. Zira's life is not any more or less valuable than my other operatives', and I can't afford to send someone digging around up there. Not now."

"Why not? You sent people to look for me in the RA. You came for me yourself."

"That was different. We knew you were alive. More importantly, we knew where to find you."

"We know where Zira is."

"We know where she *was*. We have no idea what happened after our informant left her at the lodge."

"You can't just abandon her!"

"When did it become your place to question my authority? You're letting your emotions affect your judgment. I don't think Zira would want you or anyone else risking their lives to bring her back. In fact, I'm sure she'd resent the fact that we even dared to think she couldn't take care of herself. Tensions are too high right now. If we send people over there in the middle of everything else that's happening, it will only draw negative attention and suspicion."

"If tensions are so high, then you never should have sent her over there in the first place."

Ryku's eyes narrowed. "You don't know everything, Jared. The information I choose to share with you or anyone else under my command is a very small piece of a much larger picture. I did what I thought was right, and I won't beg your forgiveness for that. If Zira is alive, she'll be back as soon as she can. If not, we'll have a funeral next week."

"Without a body?"

"It's the best we can do under the circumstances. Now if that's all you wanted to talk about, I suggest you go and find something productive to do. This is all very unbecoming of the man who's supposed to be the most elite in this unit."

Jared wanted to punch the chairman in the face, but he reigned in the better part of his temper and lashed out with his words instead. Colorful insults flew out of his mouth like a swarm of angry bees, but Ryku remained calm and still. This infuriated Jared even more, but since he didn't seem to be getting anywhere, he turned around to leave.

"Don't get any ideas about going after Zira yourself," said Ryku. "For your own good, I'm ordering you to remain here. If you leave this compound without my explicit consent, I'll have you arrested for treason."

Jared slammed the door as hard as he could.

■ ■ ■

The morning of Zira's funeral was bright and warm. The small gathering at the cemetery consisted almost entirely of people wearing black armbands. Aubreigh's red one stood out like a flare, and once Jared spotted it, he went to stand beside her.

He felt like he was walking though some kind of nightmare, wishing he could wake up to find Zira sleeping right beside him. Every hour that had passed over the last week had been torturous, and he'd spent more time than he cared to think about just pacing. Pacing the floor in his room, pacing the sidewalks around the apartments, pacing the concrete by the front gate, always hoping that he'd look up one minute and she'd be there, or that he'd glance at his CL and see an incoming call from her. After all that pacing, he'd finally had to face reality. Zira wasn't coming back, and the only reason there could be for that was that she had been captured or killed by the radicals she'd been sent to eliminate. If she wasn't dead already, she probably would be soon, and there was nothing he could do about it.

Aubreigh wiped away tears with the edge of her sleeve. Jared felt too hollow to say anything, like the place where his voice should have been had been swallowed up by some unknown void. Instead, he placed a hand on Aubreigh's shoulder, hoping to provide a little comfort. To the rest of these people, Zira had been just another face in the crowd. Only Aubreigh shared Jared's pain now, because she had loved Zira, too. Perhaps she even felt it more acutely; the two of them had been like sisters.

Ryku said a few words about Zira's dedication to the Project and her determination to be the best she could be in all aspects of her life. He seemed far too accustomed to these kinds of speeches. Jared wondered if he even still remembered exactly how many people had gone to their deaths under his authority.

A marker had already been placed, a simple gray stone with Zira's name and unit below the seal of the Project. There was no casket to lower into the ground, a clear indication that there was no body. That trivial detail was the one that tormented Jared most. Even without it, he knew she was gone.

One by one, the few who had come to pay their respects drifted away. Chairman Ryku approached them, nodding to Aubreigh and putting a hand on Jared's shoulder. "I'm sorry," he said.

Jared bristled at the touch.

In a rare display of emotion, Ryku's features softened. For the first time, he looked genuinely upset about Zira's disappearance. "You know I care about everyone in this unit," he said. "I've watched most of you grow up. I would never send any of you into a situation I didn't think you could handle."

Jared only glared back at him. He recognized the sincerity in Ryku's voice, but he was still angry. It was easier to be mad at the man standing in front of him now than at whatever unknown power or fate had allowed this to happen to Zira. Ryku frowned and walked on.

Soon, only Jared and Aubreigh were left standing in front of the headstone. Aubreigh asked the question Jared had dreaded since he saw her. "Do you know how she died?"

"Just pieces of it," he said.

"Tell me."

"I can't. I'm sorry." If anyone had a right to know what had happened to Zira, it was Aubreigh, but telling her would require him to reveal classified information about Zira's mission. Ryku had made it clear that no one outside their unit could know where she had been.

"She was doing something dangerous, wasn't she? Taking care of some problem or threat?" She spat the last words out with bitter sarcasm. Whatever problem or threat Zira might have been dealing with, Aubreigh clearly didn't think it was worth her life.

"We shouldn't be talking about this."

"Why not?" Aubreigh asked, fighting to keep her voice under control. "My best friend is dead, and I want to know why. She was eighteen years old. What kind of organization is this that sends someone so young out there just to get killed? It isn't right."

Jared swallowed hard and shifted his gaze to a tree behind Aubreigh. He couldn't look at her, and he couldn't look at the headstone with Zira's name on it. "Leave it alone, Aubreigh."

"No. I want answers."

"You wouldn't like them," he said, and walked away before she could say anything else.

CHAPTER 15

ZIRA PRACTICED WALKING WITH THE prosthesis as much as she was able to over the next few weeks. She soon abandoned the crutches altogether, and when Mei put them back in the closet, she smiled triumphantly. The road ahead was still a long one, but she was making progress. Best of all, the phantom pains subsided with the aid of an electric pressure sensor where the prosthesis attached to the implant, and Zira's mood had improved as a result.

In her impatience to do the things she used to, she experienced a few ugly falls. "This isn't as easy as I thought it would be," she admitted to Mei one evening after a particularly frustrating day.

"You'll get better," Mei said. "It just takes time."

Despite her progress, Zira didn't feel like she had much time. She wasn't a prisoner anymore, and she grew more anxious to return to the compound with each passing day. She forced herself to wait a while longer. Walking unassisted was a great accomplishment after all she'd been through, but Ryku might not appreciate it enough to let her continue working as an E-2 operative. Though she was eager to get back to her old life and see Aubreigh and Jared again, she knew she needed to get stronger.

Now that she was free to leave the room, Zira sometimes accompanied Mei into town. The fact that it was cold enough to make bulky coats and gloves a necessity served her well as it easily hid the fact that she wasn't wearing a CL, which might have raised unwanted curiosity otherwise. Since Mei liked to save her car for emergencies, they always walked. She received ration coupons for a fuel allowance each month, but it wasn't much, and she never knew when she might need it. Her house was only two miles from the outer limits of Grayridge, though it felt like much farther than that in the biting winter cold. The sun rose late and set early this time of year, so if they needed to go to town—and Mei insisted on going at least a few times a week—they only had a few good hours of daylight to make it there and back.

During these excursions, Zira saw signs of the food shortage Tripp had told her about. The most obvious was what was coming out of the distribution center in the middle of town—or rather, what was *not* coming out. Each week when Mei went in to pick up her rations, she returned with barely enough food to feed one person for three or four days. Her ration coupons should have been able to make up the difference, but even the stores couldn't keep up with the shortage. The prices of what little they had in stock had risen to an unaffordable amount. Where Mei once might have been able to exchange a single ration coupon for a sack of apples, she now wouldn't have been able to buy even one. She managed to make the food stretch for both herself and Zira, but only because they were able to supplement it with what radicals had left.

Whenever they walked to Grayridge, they each took some frozen caribou meat, fish, or canned vegetables to share with other families in the area. Zira was reluctant at first. There didn't seem to be anything inherently wrong about sharing with friends and neighbors, but Mei took great care to hide the food in a wheelbarrow under a layer of firewood when they transported it. It might not be explicitly illegal, but it did seem to undermine the Project, and that was a dangerous enough crime in itself. After all, the Project promised to take care of people and make sure everyone got their fair share. The fact that Mei had to distribute food to almost half the population of Grayridge meant the Project was failing that promise, and Zira was hesitant to accept that. Once she saw how little Mei was receiving from the distribution center, however, she became more willing to help. They couldn't get to everyone, and Mei admitted to not trusting some people enough to share with for fear they would turn her in to the Project. Still, they seemed to be making a difference. Gaunt-faced parents wept with joy whenever Mei and Zira showed up at their door, and the light that brightened the children's eyes warmed something in Zira's core like she'd never felt before.

One morning about five weeks after Zira had first come to Mei's house, someone knocked on the door. Mei stood up from the table where they'd been eating breakfast. "Go downstairs," she said. "Don't come up until I tell you it's okay."

Zira was about to ask what was going on, but Mei's frown told her this was not the time for questions. As she headed to the basement, Mei hurried to clear her plate away before answering the door. Zira pressed herself against the wall at the bottom of the stairs to listen.

"Good morning, Mei." Zira didn't recognize the man's voice. "You have something for me, I believe?"

"Of course. Here."

There was a long pause. "That's it?"

"I'm sorry, Mr. Hartman. I don't have access to—"

"That's your problem, not mine. I don't think I need to remind you of what will happen if you fail to honor our agreement."

"Please. That's all I have. That's all I can get. Haven't we been doing this long enough?"

"Long enough?" The threatening tone in his voice made Zira tense. "You don't get to say when it's been long enough. You have two weeks to get me the rest of it, and you'd better not try another stunt like this the next time I show up."

The door opened then shut again. Zira waited a few minutes for Mei to tell her it was all right to go back upstairs, but the old woman seemed to have forgotten about her. She went up anyway. Mei sat at the kitchen table with her head in her hands, frowning into a cup of tea. She was so preoccupied that she didn't even notice Zira until she was right beside her. "Oh—Zira! You startled me."

Zira sat down. "Who was that?"

Mei pursed her lips and dried her face with one sleeve. "His name is Hartman. He's the administrator at the labor camp where my son is."

There were pictures of Mei's family on the walls throughout the house. She had a husband and a son, but she never talked about them, and Zira never felt comfortable asking. Family was a somewhat foreign concept to her. She had the Project, and she had Aubreigh, but she knew that wasn't quite the same thing.

"He was asking you for something." It was more than just curiosity that fueled her desire to know about Mei's business with Hartman. She owed Mei her life, and now the old woman was in some kind of trouble. If there was any way that Zira could help her, she would.

Mei shook her head. "I shouldn't be telling you this. It's not your problem." She reached out and put her knobby fingers over Zira's. "But it's nice to have someone to talk to. It's been a long time since I had anyone who would listen."

Zira squeezed Mei's hand and gave her a small, encouraging smile. Mei sighed. "Before the war, my husband's family owned some land in a town not far from here. They'd had it for generations, and he inherited all of it when his parents died. After the war, the Project came to take it away. It was their land now, and they wanted to assign workers to farm it like they were doing everywhere else. They told us we would have to relocate, but my husband didn't want to leave. He argued with them, so they shot him, just like that."

"That's terrible," Zira said.

Tears slipped from Mei's eyes and ran into the wrinkled creases of her skin. She continued in a shaky voice. "They said he was armed, that he'd pulled a weapon on them and that's why they shot him. It was a lie. He wasn't armed. They were just talking. My son, Ethan, tried to tell the truth. I told him to let it go, but he wouldn't listen. He got one of the local papers to publish his side of the story. E-1s arrested everyone involved and sent them to a labor camp. They would have arrested me too, but the hospital here needed another doctor, so I was transferred instead."

"And Hartman is in charge of that labor camp," said Zira.

Mei nodded. "He came to me a few years after they arrested Ethan and asked me to get him some drugs. Painkillers, from the hospital. He threatened Ethan. I refused at first and tried to go to the police, but I wasn't able to speak with an officer right away. The next day, Hartman sent me some holograms from the labor camp. They'd beaten Ethan half to death. I got him the drugs he was asking for. I thought it would just be that one time, but he comes back every three or four months asking for more."

As disgusted as she was by Hartman's greed, Zira couldn't understand why Mei had allowed herself to be bullied for so long. "Why didn't you try to contact the police again? Or someone in the Project?"

"I would if I knew it wouldn't put my son in danger. Hartman will have him killed if I don't do what he says. Why take the risk? It isn't worth gambling on Ethan's life."

Anger flared up inside Zira to think that anyone would use their power to exploit and threaten someone like Mei. At her age, her son should have been around to help her and take care of her. Because of Hartman, she had to constantly worry about Ethan's safety instead. "What are you going to do?"

Mei shook her head. "I don't know. I used to get the drugs from the hospital. It was risky, but I managed. I built up a stockpile for when I retired, but it's all gone now. I have no way to get Hartman what he wants."

Zira clenched a fist. "We have to stop this."

"And what do you suggest? That we go charging into the labor camp demanding Hartman's resignation? That we rescue Ethan so he can spend the rest of his life as a fugitive?" Her shoulders slumped in defeat. "At this point, all I can do is beg for Hartman's mercy."

There was something more that Zira could do, though. A plan was already forming in her mind. Hartman had told Mei he'd be back in two weeks to collect the drugs she owed him. If she worked hard, she might be able to regain enough of her old skills and strength to put an end to Mei's problem with the man. Permanently.

She said nothing to Mei about this idea, not wanting to raise her suspicions. The less she knew about Zira's involvement when the body was discovered, the better, though Zira had little doubt that the shrewd old woman would be quick to put the pieces together. By that time, it would be too late for Hartman, and if Mei decided to kick Zira out because of her involvement in his death, so be it. Zira called it eliminating a threat, but she knew Mei would only see it as murder. Still, she was willing to face whatever consequences came after.

Zira pushed her body as hard as she could in the next two weeks to get ready for her mission. Her strategy didn't rely on a great deal of strength or speed, but if things didn't go according to plan—and she was no stranger to plans failing—she wanted to be ready. She relearned abilities she had taken for granted before and began jogging as soon as Mei cleared her to do so, but the more complicated maneuvers she'd been able to perform before would take some time to master again. Still, by the time Hartman was supposed to return for his drugs, Zira felt adequately prepared.

Mei, on the other hand, was an emotional wreck. She tried to hold herself together with fake smiles and constant activity, but there were dark circles under her eyes that no amount of makeup could cover and deepened wrinkles in her face that Zira hadn't noticed there before. Sometimes, Zira was tempted to comfort her, to promise her that everything would be all right. She didn't, though. She knew if she said anything about her plan, Mei would talk her out of it. They'd be right back where they started, and Ethan would probably be dead within the week. This was the only solution. Right or wrong, she owed it to Mei to do whatever she could to save her son's life.

It was seven o' clock on the morning of Mei's two-week deadline when Zira got out of bed and began getting dressed. The sun wasn't up yet and wouldn't be for another three hours. She slipped on a few layers of clothes to shield herself from the cold outside, then fastened the necklace Jared had given her around her neck. It was stupid, but somehow, she felt a little better having that small part of him with her, like she wasn't going into this completely alone.

She turned to the nightstand beside her bed and pulled the bottom draw open. Everything she needed to kill Hartman lay inside. Both of her handguns, which had been returned to her with her other weapons shortly after the radicals left—albeit without ammunition. A plastic bag containing the two bottles of opioids Mei had tried to give Hartman two weeks ago, which she'd stolen from Mei's room just hours ago while the old woman slept. A large syringe filled with a clear liquid that she'd mixed right after she stole the drugs, made from about a dozen crushed pills dissolved into water. Zira put all of it in the deep pockets of her coat and crept upstairs.

Mei sat at the dining room table with her back turned to Zira, staring out the window. She looked so old and fragile. Zira walked up behind her and put her arms around her shoulders. Mei seemed surprised at first, but patted Zira's hand and gave her a hollow smile. "I'm going for a run," said Zira. "I'll be back soon."

"Don't forget your gloves," Mei said. Her voice sounded more like an echo.

Zira grabbed her gloves from the table near the door, as well as a hat and a long knit scarf, then went outside. At the road past Mei's yard, she turned left, which was the direction Hartman would be coming from since the other way led to a dead end. She jogged along the desolate street, feet plunging into the snow again and again with a rhythmic, muffled crunch. She stopped about a mile from Mei's house, close enough to the main road that she could see any approaching headlights.

She pulled her hat down lower over her ears and hoped that Hartman would hurry up. The last time he'd come to visit Mei, they'd been eating breakfast, so she was counting on him showing up in the morning again. Having spent her entire life in a much warmer climate, Zira was unaccustomed to the intense winter cold of this region. Every moment she spent outside shortened her temper. She'd wait all day if she had to, but that didn't mean she had to enjoy it.

About thirty minutes later, she saw lights on the main road. The vehicle turned onto the street she stood on now. It had to be Hartman; Mei was one of just a few people living this far outside of Grayridge, and the only other house on this road had been unoccupied for years. Zira pulled a gun out of one pocket and the plastic bag of pills from the other, then walked into the middle of the street and turned to face the headlights.

As expected, the autopilot system brought the car to a halt about five yards from where Zira stood. She stepped out of the glare, then aimed the gun at the windshield with one hand and held up the bag in the other. The pale, middle-aged man inside the car beckoned her closer. He cracked the window open as she approached, and Zira barked an order before he could speak. "Unlock the door."

"Who are you?"

"If you want the rest of your drugs, you'll let me ask the questions."

That caught his attention. A few seconds later, the doors unlocked with a sharp click. Zira opened one and slid into the back seat right behind Hartman. "You're going to do exactly what I say." She nodded at the autopilot console in front of him. "Set that thing to take us to Grayridge. Somewhere on the outskirts of town, but closer than here."

"Where are the rest of my drugs?"

"What did I say about asking questions?" She pressed the gun to his temple and paused to let that sink in a moment. "Don't do anything suspicious. If you even look like you're going to try and ask for help, I'll shoot you."

He pressed a few buttons and the autopilot confirmed their intended destination. The car turned itself around and headed back to the main road. Hartman glanced at her in the mirror a few times, but seemed to have taken her threat seriously and didn't try to get any answers from her. They drove through Grayridge in silence until they reached a closed bar on the far side of town.

"You have arrived at your destination." The autopilot's cheerful voice sounded out of place in the tension that filled the car.

"Will you please tell me what's going on?" Hartman asked.

His tone was considerably more civil than it had been the first time he'd spoken to her, but that did nothing to improve Zira's opinion of him. "You make me sick."

"I—I don't understand."

"Mei. The old woman you've been manipulating." She took the painkillers out of their bag and tossed the bottles in his lap.

"I'm sorry. I have no idea what you're talking about."

"Don't give me that crap. You've been threatening her son's life so she'll get you these drugs. She's too afraid to stand up to you, but I'm not." Hartman's expression was one of angelic innocence, but Zira could see the fear behind it. Retribution had finally caught up with him. She leaned closer and jammed the gun against his head. "Well? What do you have to say for yourself?"

"This has all been a terrible misunderstanding," he said shakily. "I'm sure we can work something else out."

"Mei already tried that, remember? You refused."

"Like I said, a simple misunderstanding."

"Wrong answer."

Hartman's mouth stretched in a thin line. He wet his lips with his tongue. "If you kill me, she'll be the first person they blame."

"A nice, seventy-year-old lady? No one's going to believe that. They have no reason to suspect her. Not unless you've been going around telling people how you've been threatening a doctor in order to get drugs illegally, and I'd hate to think anyone's that stupid." She gestured with the barrel of the gun. "Set the autopilot to drive you back home, but don't start it yet."

He did. "You're just going to let me go?"

"Turn and put your hands behind your back where I can see them."

He shifted on the seat and Zira unwound the scarf around her neck. "What are you doing?" Hartman asked. Zira didn't answer. She put the gun down and worked quickly to bind his hands, not so tight as to leave an obvious mark, but tight enough that he wouldn't be able to get free.

The plastic bag that had held the drugs lay open on the seat next to her. She grabbed it and yanked it down over Hartman's head, cutting off his air supply. He kicked at the windows, but they wouldn't break. He tried to throw himself back on top of her, but Zira braced her forearm against his back and her leg against the door. It took all of her strength to hold him there as he struggled, but she managed.

A feeling that was dangerously close to guilt rose up inside Zira as she listened to his frantic gasps for air. A small part of her wanted to pull the bag off his head, let him live. Perhaps he'd be terrified enough by this whole thing to leave Mei alone.

Perhaps. Zira couldn't accept anything less than a guarantee, and that would only come once Hartman was dead.

She forced herself to watch his face in the mirror, composing her own features in an expression of cold indifference as she fought the roiling in her stomach. Hartman's eyes were wide and panicked, reminding Zira of a rabbit she'd had to snare and kill once as part of a survival training exercise. Years seemed to pass before he went still. Zira knotted the back of the bag. He was passed out; it would take a few more minutes of oxygen deprivation to kill him.

She climbed over the seat to sit beside him and untied his hands, then used the scarf as a tourniquet around his upper arm. She took the syringe from her pocket, uncapped the needle, and found a large vein in Hartman's arm. Her hands shook as she lowered the needle to his skin. A few deep breaths stilled them. She hit the vein on the first try and pushed the plunger, sending a lethal dose of opiates into his bloodstream.

She could have given him the drugs first and let him die from the overdose. Maybe that would have been a little more humane, a little less filled with pain and terror. It also would have been much slower, which put Zira at a higher risk of being seen with Hartman since she didn't dare let him go until she knew he was dead. This was the best she could do. With any luck, everyone would assume he'd died from a drug overdose based on the evidence she left behind, and that would be the end of it. An autopsy might show the true cause of death, but even if one was performed, there was nothing that could connect her or Mei to his death.

She pulled the bag off his head and removed the scarf from his arm, then sat him up straight in his seat. The bottles of pills had been knocked to the ground sometime during his struggle, but Zira found them and put them neatly in the tray of the center console beside the empty syringe. She got out of the car and leaned back inside to push the button that would start the autopilot. "Warning," it said. "Door ajar."

She closed the door and the car rolled away; it would carry Hartman safely home. She tucked the gun inside her coat and started jogging along the roadside back to Mei's house, just a regular girl out for her daily morning exercise.

CHAPTER 16

MEI SAID NOTHING TO ZIRA when she walked in the front door shortly after sunrise, and Zira offered no explanation for her whereabouts. She took a shower and put some clean clothes on, then went upstairs to help Mei with lunch. The news reports started coming in a few hours later. A relative had found Hartman dead inside his car at his home in Anchorage, and the words 'drug overdose' were already being pandered around as the most likely cause of death. All things considered, her mission had been a success. Hartman was gone, Ethan would live, and murder wasn't even being hinted at.

Mei watched the news with a flat expression. She didn't seem happy, relieved, or any of the things Zira thought she'd be upon hearing about Hartman's death. Zira's mouth went dry as she continued to watch the old woman for a reaction. Mei was smart, and Zira had known from the beginning that she would put the pieces together at some point. She just hadn't expected it to be this soon.

She turned to Zira, eyes full of disappointment. Zira lifted her chin, holding her head high and defiant against the pounding in her chest. She'd saved an innocent man from a fate he didn't deserve, and she'd saved Mei from years of threats and manipulation. She refused to apologize for that.

Mei sighed and shook her head. "You're a beautiful girl, Zira, and a good person. But if you continue down this path, it won't be long before your soul is tainted by the same blood that's on your hands."

Zira's eyes shifted to the floor, her confidence shattered in an instant. No explanation she could offer would erase the hurt in Mei's eyes, and for some reason, that crushed her more than she could have ever imagined it would. She suddenly felt very out of place in the house that had become her home over the past two months. "I'll go," she said. "I've been enough of a burden on you already. I shouldn't be here."

"If you had somewhere to go, you would have left already. I told you before that you could stay here as long as you needed to, and I meant that. No one is forcing you to leave."

Zira nodded, still unable to meet her gaze. There was so much left unsaid between them, but nothing Zira knew how to say. She went to her room, feeling Mei's eyes like icicles in her back even after she closed the door.

■ ■ ■

Despite the old woman's hospitality, Zira knew she couldn't stay with Mei forever. She didn't belong here, a fact that had become even more apparent since she'd killed Hartman. She kept Mei at a distance out of guilt and discomfort, wedging a stifled silence between them that seemed to grow with each passing day. She needed to leave, but where would she go? Physically, she didn't feel ready to go back to the Project yet, but maybe that was her only choice.

She still hadn't found an answer to that question a few weeks later when she accompanied Mei to the distribution center to get her rations. As they neared the building in the center of town, they exchanged curious glances. Something big was happening.

The street was crowded with what appeared to be every citizen in Grayridge. Armed, uniformed officers stood shoulder to shoulder on each side of the street, looking on with stoic faces. About a third of the officers wore blue bands around their left arms—the cobalt bands of unit P. Zira took some comfort from their presence. Unit P's job was to protect, and judging from the scene before her, the citizens gathered here might need a little protection. They had no weapons, but they shouted at the officers around them and pushed forward towards the distribution center. A small spark could turn into a blaze in an instant, but with unit P here to keep things under control, Zira was sure the demonstration would come to a peaceful end soon enough.

Mei pushed her way through the throng until she found a friend. Zira followed. "What's going on?" Mei asked. She had to shout her question in order to be heard over the commotion.

"It's the Murphy girl. She died last night—starved to death."

Mei's mouth turned down in a deep frown. Zira glanced behind them. They hadn't gone very far into the crowd, but it seemed to have swallowed them up somehow. More were arriving every second, but they couldn't possibly all be from Grayridge. Perhaps some of the people from neighboring towns had come as well. After all, Tripp had said this entire region was suffering from the food shortage. They might want to join the protest, too.

Protest. Zira's fingers felt numb. That's exactly what it was. The shouting crowd, the march towards the distribution center, the armed guards. Protests were considered an act of treason and punished accordingly. It was only a matter of time before the officers shut the whole thing down, by force if necessary.

Zira leaned closer to Mei. "We need to go." She searched for a way out, but she was too short to even see over most of these people. Not wanting them to get separated from each other, she took Mei's hand. "Come with me."

Mei allowed Zira to lead her. They tried to stick to the outer edge of the crowd but ended up being swept deeper into the center as the entire group marched in unison. A man pushed right through them, breaking Zira's grip on Mei's hand and nearly knocking her to the ground. This was more dangerous than Zira had originally thought. Not for her, but for Mei. The old woman was stronger than most her age, but not strong enough to avoid being seriously injured in this chaos. If she fell, Zira doubted anyone would even notice. The thought of what might happen to Mei after that terrified her.

"Mei!" Zira could barely hear her own voice. "Mei!" She raised herself up on her toes but still couldn't see anything. It was no use, and it was too hard trying to push her way through the crowd. After being almost knocked down a second time, Zira changed tactics and began walking with them. She could only hope Mei would have the sense to do the same.

After a few more minutes, they all stopped. Some started to jump, fists in the air as they shouted at the officers around them. Zira's pulse quickened. She had to find Mei and get her out of here.

She spotted a gap and darted through it to the edge of the crowd. The officers watched the protesters with darting eyes, guns raised, fingers poised on their triggers. One of the blue-banded ones, who appeared to be the man in charge, rode a sleek, silver motorcycle into the outer edge of the crowd. He held up a megaphone to address them.

"This is act of treason against the PEACE Project. Cease and desist immediately. Return to your homes. I repeat, cease and desist. This is your final warning."

The protesters yelled back at him, louder and more enraged than before. A few of them moved towards him. The officer threw down his megaphone and reached to his waist. Zira ducked on instinct.

He fired a single shot into the air, and that was all it took to unleash complete anarchy. The crowd scattered. The other officers, hearing the sound and seeing all those people run towards them, began to fire indiscriminately. A young man to Zira's right collapsed, clutching his knee and howling in pain.

She bolted into the mob, calling out with every ounce of breath in her lungs. "Mei! Mei!" Other people's screams stifled her own.

A gunshot sounded from somewhere just a few feet behind her. Zira ducked again. She passed a weeping young woman with blood on her shirt but couldn't stop to help. Seconds later, she spotted a dirty blue coat and a head of gray hair lying in a heap at the side of the road. "Mei!" She sprinted forward. *Please be alive.*

Zira skidded to a stop and knelt down beside Mei as more people thundered past them. The old woman's face was badly bruised. An alarming amount of blood dripped from her mouth onto the pavement. Zira looked for a gunshot wound, but there didn't appear to be one.

Her hands trembled as she lifted Mei's head into her own lap. Mei moaned, and the color left her face. "I'm sorry," Zira said. "I should have been right here with you. I'm so sorry." She took a breath, trying to stop the panic that crept up from her core and threatened to overwhelm her. They needed an ambulance.

She heard the low growl of an engine behind her and leapt to her feet. The unit P officer on the silver motorcycle rode towards them, weaving his way around the people still trying to get away from all of this. He clutched his pistol along one of the bike's hand grips. The weapon was pointed in her direction, though whether that was intentional or not, Zira couldn't tell. Maybe he was here to help. Maybe not. She didn't care. This was the man who had set everything in motion. He was responsible for Mei's injuries. He was responsible for anyone else who might have been hurt in the ensuing pandemonium. She wondered how many would have to be hospitalized, how many would be dead when it was all over.

The officer slowed as he neared them. Zira grabbed him by the leg and yanked him from the bike. It toppled sideways and skidded to a stop several yards away. She ripped the gun from the man's hand before he could stand and aimed it at him. His eyes widened as he took a step back, hands raised.

Zira pulled the trigger twice. The man staggered back as the bullets hit his chest.

"Zira," a faint voice said. She looked back at Mei and saw a pained look in the woman's dark eyes, a pain that hadn't just come from her injuries. Zira threw the gun away with a snarl, horrified by her own actions. She had shot a man out of pure anger and malice. He would live, protected by the bulletproof vest over his uniform, but Zira hadn't been thinking of that when she shot him. She'd only wanted to hurt him—to kill him.

There was no time to dwell on it now. Zira scooped Mei up in her arms. She was only slightly smaller and lighter than Zira, but with so much adrenaline coursing through her veins, the old woman felt weightless. She cradled Mei's head against her shoulder and began running. "Hold on," she said. "Just hold on."

An ambulance wailed somewhere ahead, and Zira hurried towards the sound. By some miracle, one of the paramedics inside saw her and stopped the vehicle. Another burst out the back doors, grabbing the gurney and running to meet them. He took Mei from Zira's arms and laid her on the stretcher.

Mei's eyes were glazed and empty. One of the paramedics felt her wrist for a pulse. It took too long. Zira knew what that meant even before the other tried at her neck, before they looked at each other and shook their heads.

One of them lifted the body off the gurney. "I'm sorry," he said, turning to pass Mei back to Zira. "We have to help the others."

Zira took the limp figure. The paramedic tried to put a hand on her arm, but she backed away. She watched the ambulance drive off in a daze, then lowered herself to the curb. Her entire body heaved, but she was too breathless and exhausted for tears as she held the old woman against her chest and tried to ignore the wails of people and sirens all around her.

CHAPTER 17

JARED SHRUGGED ON A THICK white jacket and walked outside, shoving his hands in his pockets as smoky breaths puffed from his mouth. The morning was still gray and cold, but Ryku had insisted on meeting right away. He'd probably made the chairman wait longer than he should have already, something that might have conflicted with his perfectionist-level dedication to his job before, but it didn't seem to matter anymore. Few things did.

Since Zira's disappearance, Jared had done everything he could to put her ghost behind him. A part of him still hated Ryku for not letting him try to find her, but he understood it. In time, he might even come to be grateful to Ryku for preventing him from doing something reckless. He knew the chairman would have sent someone after Zira if he thought it was a viable option; after all, he'd gone to the RA himself to rescue Jared. But Zira was gone, and Ryku had known that when Jared was still too shaken up to face the truth.

Numbness had replaced the raw emotion of it now. Throwing himself into his work helped Jared cope, but it had paid off in other ways, too. Many of his recent assignments had involved tracking down and eliminating known members of the Red Flag

Brotherhood, greatly reducing their ability to pose any direct threat to America or its citizens. His efforts had earned him a significant amount of influence and respect with the chairman, and most people in the compound believed he'd become Ryku's most likely successor. There had always been speculation, but now it seemed certain that Jared would be chairman someday. It was something he'd aspired to since he was first placed in unit E-2, something he knew he should be happy about. Instead, there was just a hollow apathy.

He knocked on the chairman's office door twice, then entered without waiting for an invitation. Ryku was, as usual, seated behind his desk. He glanced pointedly at his watch. Jared made no apology. A shadow of a smile tugged at Ryku's mouth, and he gestured for Jared to sit down. "I have a job for you."

Jared sighed. He had only returned from his last assignment the previous morning and had been hoping for a couple days off. A stupid thing to hope for; having free time meant his mind wandered more than usual, and these days, the places it took him were usually unpleasant. Another assignment might be a good idea after all. "What is it?"

"I'm sending you to the North Pacific Region. You heard about the riots in Grayridge last week, I assume?"

"Yes," Jared said. He tried to keep his face impassive at the mention of the place where Zira had disappeared. *Died,* he corrected himself. The place where Zira had died. He had to force the word, even in his own thoughts.

"I have something you should see." Ryku raised his arm and tapped a few buttons on his CyberLink. A projection popped up, and Ryku extended his arm to give Jared a better view. "Unit P just finished going through all the footage they captured during the riots. Chairman Collin passed this little clip along to me last night. It might interest you. Take a look."

He played the video. There was no audio, and even if there had been, Jared doubted they would have been able to hear anything distinguishable over the shouts of such an incensed crowd. "This was taken from the camera on a police motorcycle," Ryku explained. "One of the unit P officers was riding it. See here—a few people in the mob try to attack him. Now he's fired a shot."

The crowd lost whatever semi-organized control they might have possessed. People scattered in all directions. Jared caught a few glimpses of other officers firing their weapons and shook his head at the madness of it all.

Ryku skipped forward a couple of minutes. The officer on the motorcycle weaved through the crowd so haphazardly that it was impossible to distinguish one blur from another. Finally, he focused on something, making his way towards a small figure bent over another individual on the ground. The bent figure stood, turned around, and lunged to pull the officer from the motorcycle. The picture spun sideways as the bike toppled and hit the pavement. Then the video cut to black.

At first, Jared didn't know whether he dared believe what he'd seen before the recording cut out. It had to be a trick of his mind, brought on by memories and the mention of the place Zira had last been seen. A muscle in his face twitched as he crossed his arms over his chest. "Play it again."

Ryku obliged, this time playing back only the last few seconds of the video at half-speed. Jared squinted as he studied the few frames where a familiar face flickered into view. The images were blurry, and he looked to Ryku for confirmation. For hope.

The chairman nodded. "It's her," he said. "I had the people in unit A run it through the best facial recognition programs they have. Zira's alive."

Jared ran a hand over his face and leaned back. "I'm going to get her," he said.

"I know. That's exactly why I asked you here."

"Is she still in Grayridge?"

"Maybe. I don't know. I haven't assigned anyone to look into it further."

Jared frowned. It seemed to him that assigning an informant to look into this—if only to confirm Zira's location—was the first thing Ryku should have done. "Why not?"

"You need to understand, Jared—we don't know what we're dealing with yet. This is a delicate situation. I don't want to get more people involved than I need to."

"What are you getting at?"

"Zira has been gone for three months. In this video, she appears to be alive and well. So why didn't she come back?"

Jared caught the accusation in Ryku's question and didn't like where the conversation was headed. "I don't know, but I'm sure she has an explanation."

"Maybe. I hope so. Still, we have to consider the possibility that she deserted the Project."

"No. Zira would never do that. She didn't come back because she *couldn't* come back. For all we know, she could still be in trouble. I'm going to get her." He stood up and turned to the door.

"Listen, Jared. You need to think about this. Be rational."

He spun around to face the chairman. "You said she was dead. You wouldn't even send anyone to look for her. You abandoned her, and I *never* should have listened to you. I'm going to get her. Now. Send the rest of the information you have on this to my CL."

He turned his back and stormed out of Ryku's office without waiting for a response.

■ ■ ■

Jared wasn't able to catch a flight to Anchorage until the next morning and arrived late that afternoon. The airport was a flurry of activity and noise, but even among all the tumult, Jared found it impossible to blend in. He attracted several curious stares as he made his way through the building. One woman clutched her purse and gave him a nasty look as he passed by. He was glad to get outside and find a secluded area to go over the information Ryku had forwarded.

The most promising lead he had on Zira's current location was the old woman she'd been trying to help in the video recording. Another video from unit P had caught them walking up the street together a few minutes before the first shots were fired. It seemed reasonable to assume that they knew each other fairly well. Jared had asked Ryku to find out more about the woman. He'd done so without protest, perhaps correctly concluding that it was pointless to try to talk to Jared about all this until he knew where Zira was. Jared sifted through those files on his CL now.

The woman's name was Mei Yamada-Hunt. She'd come to America from Japan—now part of the RA—to study medicine before the war and had married a fellow university student, Kirk Hunt. After that, the couple had moved to the North Pacific Region to take over

Kirk's family's farm. Kirk was killed in some altercation with Project authorities, leaving Mei a widow. Her son was still doing time on a twenty-five-year sentence at a labor camp, and she'd been one of eight fatalities in the Grayridge riot. Aside from all that, there was nothing out of the ordinary about her.

Jared memorized the address of the home registered to Mei and shut down the CyberLink projection. He needed to go to Grayridge. He'd check Mei's house for leads first, then ask around to see if any of the locals could give him more information. Small town folks were good at keeping track of things outside the normal routine. Zira might not be in town anymore, but if she and Mei had spent any amount of time together—for whatever reason—the people in Grayridge would know about it. They might have some idea of where she went.

Jared took a bus to a car rental center and set out for Grayridge in a nondescript white sedan. Mei's house was one of two lone structures on a street at the outskirts of town, surrounded by open fields and untouched snow drifts. The car stopped in front of the house and Jared shut off the engine. The blinds were drawn, and there were no signs of activity within. He approached the door with caution and tried the knob. It wasn't locked, so he let himself in.

The house looked exactly as it must have when Mei left home the day of the riots. A kettle sat on the stove and a few dirty dishes lay in the sink. He walked through the living room and passed a muted hologram projector tuned to a news station, as if Mei had simply forgotten to turn it off that morning. A few pictures hung on the walls, but other than that, the house had little decoration. Jared continued down the hallway and entered a tidy little bedroom. He opened a dresser drawer, unsure of what he was looking for but determined to find it anyway.

The dresser yielded nothing of interest, nor did the cabinet in the closet where Mei kept an impressive stash of medical supplies. Jared was about to move on to the next room when he heard a soft click from the hallway—the sound of the front door being opened.

He swore under his breath and hurried to the window for an escape. It was too late to prevent someone from seeing the car parked out front, but if he could get outside, he could at least make some excuse about trying to find Mei out back. The window was stuck, and the footsteps in the hallway drew closer. Jared gave it one last, mighty shove, and it squeaked open on old tracks.

The door behind him burst open, and Jared whirled around to see a gun aimed at his chest. Zira stood behind the weapon. Her eyes were wide and her mouth opened a few times before she managed to find his name. "Jared?"

She wore ill-fitting clothes meant for someone at least three times her age, but she was still as beautiful as he remembered. In just a few steps, he crossed the distance between them and pulled her into a tight embrace. He buried his face in her hair and breathed in the scent of warm earth and citrus and a hundred happy memories. It was only with her there in his arms that he was convinced all of this was real.

"What are you doing here?" she asked, setting the gun on the dresser beside her.

He couldn't help laughing. "What? Aren't you happy to see me?"

"Of course, but—" She pulled back, looking up at him.

Something in her eyes worried him—something wild and afraid, like a wolf trapped in a corner. "What's wrong?" he said.

"Why are you here?"

"I'm here to bring you home."

Zira shook her head. "I can't. I'm not ready yet."

"Not ready?" Jared said, trying to keep his voice gentle. "We thought you were *dead*."

"I know."

"We buried you. You know how much that hurt us? Me? Aubreigh? She hasn't been the same since." Neither had he.

"I know," Zira said quietly. She stared down at her feet.

"Come here," Jared said, taking her hand. "Just talk to me. Tell me what happened."

Zira nodded and led him out to the kitchen. They sat down at the table and, without explanation, Zira reached down and pulled up the right leg of her pants. When Jared saw what was underneath, he began to understand why she'd been unable to return to the compound right away.

The leg was gone, amputated below the knee and replaced by a battered prosthesis. "I can't go back like this," Zira said. "I couldn't even walk at first. I still can't do everything I used to." She bit her lip and looked away. "I'm useless like this."

"Stop." The thought of everything she must have gone through to end up in such a state broke his heart, but the courage it must have taken for her to get back on her feet filled him with affection. He hated to hear her talk as if there was no hope. "You're perfect. Losing one leg doesn't change that."

Zira gave him a tight smile. "I doubt Chairman Ryku will see it that way."

"I'll talk to him. He'll understand."

"Maybe. I guess I don't really have much choice anymore." Her eyes shifted back to the floor. "I *was* going to go back. I always knew I couldn't stay here forever. But I wanted to do it on my own terms, when I was stronger. I didn't want Ryku to look at me and decide I wasn't worth fixing."

Jared reached across the table and put his hand over hers. "That's not going to happen."

"I hope you're right."

"Why didn't you just come home right when it happened? Maybe they could have saved your leg."

Zira shook her head. She backed up to the day she'd left the compound for her assignment and told him everything from the beginning. There had been more radicals in the lodge than there were in her mission file, an oversight that made Jared want to strangle Chairman Ryku all over again. It had all gone downhill from there, and by the time the radicals moved on and released her from captivity, Zira felt too vulnerable to return to the compound. In the time she'd spent with Mei, the two of them had grown close. Zira fought back tears when she told Jared about how the old woman had died. "Her funeral was yesterday," Zira said. "I meant to leave right after, but I didn't know where to go. I thought about calling you."

She didn't have to explain why she hadn't; Jared understood. After all she had been through, he couldn't blame her for being afraid to go back to the compound and face the chairman's judgment. "Ryku will understand," he said again. "He has to."

"And if he doesn't?

"He will. I'll back you up."

Zira nodded. "That will help."

"I'm sorry about all of this."

"It's not your fault. I just screwed up. Again."

"It wasn't your fault, either. You had bad information. I should have come out here to look for you, with or without Ryku's permission. We were partners. I should have been here to protect you."

"That's sweet, but it's not your job to protect me."

His hands tightened around the edge of the table. "It is! That's what people do when they care about someone—they take care of them. I should have been here. I love you, Zira."

There. He'd said it. The words had been stuck in his throat ever since their hike in the canyon, and every day that she'd been gone, he'd regretted not telling her. She met his gaze with wide blue eyes, and for a moment Jared was afraid she might bolt from him. Instead, a slow smile spread across her face and she leaned across the table to kiss him. It had been such a long time since their last kiss, and Jared savored the softness of her lips. She pulled away and rested her forehead against his. "I think I love you too."

"You think?" He chuckled. "I guess I can work with that."

She gave his shoulder a playful jab. "So what now?"

"That's up to you. We can stay here for a while, or find someplace to stay in Anchorage. Either way, I've got to get some sleep." He hadn't been able to relax since the previous morning when Ryku had told him Zira was alive.

"Let's go to Anchorage," she said. "I've already got my things packed."

She went to the basement and returned a few moments later with a small backpack. They walked out to the car. Zira paused before getting inside, turning to take one last look at the house. "You okay?" Jared asked when she slid onto the seat next to him.

"Yeah. Let's go."

He kept one arm draped over her shoulder as they drove back to the city. He needed to call Ryku and let him know what had happened, and the chairman would want to talk to Zira, but that could wait until morning. For now, he would bask in the joy he would have thought impossible just two days ago. Zira was alive, and she was coming home, and she loved him. For now, everything was perfect.

CHAPTER 18

WHEN ZIRA WOKE UP THE next morning with Jared's strong arms around her waist, she experienced a brief moment of panic before she remembered where she was. She wriggled away from him and got out of bed, smiling as she listened to his deep breaths. After taking a shower, she put on the same clothes she'd worn the day before.

Looking at herself in the mirror, she reflected on the three months she'd spent in this region and how they had changed her. She hardly recognized the person she had become, and she wasn't sure if she could go back to the Project and be the person she used to be. It wasn't just her amputated leg and all the complications that came with it that had changed her. It was the food shortage and the riots, the way the authorities who were supposed to protect people had opened fire on them just for voicing their frustrations. She'd always had confidence in the Project and her role there, certain that she was an important piece of something bigger than herself, something that was crucial in holding the world together. She'd lost that confidence at some point since coming here. The uncertain expression of the girl who stared back at her from the glass was one she didn't recognize on herself.

Mei's words about the blood on her hands still haunted her. Ryku had sent her here to assassinate a group of radicals because they were deemed a threat to the Project, but from what Zira had seen, they were just trying to survive. Tripp had told her to open her eyes, and maybe she was starting to. What she saw was that the Project itself might be the real threat. It was a treasonous thought, one she would never voice out loud. But once it was in her head, she knew it would never go away.

For a moment, she considered running away. Jared was still asleep; she could be long gone by the time he woke up. She shook her head. What good would it do? Ryku would mark her a deserter and she'd spend the rest of her life running from her past, just like Tripp. Besides, it wouldn't be fair to Aubreigh and Jared. Truth be told, she knew it wouldn't even be fair to herself. She belonged in the Project. She had her doubts, but a big part of her was eager to go back to her old life there. It was all she'd ever known, her home, her family.

Zira turned away from the mirror, away from the confusion she saw in her own eyes there. She was getting herself worked up over nothing. She needed to trust the Project. She had only seen a small piece of a larger picture, and it wasn't fair to condemn the entire organization when she didn't have all the information. Once she was back home, everything would start to make sense again.

Jared was up when she came out of the bathroom, stretching his arms in the sunlight that streamed through the open blinds. Zira went to stand beside him and he kissed her forehead. "We should call Ryku," he said. "He'll be able to get you a new CL and identification. Otherwise, I don't see how you're going to get on a plane."

Zira frowned. She'd known she would have to face Ryku sometime but hadn't planned on it being so soon. She would have preferred a face-to-face discussion. Jared was right, though, and there was no point fighting it. She nodded and Jared brought up the communications display on his CyberLink. "I'm sure he'll be happy to know you're okay."

Zira faked a smile that felt a lot more like a grimace and hung back so the CL's camera couldn't see her. Jared made the call, and Ryku's face appeared in the projection over his arm. "Did you find her?" he asked.

"She's here with me now, safe and sound. I'll let her explain everything later. Right now, we need to figure out how to get her home. She needs a new CL, identification, everything."

"Of course," said Ryku. His expression remained unchanged, and Zira couldn't tell if he was happy she was alive or angry that she hadn't made more effort to get home sooner. "I'll have the Anchorage distribution center get one ready for her. You should be able to pick it up tomorrow."

"Thank you."

"Let me talk to her."

Jared took the CL off his wrist and handed it to Zira. "Sir," she said, trying not to appear as nervous as she felt.

Ryku gave her a nod. "Zira. I'm sure you can imagine how devastated we all were by your disappearance. It's good to know you're alive and well."

"Thank you, Chairman."

"That being said, I owe it to you to be perfectly honest about where I stand on this matter. We'll talk about it more when you get back, but I don't want you to get your hopes up that everything will just return to normal. I'm concerned about the fact that you haven't once tried to contact us in all this time."

"I assure you, Chairman—"

"If you have a reasonable explanation, you have nothing to worry about, but I have a responsibility to protect the Project and the people who serve under me. Any suspicious activity has to be thoroughly investigated, and to be frank, your actions seem a little suspicious. I'm putting you on probation for a minimum of two months. I also want you to be evaluated by our psychologist."

"But that's not—"

Ryku held up a hand. "It's for your own good. Two months. After that, we'll decide what to do with you."

Zira tried to keep the frustration out of her voice, though it might as well have been written in bold, neon letters all over her face. She jerked a curt nod to demonstrate her understanding. "Yes, sir."

"I'll see you soon," Ryku said. "And Zira—I'm glad you're all right."

He disconnected and she handed the CL back to Jared. "Probation," she complained. "And a psychologist?"

"It's not a bad idea," Jared said. Zira returned this comment with a glare, and Jared backpedaled. "No, I mean, it might help. It's nothing you should be worried about. I had to see him for a while after…"

He didn't finish this thought, but Zira knew he must be referring to after he'd been held captive by the Red Flag Brotherhood. She regretted even bringing up the issue. She hadn't meant to imply that counseling was ineffective or shameful, only that she didn't see the need for it in her own circumstances.

She was about to tell him this, but he spoke first. "Anyway, the E-2 psychologist is a good guy. Dr. James. He used to be one of us, so he understands some of the challenges you might be dealing with."

"I guess," she said.

"Look, Ryku might be harsh, but he's fair. As long as you can prove yourself to him, you've got nothing to worry about. That leg of yours works, doesn't it?"

"Not as well as it should."

"Maybe you can get a better one at home. And then you've got two months to keep working and getting stronger." He put a hand under her chin and gently lifted it to look her in the eyes. "You're tough, Zira. You've got this."

Just knowing that she had his support and confidence boosted her morale. Worry and self-doubt would only slow her down, something she could no longer afford. It was time stop hiding and get to work.

Zira thought about calling Aubreigh several times that day, but decided against it. She knew her friend would be happy to see her, but she'd have dozens of questions, and Zira wasn't sure how she would answer them yet. Regardless, it wasn't the kind of reunion she wanted to do over CL. She needed to see Aubreigh in person.

She and Jared picked up her new CL the following morning and caught the next available flight to Amarillo. Zira watched the city lights and snowy landscape of Anchorage disappear below her as the plane rose into the clouds. She sighed and Jared put a hand on her shoulder. "You okay?"

"It's silly, but I feel like I'm leaving something behind. I miss Mei."

"I'm sorry. You two seemed close."

Zira bit her bottom lip. She hadn't spoken much about Mei's death until now, and it was hard to find the words. "I should have been there. She saved my life, and I should have been there to save hers, too."

"You can't blame yourself."

But she did. If she hadn't been so negligent, maybe Mei would still be alive.

"You both just got caught in the wrong place at the wrong time," said Jared. "I'm sure she knows you tried."

Despite his sincerity, she found little comfort in his reassurances. All she could think about as the plane soared through the clear, blue sky was the disappointment and pain on Mei's face as she'd died in Zira's arms.

The plane landed in Amarillo just before midnight, and the drive from the airport to the compound was quiet. Jared tried to strike up a conversation a few times, but Zira was too distracted by the knot in her stomach to talk. Her heart started to pound as they got out of the car and walked up to the huge, concrete walls. The night was dark and cloudy, and the lights atop the wall shone down like eyes boring through to her soul, exposing her vulnerabilities. Zira clasped Jared's hand for security as she followed him through the gate. She hadn't expected to feel so nervous. She was coming home, after all. She should have felt more welcome and safe inside these walls, but she felt the opposite.

Her discomfort grew as they headed to Chairman Ryku's office. She kept her pace deliberately slow, but they still seemed to arrive long before she was ready. Jared turned to her with an encouraging smile. "It's going to be fine."

She took a deep breath and forced herself to knock on the door. Ryku answered almost immediately and extended a hand to Zira. "Come in and sit down," he said. "We have a lot to talk about."

They followed him to his office and sat on the couches facing him. "I trust you had a safe return," he said.

"Yes," Jared replied. "Everything went smoothly."

"Good. Let's get right to the point, then." He turned his attention to Zira. "Please explain to me what you've been doing for the last three months."

Zira took a deep breath and started at the beginning. She told him how there had been an extra man and two children in the cabin with her targets but made no mention of Tripp specifically. He'd saved her life, and she wasn't about to betray him by telling the man who wanted him dead that she'd seen him. She hadn't told Jared, either. She claimed she didn't know his name, and when she had to refer to him in her account, she simply called him 'the one who saved my life' or 'the one who wasn't in the file.' She told Ryku about how the radicals had taken her to Mei and how her leg had been amputated before she'd had a chance to say anything about it. "Once I saw what had happened," she said, "I knew I couldn't come back here. Not like that."

Ryku raised his eyebrows. "Why not?"

Zira had expected the question and had rehearsed her answer a hundred times. It came out naturally. "I was ashamed of how weak I'd become. What use is an operative who can't even stand on her own two feet? I was afraid that if I came back, you'd decide I was no use here. I'd have to leave and become an informant or something."

"There are worse things than being an informant," Ryku said. "I rely on them just as much as I rely on the rest of you."

"I know, but that's not something I ever pictured for myself. I just couldn't give up on my life here. I had a chance to get a new leg and get back to where I was before. I couldn't leave without taking it."

"And you didn't think I would allow you that opportunity if you'd just told me about it?"

"Well—no."

"I'm sorry you felt that way," Ryku said. "I wish you'd had a little more faith in me. We would have taken care of you here. You certainly would have gotten better care and medical treatment."

"Yes, sir. I understand that now, and I'm sorry. But like I said, I just couldn't take the risk." She looked at Ryku, pleading with him to understand her. "My leg isn't exactly what it used to be, but it works. And I wasn't going to stay there forever. I was already planning to come back when Jared found me." This may not have been entirely true, but it was close enough.

Ryku glanced at Jared and he nodded. "Her bags were already packed when I arrived at Dr. Yamada-Hunt's house. A few more hours and I might have missed her entirely."

Ryku nodded and sat without saying anything for a few moments, contemplating everything he had heard. His eyes bored into Zira like lasers. At last, he said, "You're lucky to have recovered as quickly as you did. Still, I think this is only further proof that a full evaluation of your skills and mental condition is extremely important. You've been through a lot. As we discussed before, I'll be placing you on probation for a minimum of two months before you can be reinstated to your usual duties."

"Yes, sir." She still didn't like the idea, but she had little choice in the matter. The fastest way to get through all of this would be to just cooperate and do whatever Ryku deemed necessary.

He walked to his desk, pulled open a drawer, and handed Zira a black armband. "Your old apartment has already been re-coded for your use, though I'm afraid you won't find any of your old belongings inside. I made appointments for you to see Dr. James on Mondays and Thursdays at one-thirty. I also expect you to make every effort to get yourself back to peak physical condition. I'll schedule you in with some of the doctors in unit A; I'm sure they can make you a better leg than the one you have now. You can attend some training sessions with the higher-level students in the unit. I know you think you're better than that, but please, humor me. I think it will help."

Just a short time ago, Zira might have been more annoyed by the prospect of being sent back to training with the recruits. Now, she knew she needed it. "Thank you, sir."

Ryku nodded. "You're a good operative. I'm glad you're back with us. It's always hard when we have to bury one of our own."

He showed them out and shut the door. Zira turned to Jared. He hadn't said much during the meeting with Ryku, but his presence had been comforting, and he'd backed her up when he needed to. "Thanks for being there with me," she told him.

"Of course."

They walked to the apartments together, and as they passed the walkway that led to Aubreigh's building, Zira wanted nothing more than to see her best friend. "I'm going to go visit Aubreigh."

"Yeah, that's probably a good idea," Jared said. "She'd kill both of us if she found out you were back and we didn't tell her right away."

He kissed her goodnight and they parted ways. Zira knocked on Aubreigh's door and waited. It was late; Aubreigh would probably be asleep and not too happy about being woken up. Still, Zira kept knocking until the door opened.

At first, Aubreigh—still rubbing sleep out of her eyes—didn't seem to register what she was seeing. Her mouth formed a tiny, surprised 'o' as she blinked several times, as if to erase some kind of half-dream or hallucination. "Zira?"

"Hi," Zira replied. She wasn't sure what to say next.

Aubreigh stepped outside and flung her arms around her, and Zira couldn't tell whether she was laughing or crying. Knowing Aubreigh, it was probably both. "I can't believe this," she said. "How? What are you doing here? No—it doesn't matter. Come in, come in."

They sat down on the couch. Aubreigh was still gaping at her. "Stop staring," Zira said. "You're making me nervous."

"You can't blame me for being a little surprised. I thought you were dead, you know, and then you just show up here in the middle of the night. I'm still not sure if I'm really awake. What happened to you?"

Zira told her as much as she could, omitting the details about her initial assignment and the radicals. Aubreigh was just as shocked as Jared had been to see what had happened to her leg, but seemed to understand why it had kept Zira from coming home right away. She was sympathetic when Zira spoke about Mei's death, and talking to her lightened some of the weight on Zira's shoulders. For the first time since she'd been home, she felt like she belonged here.

"I was hoping I could stay here for a night or two," Zira said. "They gave me back my old apartment, but Chairman Ryku said everything had been cleared out."

"Sure," Aubreigh said. "And of course tomorrow, we'll have to go shopping and find you some new clothes. The ones you're wearing now almost make me embarrassed to be your friend."

Zira threw a pillow at her in mock indignation, but she couldn't deny that Aubreigh was right. The blouse and pants she had on now were some of Mei's old things and were more than a little worn and outdated.

"I'm exhausted," she said after they had talked for a couple hours. It had been a long day, and anxiety had prevented her from sleeping on the plane. Aubreigh lent her a t-shirt and comfortable pants to sleep in and brought out a few blankets. Zira changed and stretched out on the couch. "Thanks," she said.

Aubreigh smiled. "No problem. It's good to have you back."

"It's good to be back."

She was surprised to realize that she actually meant it.

CHAPTER 19

THE FIRST LIGHT OF DAWN creeping through the windows woke Zira early the next morning. She tried to go back to sleep, but after tossing and turning for half an hour, she gave up. A sudden, almost morbid curiosity overcame her, and she stood up, got dressed, and quietly let herself out of Aubreigh's apartment.

There were only a few people up at this hour, but they all stared with wide eyes and open mouths as she made her way to the cemetery. The compound was home to a little more than ten thousand people, but the fact that the majority had lived there since they were very young meant that most of them recognized each other by face if not by name. Zira had few friends, but everyone would have heard about her death, even if they weren't told exactly how it happened. Seeing her now must be like seeing a ghost, and Zira couldn't blame them for staring.

At the southwest corner of the compound, the sidewalk turned to grass. A green hill sloped gently down until it met the sharp rise of the wall below. The hillside was neatly groomed and dotted with at least a hundred headstones, all of them a uniform, gray rectangle with bold engraved lettering. Zira walked among them until she found her own name. She reached out to touch the cold stone and wondered what her funeral had been like. Had anyone even come to the ceremony? What words had been spoken over her grave? Who had cried for her?

At Mei's funeral, thousands of tears had been shed; it seemed that everyone in Grayridge had gone to mourn her passing. Mei had touched so many lives, brought healing and comfort to anyone who needed it. What had Zira ever done to help another person? Her own funeral had probably been small and impersonal, and the only ones who might have missed her would have been Aubreigh and Jared. The value of her own life seemed so small and insignificant compared to Mei's, and Zira found herself wondering again why fate demanded that the old woman die so violently.

A familiar voice interrupted her thoughts. "Zira?"

At first, she pretended she hadn't heard Seth. He called her name again. Taking a breath to brace herself for what was sure to be an unpleasant encounter, Zira turned. Seth came closer and stood beside her. "You here to ask me some more questions for one of your investigations, or what?" she asked.

"No, nothing like that. Someone said they saw you come down here, and I had to see for myself. Chairman Ryku told everyone you were dead."

The accusatory note in his voice annoyed Zira. "For all he knew, I was. What are you doing here at the compound? Don't you have work to do out there?" She jerked a thumb in the direction of the wall behind them.

Seth gave her a wry smile. "You're not very happy to see me, are you? That's okay—I get that a lot. Unfortunately for you, we'll probably be seeing a lot more of each other. They pulled me from my regional office, so I'm stationed here now. Something about a lack of people skills, I think, but since it was a promotion, I don't mind."

"Good for you," said Zira flatly.

They stood in silence for a while, both staring at the headstone below. "It must be strange, seeing your own grave," Seth said.

It was, but she didn't respond.

"If you ever need someone to talk to, I'm here." Zira gave him an incredulous look, wondering what she had ever said or done to make him think she'd confide in him. He smirked. "Just an idea. I'm glad you're okay. See you around."

He walked away with that awful, pompous air he had, leaving Zira to her thoughts. His presence seemed to have tainted the place with an obnoxious, nagging feeling, and Zira left a few minutes later. There were more people milling about the compound now, which meant that more people stared and whispered as she walked back to Aubreigh's apartment. This time, Zira was less tolerant and more irritated by the attention. Couldn't they all just mind their own business? How long would she have to put up with this?

Aubreigh was awake and dressed by the time Zira got back. "You ready to go? I thought we could go to breakfast in Amarillo."

Zira agreed with this suggestion enthusiastically, already dreading a meal in the cafeteria where she was sure to face more curious stares and gossip. They borrowed a car from unit C and, after breakfast, spent most of the day trying on clothes and looking for basic necessities for Zira's apartment. With a haircut and clothes of her own, Zira felt more like her old self. She and Aubreigh spent the evening hanging things in her closet and arranging her apartment so it looked almost exactly as it had before.

Jared stopped by to walk to dinner with her. He waved to Aubreigh and gave Zira a quick kiss. "You look great," he said.

"Having clothes from this decade probably helps."

Jared chuckled and handed her a slip of paper. "Ryku asked me to pass this on to you."

She glanced over it. The note instructed her to go to the unit A research facility in the morning to be fitted for a new leg. Ryku had also listed several training sessions he wanted her to attend and reminded her about meeting with Dr. James on Mondays and Thursdays. She had a very busy schedule, it seemed, but that was preferable to having excessive amounts of free time with nothing to do.

"Still running errands for Ryku, I see," Aubreigh said. There was some kind of implication behind her tone that made Zira curious. She looked at Jared questioningly.

He rubbed a hand across the back of his neck. "Just trying to help him out a little. It's no big deal."

"Oh, stop being modest. I'm not an E-2, but even I know how much you've been working with the chairman lately."

"I guess."

"Is he retiring or something?"

"Of course not. He's not even fifty."

Aubreigh shrugged. "I'm just saying what everyone else is saying. He's preparing you to take his place."

"Maybe," Jared said. He was looking at everything in the room but Zira and Aubreigh. "But it won't be for a long time, anyway."

"Why are you so embarrassed?" Zira asked. "You should be proud."

"I am proud."

"Then why didn't you tell me?"

Jared shrugged. "It's a lot of pressure. Everyone treats me differently now. It's weird."

She could understand why he might not want to make a big deal of it. He might even be worried that she would start treating him differently because of whatever new status he seemed to have attained. She took his hand and gave it a reassuring squeeze, then changed the subject. "Come on," she said and pulled him towards the door. "Let me tell you who I ran into at the cemetery earlier."

■ ■ ■

The following day, Zira went to unit A's research facility to be examined for a new prosthesis. She'd never been inside before, but it was one of the most distinguishable buildings in the compound. The exterior walls were alternating panels of concrete and glass that reflected the blue sky brilliantly. The inside was just as impressive, all sharp angles and sleek surfaces. A robot scanned her identification at the door and notified someone that she'd arrived. A few minutes later, two women in white lab coats and yellow armbands escorted her to a room with a reclining chair and numerous medical instruments.

For two hours, Zira's leg was measured, prodded, x-rayed, and thoroughly examined. The two women made notes on their CLs as they watched her walk, run, jump, and go up and down stairs. They looked at the battered prosthesis Mei had given her, shook their heads, and exchanged dismayed looks with one another. "It's too tall for you," one said.

"And so primitive," the other added.

"We could give you a robotic leg, if you like."

"No," Zira said. She was just getting used to the prosthesis and didn't want to have to start over with an entirely different kind of replacement. "Just make it like that one, only better."

They both looked slightly disappointed but agreed to Zira's request. "We'll have it done in a few days. Someone will send you a message when it's ready."

She left to go to a 10:00 physical training session with a small group of E-2 recruits. The six of them were all lined up against the wall of the training center when she arrived. Since her black armband was missing the white stripe that marked recruits, they mistook her for their trainer at first, snapping to attention and looking to her for direction as she walked towards them. They seemed confused when she took her place at the end of the line. One boy who looked to be almost her age leaned over to the girl next to him, and Zira caught the words 'dead' and 'Grayridge' in their whispered conversation. She gave him an icy stare but said nothing.

The trainer arrived, a tall woman in her thirties named Laurel who had been one of Zira's favorites when she was a recruit. She was surprisingly kind compared to most of the other unit instructors but still commanded respect and made her recruits work hard. "I'm sure you all know Zira," she said to the group. "She's going to be training with us for a while. You're lucky to have the chance to work with an active member of this unit. Pay attention and you might learn a thing or two from her."

They stretched as a group, then Laurel set them to work on some sprints across the facility floor as a warm up. Zira pushed herself as hard as she could, but she still lagged far behind everyone else. This seemed true for every activity they did. No matter how hard she tried, she couldn't keep up. By the end of the session, her stump throbbed painfully, and she limped out of the facility feeling frustrated and defeated.

Jared sensed that something was wrong when she met him for lunch that afternoon and asked her about it. She told him about the training session. "You'll get stronger," he said. "That's the whole point of this. Don't give up."

"I'm not giving up. It just pisses me off that I can't do this."

"You can."

"Yeah?" Zira growled "When?"

"It's going to take time—you know that."

"What if I don't get better?" Zira asked, voicing a fear that had tormented her from the moment she saw that her leg had been amputated. "What if this is the best I can do?"

"We'll figure that out when we get there. For now, just keep working at it. You're getting a new leg in a few days—a better leg. That should help. Just take it easy until then. Don't kill yourself. If you get hurt, you'll just have to start all over."

After lunch, Zira had to hurry to the medical station for her meeting with Dr. James. The scrawny, freckle-faced man sitting in an armchair hardly looked like the type who had once been an E-2 operative. He stood up when Zira entered and shook her hand. "Hello, Zira. I'm Dr. James." He gestured to a couch for Zira to sit on and returned to his own chair. Zira slumped into the couch, trying not to dwell on all the better things she could be doing right now.

For the next hour, Dr. James asked her dozens of questions about her life and any factors that might be affecting her stress level. She gave the shortest answers possible. She didn't know Dr. James; by default, she didn't trust him. Did he really expect her to open up to him completely? Judging from the questions he was asking, that was exactly what he wanted. Zira just wanted to get this over with as quickly and painlessly as possible.

Finally, he leaned back in his chair and sighed. "You know I can't help you unless you talk to me."

"I am talking," Zira said. "And I don't need your help."

"You might be right about that. I'm going to level with you here, Zira. I think this is as much a waste of my time as it is yours. But Chairman Ryku wants me to evaluate you, so that's what I'm trying to do. And you need my evaluation to get back to work, correct?"

"Yeah."

"So do yourself a favor and help me out. You can talk to me. Nothing you say here ever has to leave this room."

Zira's eyes narrowed. "But you have to report back to Ryku about me."

"I just have to tell him whether or not I think you're mentally and emotionally prepared to go back to work. The specifics don't matter."

Zira looked out the window in silence, considering for a moment that Dr. James might actually be able to help her. There was so much that she still needed to sort out in her head. Mei's death, the things she'd seen in Grayridge, her doubts about working for an organization she no longer trusted completely. Dr. James was almost an outsider, and perhaps that gave him a clearer view of things than Zira or Jared or anyone else in the unit. Jared had spoken highly of him, so maybe she *could* trust him. Maybe.

Before she could respond, Dr. James stood up. "We're done for today. Just think about what I said."

After that meeting, she had more PT with the same group of recruits as before, this time led by a bulldog of a man named Fuller who was much less understanding of Zira's condition than Laurel had been. Insults flew out of his mouth like water out of a fire hose. He seemed to take a special interest in Zira, laying into her even more than she remembered from when she'd been a recruit. She could hardly concentrate with him breathing down her neck, and she barely managed to reign in her frustration by picturing herself punching him in the face. By the time the session was over, she wanted to scream at someone herself.

This, of course, only made Seth's timing worse than usual when he approached her near the apartments. Zira didn't even have the energy to fake courtesy. "Goodbye, Seth," she said through gritted teeth as he matched her stride.

Seth was undeterred. "I was hoping we could talk."

"Now's not a good time."

"Oh, okay. When would be a good time, then?"

Zira unlocked her apartment door and stepped inside. "Never," she said, and slammed the door in his face.

CHAPTER 20

THE NEW LEG UNIT A constructed for Zira was an impressive piece of equipment. Black and somewhat tactical in appearance, she could tell it was far superior to her old one the instant she put it on. It felt more balanced, and the flexible ankle joint responded to pressure almost as well as her real one had before. With this, she was more confident than ever that she could get back to her old physical capabilities.

She attended all of her required training sessions without complaint in the next several weeks. Climbing over walls, rolling into cover, hand-to-hand combat—all of it was new to her with her new leg. She didn't see improvement right away, but in time it seemed the frequency of Fuller's screaming decreased, and she didn't lag so far behind the others.

Jared celebrated each success with her and encouraged her to stay positive when she'd had a particularly bad day. They spent as much time as possible together, which wasn't as much as they might have liked since he was often with Chairman Ryku these days, attending joint unit meetings or putting together assignments for other operatives. Zira noticed the changes he'd mentioned in the way people treated him. When they were alone, he was the same Jared she had known and befriended six months ago, but there seemed to be something different about him when others were around. It might have been the way he carried himself. It might not have even been anything inherent about him, but she could easily see the increased level of respect he commanded around the compound, especially from their fellow E-2 operatives. It was something in their eyes and the way their bodies straightened whenever he walked by. They looked at him in much the same way as they looked at Ryku, with a mixture of deference, awe, and fear.

Zira also tried to keep up on the news coming out of the North Pacific Region. The Grayridge riots were briefly discussed by the media when she first came home, but always with a slant that painted the protesters as ungrateful troublemakers stirring up unwarranted conflict. There was no mention of the food shortage that had started it all, nor of the little girl who had starved to death, nor of any victims killed by officials trying to shut down what they called a riot. The unit P officers and other authorities were always portrayed as heroes, putting a peaceful end to the chaos brought on by the deluded citizens of the region. After a few days, the media stopped talking about it altogether.

She asked Jared what he thought about the situation one night as they walked back from the shooting range. It felt safer to talk about such things here outside the wall. She wondered if he even knew the truth. "Do you know why the people in Grayridge protested?"

Jared shrugged. "I know they claimed they weren't getting enough food."

"They weren't. Mei and I used to take some of her extras around to help the others."

"How did she have extra?"

"The radicals left it with her before they went away. Caribou meat, mostly, and some other nonperishables they'd stockpiled."

He nodded and thought about this for a moment. "I'm sure it wasn't as bad as they made it out to be."

"A little girl died. She starved, or maybe she was just malnourished. Either way, people blamed the Project. That's why they started protesting."

Jared looked at her, head tilted to one side. "That wasn't in the news."

"A lot of things aren't in the news." They walked in silence for a few more minutes before she dared to say the thing she'd been thinking ever since Mei died. "Maybe the radicals are right in trying to get away from all this. We control so much of their lives, and then when something bad happens, we try to erase it." She thought of something Tripp had said, his reasons for leaving the Project. Too many lies. Too many secrets. *Open your eyes.*

"If we control them, it's only to keep them safe," Jared said. "Before the war, there wasn't enough control, and look what happened. Our grandparents and great-grandparents nearly destroyed the world."

"It just seems excessive sometimes. Ryku asked me to kill those radicals, but they didn't even seem like a real threat. Not like Feng or Li or even the ones we saw at the factory. They were just trying to survive. Two of them were just kids."

"The kids weren't supposed to be there."

"Yeah, but why were any of them targets at all?"

Jared stopped walking and gently pulled her around to face him. His eyes darted across hers, trying to understand. "Where is all of this coming from?"

"I don't know." She shook her head. "Never mind. Just forget about it."

She didn't mention her doubts to him any more after that. Instead, she made an effort to open up to Dr. James during their bi-weekly meetings. The man was surprisingly helpful, though Zira would never admit that to him. They talked about Zira's frustrations over her slow recovery, and eventually, about Mei's death. It was a sort of test Zira had devised to determine how much she could really confide in him. He'd done well so far, and though she still wasn't sure she could trust him completely, she decided it was time to tell him what was troubling her most.

She blurted it out one afternoon like a lighting strike, sudden and sharp. "I don't trust the PEACE Project anymore."

Dr. James hadn't even settled into his chair yet. He paused, then sat down and adjusted his tie. Zira backed up to the day she'd received her assignment to kill the radicals. She wasn't sure how much he knew already, but she told him everything. He listened in silence, not even bothering to jot notes on his CL as he usually did. When Zira had finished, he just said, "That's quite a story."

"It's not just a story."

"I know; sorry. But you do realize the seriousness of your accusations, don't you? The PEACE Project can't be trusted. Chairman Ryku sent you to kill people who weren't really a threat. Unit C's mismanagement of the distribution center caused a child to starve to death. Unit P opened fire on a group of unarmed civilians. It all goes against everything the Project is supposed to stand for."

"I know. That's why it bothers me so much."

"Have you talked to anyone else about this? Besides Jared?"

"No. Just him, and now you."

"From what I understand, Jared is close to the Chairman."

"He is."

"And you haven't told Ryku any of this?" Zira shook her head, and Dr. James leaned forward with his elbows on his knees. "If I were you, I would talk to Ryku before he hears about this from someone else."

Sensing a threat, Zira glared at him. "What about that client confidentiality you're always talking about?"

Dr. James shook his head. "I promise you, he won't hear it from me. But one thing I've learned about chairmen's dogs over the years is that they're always more loyal to their masters than they are to anything else."

Zira clenched her fists. "Jared wouldn't say anything. He loves me."

"That may be, but if it came down to duty or love, do you know which one would he choose?"

As much as Zira wanted to say that nothing would make Jared betray her trust, she couldn't. He was ambitious. That was how he'd earned so much of Ryku's esteem in the first place. She didn't think he would tell the chairman anything without being prompted, but she suspected that Ryku didn't fully trust her. If he wanted information about her, Jared would be the obvious first choice for questioning.

"Zira," Dr. James said, "I'm only here to try and help you see all of your options. I can't make the choice for you, and I can't pretend to know Jared any better than you do. But Ryku is a dangerous man. He doesn't like secrets and half-truths from his people. Just think about what I said. If you won't confront him to protect yourself, at least do it so you can move on with your life. You've been through hell, and you deserve an answer. You'll always wonder if you don't ask."

Zira sighed. She hated the idea of confronting Ryku about the Project's questionable methods. There was no way to say it without it sounding like an accusation. But Dr. James was right; she wasn't getting anywhere by keeping her doubts bottled up inside. "Thanks for the advice."

He shook her hand as she stood up to leave. "You're welcome. I'll see you next week."

She walked out of the building and, before she could talk herself out of it, went straight to Chairman Ryku's office. He didn't answer right away. She almost lost her nerve and left, but forced herself to knock again. Ryku opened the door, looking mildly surprised to see her. "Zira—to what do I owe the pleasure?"

She had never hated his stiff formalities and false politeness more than she did now. "I need to talk to you about something."

"Unfortunately, I'm rather busy right now. Can it wait until tomorrow?"

Zira almost agreed to the suggestion, but she would only be doing so out of fear, and she wasn't about to let her fear control her actions any more than it already had. "It's important."

Ryku's frown deepened. "Very well, then. Come in." He led the way in to his office and gestured to the couch, but Zira stood firmly in front of him. "Well, what is it?"

"I wanted to talk to you about what happened in Grayridge," Zira said.

Something like a smile crossed Ryku's face for a moment. "I was wondering when you might get around to this. I knew you must have seen things there that raised some questions."

It was uncanny, sometimes, just how much the chairman seemed to know. Zira felt a chill in her spine, and a muscle in her face twitched. She didn't dare ask him about the food shortages or why unit P had put down the protests so forcibly. It would be too accusatory, bordering on treasonous, and Ryku would just tell her it was none of her concern how the other units chose to handle their responsibilities. She could ask him about her targets, though—the reason all of this had happened to her in the first place. "You sent me to kill three people over there. Radicals, we call them. People who oppose what the Project's doing."

"Yes." Ryku looked at Zira in a way that reminded her of a tiger she'd seen on an old educational program as a child. Predatory. Dangerous.

She chose her next words carefully. "They didn't really seem like a threat. I guess I just don't understand why you wanted me to kill them."

"You don't trust my judgment."

Zira didn't respond, afraid that any misstep would push her further into some kind of trap.

Ryku crossed his arms. "Zira, I am the chairman of this unit, which means I have access to information the rest of you do not. What you know about a target is not the same as what I know, and I disclose information to you at my own discretion. It's not your place to question my authority or your orders. You do what you're told—that's it."

A surge of hot anger replaced Zira's fear. It flew out of her mouth before she had time to curb it. "That's not good enough! You have no idea what I lost on that assignment. I almost died, and I want to know what for. You owe me an explanation."

"I owe you *nothing*," Ryku hissed, drawing himself up to his full height. For an instant, Zira saw the formidable young operative he must have been years before. She'd never felt smaller in her life, but she held her ground. She wouldn't leave until she had answers.

Ryku waited a few seconds before speaking again, searching her face for something, perhaps some sign of weakness. Zira refused to give him any such sign. "Since you asked," he said, all traces of anger vanishing from his voice, "and since the matter is obviously important to you, I'll tell you. It's true that the radicals you failed to kill were not as dangerous as most of our targets. Some might even call them innocent. However, their very existence undermines everything this Project stands for. They oppose our laws and refuse to contribute to society, yet they expect the Project to give them the rights and resources they're not entitled to. One or two or even a dozen of them might not be a threat, but a hundred or a thousand could cause significant damage to everything we've worked so hard to build. If they had their way, this country would dissolve into complete anarchy. They're as much a threat to our peace and security as any other target you've eliminated."

Zira could hardly believe what she was hearing. She had expected the chairman to produce evidence that showed the radicals were planning some kind of attack on the Project or trying to recruit the masses to their cause and start a rebellion. Instead, he was admitting that he'd orchestrated their deaths not because they were a threat, but because they had the mere potential to become one.

"Not what you were hoping to hear, is it?" Ryku asked.

"Not what I was expecting," she said. "Not after all the years we spent learning that a life should only be taken as a last resort, when the person would harm others if they were allowed to live."

"But they would have harmed others," Ryku said. "Perhaps not directly, but their extremist ideas might have become a problem had they been allowed to spread."

"And they deserved to die for that?"

Ryku sighed and rubbed a hand over his eyes. He spoke with the tone of an adult explaining a difficult truth to a young child, condescending, impatient. "I know this is hard for you to understand, Zira. You're young, and you have a lot to learn and experience before you can begin to see the world clearly. Things aren't always black and white. Sometimes the choices we have to make seem wrong, but in the long run, they are the only right choice."

Nothing Ryku was saying convinced her that his decisions had been any less wrong, and his patronizing tone only upset her even more. "You could have just had the E-1s arrest them."

He shook his head. "It's not that simple. I'm not happy with all of the choices I have to make as the chairman of this unit, but they are *my* choices. At the end of the day, I can hold my head high knowing I made the best possible decision that I could for the peace and safety of this country. I hope you can understand that."

Zira swallowed her anger, realizing how unwise it would be to let Ryku see her true emotions. She tried to pretend that she accepted what he was telling her, but she would never understand how a person could justify taking a life on those terms. With a dry throat and a heart made of lead, she thanked the chairman for his time and walked out of the office.

She had almost reached her apartment when Jared put his hands on her shoulders from behind. "There you are," he said. "I've been looking for you." Zira didn't respond; she was in no mood for company. Jared took her hand gently and asked, "What's the matter?"

"Nothing," Zira said. She managed a small smile and kept walking.

"It's a beautiful day, and I'm free the rest of the afternoon. I was thinking we could go for a hike."

Zira shook her head. "Maybe another day."

She wished he would just go. She couldn't talk to him about this even if she had wanted to. Dr. James had been right when he'd suggested that Jared's first loyalty was to Chairman Ryku and his unit, not to her. The truth of it irritated her so much that she could hardly tolerate his presence right now.

Jared didn't say anything else until they had reached Zira's apartment. "What's wrong?"

"I'm just tired, I guess."

"That's a lie."

Zira flung the door open and stepped inside, whirling around to block him from following her. "Just let it go! I'm fine."

"Sure had me fooled," he muttered.

Zira slammed the door and flung herself on the couch. She shouldn't have been so snappy with him. None of this was his fault, but he worked so closely with Ryku these days that it was hard to separate Jared her friend from Jared the chairman's dog. It felt like a betrayal somehow, though Jared hadn't really done anything wrong. If anything, *she* was the one who was wrong here. Hot tears pricked at her eyes, but she blinked them away before they could fall. Nothing made sense anymore, and she tossed and turned for hours that night, trying—and failing—to make sense of everything Ryku had told her.

CHAPTER 21

JARED HAD AN ASSIGNMENT, AND Zira didn't have the opportunity to talk to him again before he left. Aubreigh was also gone, but Zira knew she couldn't tell her friend any of this even if she'd been around. Instead, she confided in Dr. James once more.

"Did you talk to Chairman Ryku?" he asked at their next meeting.

Zira told him about their conversation and what she had learned. She was still so conflicted about everything that her head spun just thinking about it. She hated that she felt this way. She had killed people before and never had any major qualms about it. In many ways, Ryku's justification for targeting radicals even made sense. "Do you think he's right?" she asked Dr. James. "Maybe I'm just being too sensitive about it."

"A moral question," he said. "Which of course means that there are countless answers, and none of them are completely right or wrong. I understand his reasoning, but I can also understand your misgivings about it. It might take some time for you to come to terms with what you've learned. The important thing is that at least you've put it out in the open. That's a good start."

"I guess so."

"You don't sound very relieved."

"I'm just confused." All this time, she had believed that she and her fellow operatives were doing the right thing. It was awful and harsh, and as Ryku had said, things weren't always black and white. But ultimately, they were doing the right thing. They were protecting people, preventing catastrophe before it happened. Maybe that was still true, and she just needed to shift her focus in order to see it. But it seemed that every time she tried, she remembered the look in Mei's eyes when she'd returned to the house after killing Hartman, when she'd shot that officer in the Grayridge protest.

"Confusion is a natural response," said Dr. James, "but you need to ask yourself if you're prepared to accept what you've learned. Can you live with it?"

Zira let out a short, humorless laugh. "Of course I can. What other choice do I have?"

"There's always a choice, Zira."

As much as she would have liked to believe him, she couldn't. She had nothing else but the PEACE Project. She couldn't run from it, couldn't simply choose another life. Once you were in the Project, you were in it for life. The walls of the compound had been built to keep people in as much as they were intended to keep people out. The few who had dared to desert the Project over the years had been hunted down and captured or killed by members of units E-1 and E-2. Even Tripp, who'd managed to survive fifteen years on the outside, would spend his entire life on the run, wondering when Ryku's assassins would finally catch up to him. Unless she wanted to share that fate, Zira had about as much choice in the matter as she'd had to be born with blonde hair.

Aubreigh came home later that week. They were eating lunch together in the cafeteria when she said,

"Seth's been looking for you. He was trying to talk to me this morning about what you'd been doing when you, well, you know, *died*."

"What did you tell him?"

"Nothing," Aubreigh said. "Actually, I told him to shove off and mind his own business. It's not like I could tell him anything even if I wanted to. I barely know anything myself."

"Aubreigh, I'm sorry. You know I can't—"

She waved a hand. "No, no. I get it—really. Besides, I'm not sure I want to know anymore." She looked past Zira and jerked her chin forward. "Speak of the devil."

Seth plunked his lunch tray on the table next to Zira before she had time to make a hasty retreat. "Hello," he said cheerfully.

Zira said nothing. Aubreigh smiled at Seth, but it was perhaps a less friendly smile than it might have been a few months ago.

"How have you been, Zira?" Seth asked. "I heard you've been training with some of the E-2 recruits since you've been back."

"I'm fine," she said.

"Good. You're adjusting back to life here?"

"Yes."

"Glad to hear it. Look, I've really been wanting to talk to you about what happened while you were gone. I know you're busy, but it would mean a lot to me if you could just give me a few minutes."

"Why do you think it's any of your business what happened to me?"

"I'm just doing my job. Investigating. The whole thing was a little suspicious. Did you know there was some kind of explosion in the North Pacific Region around the same time you were pronounced dead? It happened in the same area, too."

"You don't know where I was. You don't know anything."

A clever smile spread across Seth's lips, and Zira realized too late that by reacting so defensively, she'd given him the information he wanted. "Your chairman abandoned you over there. He barely even bothered with a search party, and he certainly didn't try to recover your body for the funeral."

"Shut up, Seth!" said Aubreigh.

Zira drew a breath and clenched her fists under the table. "Again, Seth—none of this is any of your business."

"I know you don't want to talk to me. I know you think you're doing the right thing by not answering my questions, but we're on the same side here." He lowered his voice to a whisper and leaned towards her. "I've got a bad feeling about some of the things going on in this Project, and I could really use your help."

If only he knew. She picked up her tray and stood to leave.

Seth grabbed her arm. "Please. Just tell me what happened over there."

"You want to know what happened over there?" Zira wrenched her arm away from him and slammed her tray back on the table. The cafeteria went quiet as everyone turned to watch the confrontation, but she didn't care. She hitched the right side of her pants up to show him her leg. "This. *This* happened over there. And if it's okay with you, I don't want to talk about it. Leave me alone."

She left him standing there with his mouth agape. Aubreigh started yelling at him as Zira walked away. She hurried back to her apartment, and as soon as she shut the door behind her, sank to the floor with her arms around her knees. Why was she so upset? Why did everything continue to get worse when it should have been getting better? Coming back to the compound was supposed to be a good thing. It was what she'd wanted, wasn't it? To be back at home? But it didn't feel like home anymore. She felt like a prisoner waiting to be sentenced, but she didn't know what crime she had committed.

Jared came home after two weeks. By this time, most of the initial anger she'd felt during their last conversation had gone out of her. When she found him standing outside her door after a training session, she wrapped her arms around his waist and rested her head on his chest.

"I'm sorry for the way we left things," he said. "I should have just given you some space."

"It wasn't your fault. I was mad about something else."

He pulled back to look her in the eyes. "Do you want to talk about it?"

She considered this, unsure of how he would react to her doubts and everything Ryku had told her. But she trusted him, and maybe he could help her make sense of it. She nodded and opened the door to her apartment.

They sat down on Zira's couch and she told him about her last conversation with the chairman. She'd expected him to be just as disturbed by the truth as she was, or at least surprised, but his face remained expressionless. "I'm not sure what you want me to say," he said after she'd finished.

What *did* she want him to say? She wanted him to rage at how wrong Ryku's justification was, to march to the chairman's door and demand answers. She wanted him to wring his hands and pace the floor trying to understand the implications of this. She wanted him to explain it in a way that would clear her own head, and at the same time, she didn't. In short, she wanted him to feel all the turmoil she felt, not because she needed his support or his empathy, but because she needed to know she was *right* to feel that way. She needed to know she wasn't just losing her mind.

"I just don't know what to think anymore," she said. "What are we doing here, really? What's the point of all this? We say we're only killing people who pose a real threat, but is that actually true?" She shook her head. "I feel like I crossed a line somewhere with those people in that cabin. I didn't kill them, but I would have, and I don't think they would have deserved it. I just don't know if I can do this anymore."

"You didn't tell Ryku *that*, did you?"

"Of course not." She knew as well as he did that telling the chairman such things would only make her situation worse.

"I know this is confusing, Zira, but you have to try to understand it. Give it some time; things will sort themselves out. You just have to look at the big picture."

Zira nodded, wanting to believe that he was right, that it could really be so simple. If she was going to have any sort of future here, she *needed* to believe it—sooner rather than later. She had less than three weeks left in her probation and needed to pass Ryku's evaluation, which would doubtless be based in part on whether or not he thought she could accept what he'd told her.

She finished out those last days strong, having made significant improvements in her physical abilities. She easily kept up with the rest of the group during PT and could best any one of the recruits when they sparred. Fuller ignored her entirely during her final week, and as she walked out of the facility on her last day, he shook her hand. "You did good," he said. "I'm going to miss having you around to show these other idiots how it's done."

She grinned at him as she walked out into the cool night air and almost ran right into Chairman Ryku, who had walked out of the shadows so quietly he could have been a ghost. He held a large tan envelope in his hands and handed it to Zira. She stared at it, her mouth hanging open. "Is this—?"

"An assignment, yes," Ryku finished. "Dr. James and your trainers spoke very highly of your performance. They have full confidence that you'll continue to be an asset to our unit. Welcome back."

He walked away as quickly and quietly as he had appeared, and Zira headed for her apartment with the file clutched against her chest. She couldn't decide whether or not she was happy about the assignment. In spite of her misgivings about Ryku, she still valued his opinion of her and was pleased that he thought she'd done well since returning to the compound. Maybe an assignment was what she needed to sort out her uncertainties. If she completed this mission, maybe things would go back to the way they'd been before—the way they should be.

Zira opened the door to her apartment, set the file on the table, and got a glass of water. She had to stop dwelling on things she couldn't change and find her place in the Project again. If Ryku thought she was ready for an assignment, then why shouldn't she be? She opened the file and began planning how she was going to take out her target.

CHAPTER 22

THE COASTAL CITY OF DAVINSPORT was much colder than the mild early-spring climate Zira had gotten used to at the PEACE Project compound, but not nearly as cold as it had been in Grayridge. Cool sea breezes that might have been pleasant in the summer pierced through her jacket like icicles as she waited at the bus stop. She clenched her jaw to keep her teeth from chattering.

Her target was Albert Randolph, a wealthy man who owned several massage parlors that served as fronts for a vast human trafficking operation. He'd been arrested a dozen times but never convicted of anything, and unit E-1 had passed their evidence on to Chairman Ryku. It was enough to convince Zira that Randolph was guilty, and she was grateful Ryku had chosen such an obviously corrupt target for her first assignment since coming back. She had no misgivings about putting a bullet through Randolph's skull.

The bus arrived right on time, and Zira was grateful for its warm interior. She took a seat in the back, shoving her large, pink messenger bag under her feet. The bag looked almost as innocent and charming as Zira did with her youthful face and naïve smile. Inside it, though, was the disassembled rifle she would use to take out Randolph. The rifle had been Jared's suggestion. "You've always been a good shot," he'd said. "This way, you won't even have to go near the target." Ryku hadn't specified that the kill needed to be especially clean or look like an accident, so she'd decided to take Jared's advice.

She got off the bus in the center of town. Tall buildings lined the streets, and it didn't take Zira long to find the one Randolph lived in. She brought up the apartment building's three-dimensional blueprint on her CL and compared it to the structure in front of her. Once she figured out which balcony was Randolph's, she began searching for a good place from which to take her shot. There weren't many other buildings tall enough to provide a good vantage point, but she finally found one a few blocks down the street. After that, it was a simple matter of gaining access to the rooftop, which she accomplished by telling the janitor she just wanted to watch the sunset and take some pictures.

Once there, Zira crouched against the wall of a utilities shed in the corner and began piecing the rifle together. It took her less than a minute, and once the shot was taken, she'd disassemble it even faster. She'd be on a bus back to the airport long before the police showed up.

She checked to make sure the scope was mounted properly, then made a few quick calculations and adjustments to account for the wind. She got down on her stomach and pushed the rifle against her shoulder, sliding a single bullet into the chamber. The scope gave her a clear view through the windows of Randolph's apartment.

An hour passed before she saw any signs of movement. Her nerves were frayed, and her body had stiffened in the cold. As soon as Randolph's face appeared in her sights, though, Zira forgot about everything else. She shifted the rifle more snugly against her shoulder. She had the shot from the bedroom window right now, but the bullet's impact against the glass could shift its course. Not much, perhaps, but enough that Zira didn't want to take the risk if she didn't have to. She would wait for him to go out to the balcony. If that meant she had to wait for hours or even come back the next day, so be it. She had all the time in the world, and she didn't want to mess this one up.

Dusk began to settle over the city, lengthening the shadows and painting everything in a dramatic contrast of light and dark. Zira barely noticed it; her entire world was contained in the ring of her scope. In her cross-hairs, Randolph poured himself a glass of wine from an expensive-looking bottle. Zira wondered how many human lives he'd sold to pay for it. He stretched and loosened the tie around his neck, then walked through the living room and out to the balcony.

This was it—the perfect shot, the moment where Zira would earn her place back in the Project and prove herself a devoted E-2 operative. She took a deep breath and let it out slowly, steadying the cross-hairs on the back of Randolph's head. She inhaled again, held the breath, put pressure on the trigger.

Another figure entered her sights, so small that his head bobbed just along the bottom of the circle that was Zira's world. She watched as Randolph lifted the boy in green pajamas and spun him around. Father and son both laughed. The pure innocence of the scene was enough to pull Zira's finger away from the trigger.

She tried to put it back, but her hand wouldn't obey. She remembered Tripp, Alma, Nate, Liza, the kids.

Could this be the same thing? Was Randolph really the man Ryku claimed him to be? Or was he the man Zira saw in front of her now, a devoted father with a son who obviously adored him? He was probably both.

It didn't matter. She had her orders, and she had no choice but to follow them.

There's always a choice. Dr. James' words cut through her mind like a knife.

Immediately after came Mei's voice. *It won't be long before your soul is tainted by the same blood that's on your hands.*

Open your eyes.

Zira put her finger back on the trigger. She reminded herself of everything that had been in Randolph's file—all the faces of missing people he was suspected to be responsible for. They deserved justice, or at the very least, vengeance. She could give them that, and all it would take was to pull the trigger and send a bullet straight into Randolph's skull.

But it was Ryku who had put that file together, just as he had put the radicals' file together a few months before, with information that had been manipulated to make them all look like a threat. How could she justify murdering Randolph in front of his own son when she didn't even know if she could trust the man who'd ordered his execution?

The boy took his father's hand, and the two walked back inside together. One by one, the curtains of the windows were drawn, leaving Zira blind. Her moment had come and gone. There was nothing more she could do.

Cursing, she sat up and leaned back against the wall. She took apart the rifle and shoved the pieces into the pink bag. For a moment, she entertained the idea of coming back to try again tomorrow, perhaps earlier in the day when the kid would be at school. If it hadn't been for the kid, Randolph would already be dead.

Deep down, she knew that wasn't true. She was an assassin, but she wasn't a cold-blooded killer, and she wasn't a blind follower anymore, either. If she couldn't shoot Randolph today, she wouldn't be able to do it tomorrow or the next day or a week from now.

Ryku had been wrong. She *wasn't* ready for this. But he would never understand that, and Zira knew she would have to come up with some excuse for her actions when she got back to the compound in order to buy herself some time. If she had no real future in her unit anymore, she was going to have to figure out something else, and she had no idea where to even begin.

She was playing a risky game with a dangerous man, and it was only a matter of time before her luck and her excuses ran out.

CHAPTER 23

BY THE TIME ZIRA GOT back to the compound the next day, she felt more conflicted than ever. She stood by the decision she'd made on the rooftop, but a small part of her screamed at herself for not completing her assignment. She'd turned her back on the best chance she had to get her old life back, and in doing so, she'd put herself in a precarious situation. There was no way to know how Ryku would react when he found out what she'd done, but he wouldn't be happy. Not that Zira planned on telling him the truth—that she'd lost her nerve. She'd already concocted a number of excuses to write in her mission report, all of which revolved around the idea that an opportune moment had never presented itself. She hoped the chairman would take her history of botching recent assignments into account and assume she was being extra cautious. It was the best she could do for now. Later, she might be able to request a transfer outside the compound to work as an informant. A bitter irony, since that had been the last thing she'd wanted just a few short months ago. Now, though, the only thing Zira knew for certain was that she never wanted to kill someone on Ryku's orders again.

She wrote up her report as quickly as she could and took it to his office before she could change her mind.

Jared was on his way out when she got there. "Back already? How did it go?"

"Fine," Zira said. "Everything went fine."

She had already decided not to tell him what had happened, partly because of what Dr. James had said about chairmen's dogs, and partly because she just didn't want to face his inevitable disappointment in her. Lying to him made her uncomfortable, but not quite as uncomfortable as trying to explain herself when she knew he wouldn't understand. Jared's first loyalty was, and always would be, to his unit. He'd devoted his life to serving the Project and had complete confidence in its every principle. That was what made him the perfect operative. Not his size or his strength or his calculated decisions, but his unwavering dedication to his work, his readiness to follow every command without question.

Once, she'd admired that about him. Even now, she envied him. Everything would be so much easier if she could just believe in Ryku's skewed morals, if she could accept his justification that sometimes eliminating threats meant hurting otherwise innocent people just because they stepped out of line. She might have been able to accept it before, but something inside her had changed while she was in Grayridge. Maybe it was the fact that she'd almost died and realized how fragile life was. Maybe it was Mei, with her deep-seated beliefs about the value and sanctity of life. Maybe it was Tripp's prompting to open her eyes and see the same truths that had caused him to leave the Project. Maybe she was just a coward. It didn't really matter what it was, because in the end, it all meant the same thing.

She couldn't do this anymore.

Zira took a step past Jared to enter Ryku's office, but Jared shook his head. "He's not here. All the chairmen went to talk to the people in the North Pacific Region and straighten things out."

Zira wondered if talking was really all they were doing. "I'll just keep it until he gets back then."

"You sure? He asked me to do some of the paperwork that comes in while he's away. I can take a look at it."

"No, that's ok. I wrote it up pretty fast; it's probably a little sloppy. I'll fix it before he gets back."

She did no such thing, however, and instead put the report under her mattress like a child hiding a secret diary. The week that followed was a painfully long one for Zira. A weight the size of a boulder settled deep inside her as she waited for Ryku's return. She went from dreading what the chairman might think of her failure to just wanting to get the whole thing over with.

Apprehension kept her up at night. When she couldn't sleep, she watched the news. The same clips kept playing over and over again. The five chairmen stood together in front of a crowd, making some speech about unity, individual contribution, and keeping the peace. The smiling onlookers cheered them enthusiastically. Zira noted that everyone in the crowd looked healthier and better-dressed than anyone she had seen in Grayridge.

On the morning the chairmen were expected back at the compound, Zira slipped her report under Ryku's door. Jared had finished going through all of the other mission reports the night before, so she doubted he would come back and look over hers before Ryku returned. As she turned to leave, she nearly ran into Cecilia and Lucas standing just behind her.

She tried to step past them, but Lucas matched her movements to block her path. She clenched a fist; this was the last thing she needed right now.

"Hold on there, runt," said Cecilia. "I've been meaning to check in on you since you got back. How's that brand new leg treating you?"

"Like you care," Zira muttered.

Cecilia smiled. "No, I don't. It's so cute that Ryku gave you an assignment even though you're crippled. I doubt it was anything very important, but still, it's nice of him to try and make you feel like you're doing your part." She laughed. "I've missed you, runt. I'd forgotten how much fun this was."

Zira rolled her eyes. "Are we done now?"

"Not quite." She held a folder in one hand and tapped the edge against her other palm. "You know what this is?"

"A mission report."

"Not just any mission report." She and Lucas exchanged a smirk. "We just got back from the North Pacific Region. A little town called Grayridge. You've probably heard of it."

Zira crossed her arms and took a step back from Cecilia. "Yes."

"Our target was the guy who started the riots. Man by the name of Murphy, I think."

Zira's nails dug into her arm. Murphy was the last name of the girl who had died because of the food shortage.

"You know him or something?" Lucas said.

She didn't answer, and Cecilia took a step towards her. "This guy had a kid. A boy, maybe thirteen or fourteen years old. He came at me with a kitchen knife."

She made a gun with her fingers and aimed it at Zira, then shrugged. "You know how it is—self-defense. I just thought you should know, since you loved that place so much." She held the file out to Zira. "You want to take a look? Pay your respects? Maybe they were friends of yours."

Once, Cecilia's abuse might have rolled off Zira's back with ease. Now, she'd heard enough. Her temper snapped. She threw herself at Cecilia and pulled her to the ground. Pages from the file scattered as Zira straddled the older girl and slammed a fist into her jaw. Cecilia cackled, exposing teeth stained red with blood.

Lucas came at Zira from behind. He yanked her off Cecilia and tried to grab her wrists, but she slipped away. He came at her again. Zira's foot connected with his ribcage and he doubled over.

Cecilia was on Zira before she could turn and wrenched her head back by the hair. Zira thrashed to break free, screaming like some kind of wild animal. Lucas kicked the breath out of her chest while Cecilia used her free hand to punch Zira in the face.

Stunned, it took Zira a moment to compose herself and let her training kick in. She reached for the pocketknife in her boot and slashed behind her, catching Cecilia off guard. She used the distraction to scramble away, then whirled to face the pair. Both were armed with their own blades now, and all three of them were surrounded by a small crowd that had gathered to watch. Lucas took a step towards Zira. She braced herself for the attack.

Someone pulled her back and pinned her arms at her side. She twisted her head around and was enraged to see that the new assailant was Jared. She struggled to break free, but he held her tight. "Let go!"

Jared paid no attention to her. "Get out of here," he said to Cecilia and Lucas.

"But—" Lucas began.

"Now!" Jared barked. "You know fighting isn't allowed. Go, before any of the chairmen see this." He turned to the spectators, raising an authoritative voice. "That means all of you!"

Zira continued to strain against Jared's grasp as the audience dispersed. "Let me go!" She cursed at Cecilia's retreating figure. "Murderer! Coward!"

"Look at yourself!" Jared said. "You're acting insane. What's your problem?"

"What's *your* problem?" she retorted, turning her rage on him.

He released her. "I just saved you from ruining everything you've worked for." His eyes were cold and hard. "Fighting with people in your own unit, right here in the compound for everyone to see? What were you thinking?"

"She killed an innocent kid. She told me all about it, like she was proud of it."

"So you attacked her?"

"I couldn't just let it go."

"Yes, you could have. We all do what we have to do. It isn't always pretty, but somebody has to do this job. You know that. Or you used to." He sighed and ran a hand over his face. "What happened to you?"

"We're supposed to be working for peace. Killing some defenseless kid doesn't accomplish that."

Jared shook his head. "You don't get it anymore, do you? We *are* killers. You can't just ignore that and hope it will go away. We kill so that other people don't have to die, because it's for the greater good. No matter the cost—do you remember that? No matter the cost."

"That doesn't apply to taking innocent lives."

"It applies to everything."

"How can you justify it like that?" She couldn't believe what he was saying. How could he see things that way? In a renewed surge of anger, she said, "You're just as bad as any of our targets."

Jared's patience evaporated in an instant. "Screw you," he said. His voice was low and thick with venom. "Screw you and your self-righteous attitude. Stop trying to pretend that everyone else is the villain and get your act together."

He turned his back and walked away from her. She knew he was furious—knew that this could be the breaking point in their relationship—but she didn't care about that right now. She felt betrayed. He was supposed to understand her, but he wasn't even hearing anything she was trying to tell him. She returned to her apartment to be alone, struggling to contain the heat that still boiled inside her.

At lunch that afternoon, Aubreigh hurried to Zira's side as soon as she walked in the door. "Are you all right? Everyone's been talking about your fight. Oh—your eye!" She covered her mouth with her hand as she examined the bruise that covered most of the left side of Zira's face.

"I'm okay," Zira muttered, glancing across the room as people stared at her and whispered. Cecilia and Lucas sat in the far corner with a group of friends. Cecilia winked and blew her a kiss. Zira bristled, but she knew better than to start another fight. She kept her head down and tried not to look around as she and Aubreigh went through the food line.

"So what happened exactly?" Aubreigh asked after they sat down.

Zira hunched over her tray and picked at her food. "Same old Cecilia. Still gets a kick out of other people's problems."

Aubreigh frowned. "You know she just likes to provoke you."

Zira shook her head. It was more complicated than that, but she couldn't tell Aubreigh the real reason the fight had started. "I know, but—it just happened."

"It looks like they got you pretty good."

"It probably would have been worse if Jared hadn't stepped in." She hated to admit that, but it was true. Cecilia and Lucas were both more experienced than she was and just as well-trained. Taking both of them on at once had been stupid.

"Where is he, anyway?"

"I don't know. We had a fight. I think we might be done." It hurt to say it out loud. This was exactly what she'd been afraid of when they started this relationship. This was why she hadn't wanted to push things any further than friendship. Jared was one of just a few people who really understood and cared about her, and she didn't want to lose that. With the way things were going now, though, she might have lost it anyway.

"I'm really sorry, Zira," Aubreigh said. "Is everything all right with you? I mean, besides Cecilia and this thing with Jared. You've just seemed different since you got back."

"Honestly?" Zira gave up on her food and pushed the tray aside. "No—everything is not all right. Everything is really screwed up right now, actually." She took a breath, knowing that Aubreigh was going to react badly to what she had to say next. "I don't belong here anymore. I'm going to ask for a transfer."

Aubreigh looked confused. Zira couldn't blame her; transferring out of the compound was almost unheard of and only allowed under special circumstances. "How? Where?"

"I don't know. Anywhere. Ryku has all these informants on the outside, people who pass him useful intel. Maybe I could do that. A lot of them are damaged goods anyway, so I at least have the leg for the job."

Aubreigh didn't seem to find her joke amusing. "You don't have to leave. There has to be a way to fix whatever it is that's wrong."

"I've been trying," Zira said. "I've tried to get back to how it all was before. I've tried to understand. I just can't do it anymore. I have to get out of here."

Aubreigh's brows drew together. "If that's what you really think is best," she said quietly. "I don't understand, but I know you've got to do what you think is right."

"We'll still see each other. I promise." It was a promise she didn't know if she could keep, but if there was any possible way to keep Aubreigh in her life after this had all settled down, she'd find it.

Aubreigh nodded and put on a brave smile, but her eyes were wet as she glanced around the cafeteria, looking at everything besides Zira. Zira felt bad for dropping this on her so suddenly, and she was going to miss her best friend. But like Aubreigh had said, she needed to do what she thought was right.

As she left the cafeteria, a gentle vibration from her CL alerted her to a new message. It was from Jared. Her heart turned to ice in her chest as she opened it.

Something's come up. I have to leave for a couple days. When I get back, we need to talk.

I'm really trying to understand. I still love you. I'm sorry.

Zira closed the message, too dispirited to write back right now. It was for the best that he was gone. They both needed some time apart to clear their heads, and things were going to change if Zira left the compound to become an informant. She didn't know what all those changes would be yet, but her mind was made up. As soon as she got back to her apartment, she sent a message to Chairman Ryku with her request.

CHAPTER 24

ZIRA HEARD NOTHING FROM RYKU that day or the next. She saw two of the other chairmen walking around the compound that afternoon, though, and assumed they all must have come back together. Between the fight she'd had with Cecilia and Lucas, her failure to kill Randolph, and her request to be transferred, she and Ryku had a lot to talk about. She wasn't sure what was taking him so long, but she wasn't about to go hunting him down to instigate the conversation.

She ate dinner alone that night since Jared was still gone and Aubreigh was stuck in her office finishing up some work. As she went to return her tray, Seth spotted her across the room and came to meet her. "We need to talk," he said. "Now."

"We've already talked. I have nothing else to say to you."

She started to walk away, but he grabbed her arm. "Zira, please. You need to hear me out."

The way he lowered his voice and the almost desperate look in his eyes caught her attention. "Fine. What is it?"

"Not here."

She grumbled, but followed him outside anyway. They went to a shaded area between the cafeteria and another building. Seth kept looking around suspiciously even though no one was anywhere near them. "What is it?" Zira asked.

"You're not safe here."

"What makes you think that?"

He tapped a few buttons on his CyberLink and projected some sort of document. "This."

She glanced at it but didn't bother trying to read the whole thing. "What is it?"

"Ryku sent it to us this morning. It's a security block; we're supposed to cut off your access to everything. The Net, vehicles, the compound gate. You're on lockdown."

Zira looked at the document closer. It was exactly as Seth said, and Ryku's signature was scrawled across the bottom. She gnawed at her lip as Seth withdrew the projection. "I asked for a transfer," she said. "I wanted to work on the outside. It's probably just something to do with that."

"If you were going to transfer, you'd have to be able to get out of the compound. You can't do that if your gate access has been cut off." He paused and leveled his gaze at her. "Zira, you're a threat. He's going to eliminate you. He did the same thing to Tripp just before he left the Project."

Zira tried to conceal the shiver that ran up her spine at the mention of that name. For a moment, she considered that this might be some kind of trap. If she admitted to knowing Tripp and not telling Ryku about it, she'd be guilty of treason and slated for execution. On the other hand, if what Seth was saying was true, she'd already been sentenced. She had always considered him an enemy, but now, he might be the only person in these walls she could trust. "You know Tripp?"

"I've been in contact with a rebel group for several years now, passing them whatever information I could. I've never met Tripp personally, but he asked me to keep an eye on you when you got back here. He wanted me to find out if you told Ryku that you'd seen him. I tried to get you to talk to me about it a few times, but you didn't want to."

Zira remembered how persistent Seth had been in trying to talk to her about Grayridge ever since she'd come back. He'd even mentioned that they were on the same side and that he was suspicious of some of the things going on in the Project, but she'd been too angry to even consider that he might be an ally. "Why are you telling me all this? I could run straight to Ryku and tell him everything. Maybe if I just proved my loyalty, he'd give me another chance."

Seth gave her a thin smile. "You're not going to do that. You have no loyalty—not anymore. And even if you did, do you honestly think Ryku wouldn't kill you anyway? You're a threat, Zira, and all threats must be eliminated."

Zira's mind began to run in a hundred different directions at once. She had tried so hard to make this work. It didn't matter; of course Ryku wasn't going to give her another chance. She should have been more careful. Now she was a target, and she was trapped. Another operative could be coming to kill her right now.

She had to fight to keep her breath steady; panicking now was only going to make things worse. "What do I do?"

"I know how to get you out of the compound," Seth said, and he handed her a folded scrap of paper. Zira glanced at the writing inside. It was an address in the North Central Region. "That's where Tripp is. You'll have to get yourself there, which might be difficult since you won't be able to use any of the usual methods of transportation. Once you're gone, Ryku won't waste any time sending someone after you."

She'd spend the rest of her life looking over her shoulder, waiting for Project assassins to catch up with her. It was a daunting prospect, but better than dying—though that could very well be in her near future if she wasn't careful. Still, Tripp had survived fifteen years in the same position. She could survive, too, especially with his help. "Tell me how to get out of here."

"There's a food delivery scheduled for four A.M. tomorrow. You'll have to sneak onto one of the trucks before they leave. I don't think I need to tell you how unwise it would be to talk to anyone about this."

Aubreigh. She wouldn't get a chance to say goodbye. And what would Jared think when he found out she'd betrayed her unit and run away? She wouldn't even have a chance to explain things to him. He'd hate her. Seth was right, though. Telling her friends was a bad idea, and dragging them into the middle of this could put them in danger, too. "I understand," she said.

"Good."

He started to walk away. "Seth," Zira said, and he stopped. He had risked a lot by even telling her all of this and had nothing to gain from helping her. She had misjudged him. "Thank you."

He looked over his shoulder at her and nodded. "Watch your back."

"You too."

Once Seth had gone, Zira returned to her apartment. She tried not to walk any faster than normal, but every time she passed someone with a black armband, her entire body tensed. She was sweating by the time she closed her door behind her and had to check every possible hiding spot in her apartment before her heartrate returned to normal. She pulled a backpack out of her closet and began shoving things inside as fast as she could. She only took two extra sets of clothing and some other basic necessities, not wanting to be slowed down. Every weapon she owned also went into the pack. It wasn't much—a few knives, a handgun, and a single 50-round box of hollow-points. Most of the weapons she used on assignments belonged to the unit, and she doubted she could just waltz into the training center and request to borrow weapons and ammo right now.

She glanced at her CL; it was only eight o' clock. She had a long night ahead of her and didn't dare fall asleep. Instead, she pulled a chair to face the door and sat with her gun on her knee to wait out the long, dark hours ahead.

Every noise made her skin prickle. Somewhere around midnight, her CL beeped with an incoming message and she nearly jumped out of her chair. It was from Jared.

I'll be home tomorrow.

Zira's throat tightened. He still wanted to talk. She hated to leave like this without giving him any sort of warning, but really, what could she say? Even an apology seemed inadequate at this point. She didn't even think she *was* sorry anymore. Why should she be? The Project had betrayed her first. She closed the message without responding and settled back into her chair.

At 3:55 A.M., Zira removed her CyberLink and placed it on her bed. She cracked open her apartment door. No movement in sight. She put the gun in the deep pocket of her jacket, slung her backpack over her shoulder, and walked outside. Two delivery trucks rolled into view, heading for the back of the cafeteria where they would be unloaded. Zira followed them, moving quickly but trying not to act suspicious.

She stopped in the same narrow space between two buildings where she'd conversed with Seth just hours before and peered around the corner. The cafeteria cooks and their bots unloaded boxes one by one. The truck appeared to be automated; Zira didn't see a driver. When the final box was unloaded, the back of the truck began to slide shut. Zira crept forward, keeping one eye on the man carrying the last box inside. Once he'd shut the kitchen door, she bolted for the truck and just managed to slip through the narrowing gap. The door closed, leaving her in total darkness.

Zira fumbled her way to the back corner of the cargo area as the truck began to move. She sat on the floor and braced herself against the wall, her gun pointed at the door. A few minutes later, the truck stopped again. Over its engine, Zira could hear the mechanical sound of the compound gate opening. She held a breath and checked the safety on her pistol.

The truck rolled on. Zira let out a long breath, put a hand over her smile, and tilted her head back. She was free.

■ ■ ■

Zira walked along an old highway under the midday sun, periodically glancing over her shoulder for approaching headlights. The supply truck had parked itself in a lot filled with other trucks a few hours before, and after fiddling with the inner control panel for an hour, she'd finally managed to let herself out. Local signs told her she was in a town called Montecito, west of the compound. She had a long way to go to make it to Missoula, the city in the North Central Region where Tripp was. She couldn't rent a car, get on a bus, or take an automated taxi without her identification, which was stored on her CL and would have been restricted even if she hadn't discarded it. She would walk the entire distance if she had to, but hoped that someone on the road might be willing to pick up a hitchhiker. It wasn't the most advisable strategy for a young girl out alone in the world, but Zira was more than capable of taking care of herself if someone picked her up with ill intentions. One car had already passed her by, but that had been over an hour ago and she hadn't seen anyone since. It might turn out to be a very long walk.

Her feet dragged on the pavement. The warmth of the sun in her hair was relaxing, and having not slept at all for something like thirty hours, she struggled to keep her eyes open. She didn't want to stop yet; she was still so close to the compound, and depending on how soon Ryku discovered she was gone, assassins could be closing in on her already. She walked another mile before she heard the soft rush of tires in the distance.

She turned to face the approaching car and began to wave her arms in an attempt to flag it down. She could have just walked into the middle of the road the way she'd done with Hartman's car in Grayridge; the safety features of any standard autopilot system wouldn't allow the vehicle to hit a pedestrian. That was a rather threatening way to ask a favor from someone, though. Zira needed them to stop on their own, and she was relying on her youthful, innocent appearance to catch someone's attention and convince them she wasn't dangerous.

The car slowed and the window rolled down. A grizzly old man with a hat straight out of an old western film leaned out on his forearm. "Where you headed?"

"As far north as you can take me."

He waved her over. "Hop in."

Zira slid into the back seat, setting her backpack at her feet within easy reach. She still had the handgun in her jacket pocket and a knife in her boot, just in case. "Thanks," she said as the car began moving again.

"What's your name?" The man's cowboy accent matched his hat.

"Zira."

"Nice t'meet ya. I'm Bill." He took a drink of water from the bottle in the center console and offered it to her. She shook her head. "Awful strange to see a girl walking the road on her own like that." He gave her a prying sidelong glance.

"I don't have a car." She tugged at the sleeves of her jacket, making sure they covered her wrists to hide the fact that she wasn't wearing a CL.

Bill grunted. "Me neither. This one's just a rental. I've got to get to Wyoming for my mama's funeral."

"Wyoming?"

"Oh, right—sorry. I forget they don't teach you kids that old geography no more. One of the fifty, you know. From before the war."

It took her a moment to realize that he was talking about the fifty United States. "Oh."

One side of his mustache lifted as he gave her an amused smile. "What's up north for you?"

Zira rested her head against the car window and looked at her translucent reflection in the glass. "A new start."

■ ■ ■

Bill let Zira out of the car in a rural town just past a city called Casper with a tip of his hat. He'd offered her a room in his mother's old house, but she'd declined, saying she'd find a hotel in town. She slung her pack over her shoulders and kept walking. It was past midnight. The cold air was biting, and she was still exhausted. She had dozed off a couple of times on accident in Bill's car but hadn't dared fall asleep completely. A hotel room was out of the question since that also required ID she didn't have, but maybe she could find an old building to take shelter in somewhere close by.

A few of the houses on this road had barns, but she could hear animals moving around inside and knew the houses would be occupied as well. She walked a few more miles and found a barn that was empty, and the land surrounding it looked like it hadn't been cared for in decades. Zira had to break a window to get into the house. It was dank and dusty and still cold, but at least it offered some protection from the wind. An empty room upstairs had carpet floors that made a reasonably comfortable bed. She lay down with her backpack under her head, threw her jacket over herself, and fell asleep in seconds.

CHAPTER 25

IT WAS NEARLY MIDNIGHT WHEN Jared arrived back at the compound, and he could think of no reason why Chairman Ryku might be in the guardhouse talking to the gatekeeper at such a late hour. As soon as he saw Jared, he exited through a side door and fell into stride beside him.

"You've been waiting for me?" Jared said.

"Something urgent has come up. I wanted to make sure I was the first person to see you when you got back."

Jared shifted his bag over his shoulder with a sigh. Being the chairman's right-hand man had its perks, but it was also rather tiring. Whenever Ryku had a problem or a particularly difficult assignment, he went to Jared first. "What is it?"

"We'll talk about it in my office."

They said nothing more to each other as they walked, and Jared's thoughts drifted to his argument with Zira. He had done everything he could to put it out of his mind while he was on his assignment, but now it was time to face the aftermath. He had said some cruel things—they both had—and although he was sorry to have hurt her feelings, he'd meant what he had said. Perhaps there was some truth in her words, too. Jared just didn't understand what had happened to make her change so much. He needed to talk to her and try to sort it all out, but knowing Zira, that wouldn't be easy, assuming she would even speak to him at all. He knew how much she hated opening up about her feelings, even to him.

Not now, though; he was too tired to fight that battle tonight. The conversation would have to wait until morning.

Ryku opened his office door and Jared followed him inside. The room was hot and stuffy, with an eerie, red glow emanating from a seldom-used fireplace in the corner. The flames were the only source of light in the room, casting dramatic, flickering shadows all around. Ryku didn't bother to switch on the overhead lights. "Please, have a seat," he said. "Would you like something to drink?"

Jared sat on the couch. Typical Ryku, to bother with such hospitable formalities when there were more pressing matters to discuss. "No, thanks."

Ryku took up a place in front of his desk, leaning back against it with his hands on either side. "I have something important to tell you, but first I need your word that you won't speak to anyone else about this. This is to remain between us."

"I understand," said Jared, his interest growing.

"Good. We have a problem in our unit—a former operative who has jeopardized the security of our work. Some recent experiences seem to have caused her to lose faith in this Project, and despite my best efforts to rehabilitate her, she remains unstable. She's a threat, and now, she's committed treason by deserting the Project."

Jared's palms became sweaty in the stifling red heat of the fireplace.

"I care about everyone in this unit like a father cares for his children, but I care about the Project most. I can't let one of my own endanger the peace we've worked so hard to create and maintain. I've considered this long and hard, but there are no other options. This person must be eliminated."

Jared's stomach plummeted. He had to ask, just to be sure. "Who are you talking about?"

"You already know the answer," said Ryku. There wasn't even a hint of sympathy in his voice. "And what does it matter? She's a threat. If she were a stranger, this would play out the same way."

Jared stared at the floor, forcing out her name. "Zira."

"You must have noticed it too, how much she's changed since coming back from Grayridge."

"Yes," he said, trying to figure out how Ryku had come to such an extreme conclusion. It didn't make sense; he thought Zira had worked past this. And there was something else the chairman had said that didn't make sense, either. "She deserted the Project? What do you mean?"

"She turned in a request asking me to make her an informant, but she disappeared before I could give her my answer."

"She's just scared, then. Let me talk to her."

"This is more than just fear, Jared."

He rubbed a hand over the back of his neck. "Look, I know she's changed. But hasn't she proven herself? She did everything you asked—all the training and the counseling and everything. You approved all of that. You gave her an assignment."

"Yes, I did. An assignment which she failed to complete."

"What?"

"She didn't tell you." He took a file from his desk and passed it to Jared. "She didn't kill Randolph. Instead, she gave me a bunch of excuses for why he isn't dead."

Jared flipped through the report, barely registering what he was reading. It was all there, just like Ryku had said, and all written in Zira's hand. "Maybe she was just being careful," he said.

"It was a very basic assignment. All she had to do was shoot Randolph and get out. She could have killed him openly in the street for all I cared. But she didn't. She wasn't even there a full day before she decided to let him live. It wasn't a mistake—it was blatant disobedience."

"And she deserves to die, because of that?"

"It's not just that. It's her refusal to accept what happened in Grayridge, the fact that she's picking fights with people in her own unit."

"That happened one time," Jared said. "And Cecilia started it."

"She's unstable—a ticking time bomb just waiting to explode. We can't afford any weak links. Every moment she's out there puts the rest of us in danger. You have to eliminate her."

Jared's heart thundered in his chest. How could Ryku expect him to do this? Why was he even asking him? He looked up at the chairman and spoke in the most sincere and pleading voice he could. "Please, Chairman, please don't do this. I know it's not my place to question you, but Zira is—"

What?

Misguided? Certainly. A threat? Possibly. He didn't want to believe it, but after the things she'd said following her fight with Cecilia and Lucas, Jared had to consider the option. He saw the way Ryku's eyes flickered at his hesitation and hurried to correct himself. "Please, Ryku, I can bring her back if you'll just give her another chance. She needs more time. I'll work with her myself, make her see things the way she used to. Please."

Ryku frowned and looked down at Jared. "The decision has already been made. She's completely fallen apart, and there's no telling what she might do out there. She knows too much. I can't allow her to stir up trouble. How can we expect to protect the peace of this entire country if we can't even keep our own people in line?"

Jared knew the chairman was right. Still, he looked down and shook his head. "I can't."

"This is not a choice, Jared," Ryku said, his voice rising in a sharp command. "It's an order, just like every other assignment you've ever had. Failure is not an option. *Refusal* is not an option. You can't let your emotions get in the way of your duty."

Jared clenched his jaw. Why was this happening to him? He silently cursed Zira for her skewed perceptions, then cursed himself for not doing more to help her. He should have seen this coming. Maybe he could have changed her. No—that would have been impossible. Zira was too strong-willed for that. But at least he could have warned her. Now it was too late.

"Will you do it?" Ryku hissed. "Because if you won't, I'll find someone else, and you can consider yourself just as much a traitor as she is."

It seemed that walls had risen up all around Jared. There was no way out, no way he could change the chairman's mind or refuse this assignment—not unless he wanted to condemn himself to death. He answered reluctantly, feeling detached from his own words. "I'll do it."

Ryku sounded pleased. "Good." He pulled up a projection on his CyberLink—a map with a blinking, red dot in the center. "She took off her CL before she left, but I had unit A put a tracking chip in her new prosthetic leg." It was a dirty trick, but Jared supposed he shouldn't be surprised by anything the chairman did anymore. "She's headed north. I'll send you the signal for her tracker. Find her. Once you see an opportunity—"

"I know," Jared growled. "I'll get it done."

Ryku nodded. "I know this won't be easy, but you're doing the right thing. Your dedication and service to this unit is appreciated. I have complete confidence in you."

Jared stood and turned sharply on his heel. It took a tremendous amount of self-control to refrain from slamming the door on his way out.

The cold air outside did nothing to cool his emotions. When he reached his apartment, he let out a yell like an enraged animal and grabbed the first thing he saw, flinging it against the wall. The lamp shattered with a satisfying clatter.

Jared sat on the bed and projected all the photos he had on his CL of himself and Zira before she'd gone to Grayridge. They'd been so happy and carefree. Things had been less than perfect since her return, but still, they'd been happy. This thing Ryku had ordered him to do seemed impossibly cruel. He'd told the chairman he would do it, but he wasn't sure he had meant it. Even if he wanted to, he didn't know if he could. This was the girl he loved.

But what other choice did he have? He could try to warn her, but what good would that do? She'd spend the rest of her life being hunted by E-2 assassins like some animal. If he chose to simply ignore Ryku's orders, he'd become a target just like her, and Ryku would find someone else to do the job. Any number of operatives would be willing to accept the task if it meant getting into his good graces.

All of that was irrelevant. He was wasting his time weighing meaningless options to avoid the heart of the problem. The truth was that Ryku was right. Zira had become unpredictable. Everything she had once believed in was crumbling away bit by bit, replaced by doubt and unreasonable idealism. Such mistrust was dangerous in an organization that relied on unwavering obedience from its members. Her failure to kill Randolph meant that she obviously wasn't cut out to be an operative anymore. Even if she became an informant, her shifting beliefs could be dangerous to others in the unit; she might not remain objective in the information she chose to provide about a target, and that could get operatives killed under the wrong circumstances. The fact that she had run meant that she'd given up on the PEACE Project altogether, and there was no coming back from that.

This wasn't about love or friendship or whatever other ties he might have to Zira. He had always put his duty to the Project first, and that was exactly what he needed to do here. If this had been anyone else, Jared wouldn't have hesitated or questioned Ryku's orders at all. He simply would have done what was expected of him, because he trusted that Ryku was doing what was best for the entire unit—for the entire country. He still trusted that. He didn't like the decision the chairman had made, but he trusted that it was a sound one. When he looked at it from that angle, the answer became clear.

Zira was a threat, and that made her an acceptable target.

He threw himself back on his bed. He couldn't remember the last time he'd cried. Even when Zira had been pronounced dead, he hadn't shed a tear; he'd been too angry and shocked to cry then. He was angry now, too—more so, in fact—but the anger was numbed by self-loathing and regret. It was enough to melt away every barrier he'd built around his heart. Jared drew in a hitched breath, put a hand over his face, and wept.

CHAPTER 26

ZIRA WOKE UP REFRESHED AND alert late the following morning. She smiled as she looked out the window. She had done the impossible. She was over five hundred miles from the Project, and she was alive and free.

In order to stay that way, she needed to figure out how to cover the remaining half of her journey. She could steal a car, but that just seemed like a good way to attract bad attention. Hitchhiking seemed the safest bet, but this was a sparsely populated region and it might be difficult to find a ride. She'd end up covering a lot of the distance on foot, and for that, she needed warmer clothes. She found some old coats hanging in one of the closets in another room and picked the heaviest. She also needed food, but that problem was solved when she explored the kitchen pantry and found a few dozen cans of vegetables the previous occupants had left behind. An old pre-war map was buried under a stack of papers in another drawer. She traced a path to Missoula with her finger and stuck the map in her back pocket.

She decided to spend another night in the house before resuming her journey. It seemed like a safe place to rest, and she didn't know when she'd be able to find shelter again. She ate a can of beans for supper and put the rest of the food in her backpack with her gun and ammunition, then slept.

It was still dark outside when Zira woke up, but she no longer felt tired. She picked up her pack and walked outside, then consulted her map to figure out how to get back to the highway. She heard the soft, muffled crunch of footsteps on the snow somewhere to her right. Whoever or whatever approached was moving slowly. Zira turned but couldn't see anything, and the noise stopped. It was probably just some animal; she'd seen deer tracks near the house earlier. She put the map back in her pocket and started walking. She hadn't gone more than a few steps when she heard the noise again, faster this time—and close.

Zira dropped her pack and whipped out the long knife strapped across her chest. A huge, dark figure came rushing at her from the patch of trees to her right.

Jared's mouth was set in a hard line, his eyes cold and dark, brows furrowed in fierce concentration. It took Zira a few moments to register the expression, and by that time he was nearly on top of her. She jumped aside at the last second, still close enough to feel the knife slice through the air where her throat had been.

Jared came at her again, but this time she reacted sooner. "What are you doing?" she shouted. In answer, he swung at her again. Zira ducked.

He was trying to kill her.

Of course he was. She had deserted the Project. It only made sense that Ryku would have sent his best man to eliminate her. Zira's knife hung limp at her side. Her legs danced away from each attack with movements that had become automatic after years of training, but she couldn't bring herself to raise a weapon against him.

He slashed through her coat and the edge of his blade bit into her side, opening a long, thin gash. The pain dragged her back to her senses. She forced herself into the fight. This was not a game or some kind of test. Ryku had sent Jared to kill her, and from the look on his face, that was exactly what he intended to do.

Jared lashed out with the knife again. Zira barely managed to deflect the blow without losing her balance. He was stronger than she was—so much so that she wondered how she could ever expect to beat him. But she was quicker. When the next strike came, she used that speed to twist around behind him, far out of his reach.

For a moment, she had a chance to strike at his unguarded back. She hesitated, and the moment passed. Jared's foot caught her in the chest. She staggered, gasping for air.

This could only end in death for one of them. Most likely hers. Jared could have killed her more than once already. He'd had several chances to overpower her with sheer strength and skill. He could have done it with a single bullet from a distance and avoided a confrontation altogether, but he hadn't. Why was he toying with her?

His knife came whistling at her again. Zira had no time to dodge the attack. She raised her own weapon defensively and for an instant, the blades locked. Zira stared up at the man who was suddenly a stranger to her, searching his eyes for some kind of answer. Jared's face was emotionless. He shoved her back and pulled a second, shorter knife from his belt. Wielding one in each hand, he charged her.

It was all Zira could do to avoid being cut into pieces. She was wearing down quickly, but Jared seemed tireless. Her resolve weakened with each labored breath she took. Even if she managed to survive this, Ryku would send others to finish the job. A small voice whispered that fighting was pointless. It grew louder with each passing second, but Zira refused to listen.

She stumbled, and as she scrambled to recover, Jared's knife slashed across her shoulder. She cried out in pain and tried to run, but Jared swept her legs out from under her with a well-placed kick. Zira caught herself on both hands. She reached for her dropped knife, but Jared flicked it away with his toe.

She rolled over to face him. If he was going to kill her, he would look her in the eyes when he did it.

He stood over her, knife poised for the kill. Zira's eyelids shut involuntarily. She tried to open them again but couldn't. She was a coward. She'd always promised herself that when death came, she would look it in the face, defiant and fearless. Now she couldn't bring herself to do so.

She counted the last seconds of her life.

One. Two. Three.

Look at him!

Four. Five.

Tears ran down her cheeks, burning as they melted into a small cut on her face. Why didn't he kill her already? She finally forced herself to look up at him.

Jared's hands shook. His eyes were full of a suffering Zira did not understand. He dropped his weapons and fell to his knees in the snow before her. "I can't." His voice was ragged. "I just can't."

Nothing about this made any sense, and she didn't know whether to be angry or heartbroken or just confused. He was having second thoughts *now*, after he had worked so hard to kill her?

Except that he hadn't—not really. If he'd really wanted to kill her, there were easier, cleaner ways to do it. For whatever reason, he'd given her the chance to fight back. Perhaps a part of him had even hoped she'd beat him.

He had his face in his hands now, and his body heaved. "I'm so sorry, Zira. I didn't know what to do. I didn't have a choice, but—I shouldn't have done this. I'm sorry."

Zira didn't know what to say. This was all wrong. Her heart felt like it was shredding itself into a thousand tiny pieces.

"I love you," Jared said. "I'm sorry."

She no longer believed him. She just wanted to go. Her legs shook violently as she stood up and looked at him.

He wouldn't meet her gaze and instead stared at the red patch of snow where blood had trickled down her arm and dripped from her fingers. "Wait," he said. "There's a tracker in your prosthesis. If you give it to me, I'll bury it somewhere and tell Ryku you're dead. They won't look for you."

Zira picked up her blade from the red-stained snow. She leaned against a tree and used the knife to loosen the screws that bolted the prosthesis to the post in her leg. Once it was removed, she peered into the hole where the post fit. Something metallic gleamed inside. She pried it loose and tossed it onto the ground in front of Jared, then reattached the leg.

"Find somewhere safe," he said.

He looked so small kneeling there below her, hunched over like he was trying to collapse in on himself. For some inexplicable reason, Zira pitied him.

Before he could change his mind, she retrieved her pack and ran blindly into the darkness ahead.

She was still crying when her strength ran out and she fell into the snow. She retched. Vomit spewed from her mouth, steaming on the cold ground. Shivering, she tore strips from a shirt in her backpack to bind her wounds.

What had happened between her and Jared that would make him do this? She had never imagined his dedication to the Project would be tested in such a cruel manner. She knew how seriously he took his job, but shouldn't his feelings for her have won out over his duty? They had in the end, but Zira couldn't forget the hardness in his eyes and the sting of his blade. Ryku's orders had been Jared's first choice. Not her.

After she had cried as many tears as her eyes would allow, Zira picked herself up and wiped her face with her sleeve. She straightened and continued walking as dawn broke over the horizon.

CHAPTER 27

JARED HAD NOTHING TO BRING back to the compound as proof of Zira's death except his word and a heavy heart. His grief was real enough to convince the chairman, even if Ryku didn't know the true reason behind it.

"You did well," Ryku said. "I know this was difficult, but you did the right thing. The Project appreciates your service, and I want you to know how much I personally value your loyalty."

Under other circumstances, Jared would have taken pride in Ryku's words. Now, he hated them. They only reminded him of the betrayal he'd committed against the one person he loved most in this world, and simple praises were poor compensation for that.

The part that stung the most was knowing he couldn't blame Ryku for everything that had happened. Jared was the one who had chosen to carry out the assignment. He'd told Zira he didn't have a choice, but that wasn't exactly true. He could have refused. He'd be dead, but at least he might have died with a little more honor and self-respect than he had now. He could have gone with her. He'd be a traitor to the Project, and perhaps that would have been a more difficult kind of betrayal, but he wouldn't have had to hurt Zira.

He couldn't erase the image of her lying broken and bleeding as he stood over her, tears running down her face. She had shut her eyes like she was too disgusted to even look at him. He would never forgive himself for that. The guilt was so sickening that he could hardly stand to be in his own skin anymore.

He took some small comfort in knowing that Zira was alive, at least. That wouldn't have happened if Ryku had sent someone else to kill her, or if Jared's conscience hadn't gotten the best of him in the end. All he could hope for now was that she would find somewhere safe to grow old and live the rest of her life in peace. She deserved that, after everything she'd been through these past months.

As Jared walked away from Chairman Ryku's office, someone called his name. He turned towards the sound and Aubreigh hurried to catch up with him. She was the last person he wanted to see right now, but he couldn't avoid her forever.

"Where have you been?" she asked. "Have you heard from Zira? She asked for a transfer—somewhere outside the compound. I think she's gone already, but you really need to talk to her. She was pretty upset about the way you guys left things."

It would be so easy to let her keep believing that Zira had simply transferred out of the compound, but Aubreigh would start missing her friend and try to contact her eventually. That could be dangerous for someone who was trying to pretend to be dead. Jared didn't think Zira was stupid enough to stay in touch with people from her old life, but he also didn't think there was anything she wouldn't do for Aubreigh. The best way to keep her safe was for her to stay dead, and that meant Aubreigh had to believe it, too.

Jared looked her straight in the eye and lied as convincingly as he could. "Zira's gone," he said. "None of us can talk to her anymore."

Aubreigh's face fell. "What do you mean?"

"She's dead," said Jared. He didn't have to fake the gruff rasp in his voice.

Aubreigh shook her head. "There could be a mistake, like last time. Maybe she's still alive somewhere. They're going to look for her, right?"

"No," Jared said. "This time it's true. She's dead. They have proof."

Tears welled up in Aubreigh's eyes, and she covered her mouth with her hands. She kept shaking her head. Jared stepped closer and hugged her as she sobbed into his shirt. He patted her back and told her he was sorry, told her that everything would be all right. He added the lies to a growing list of things he would carry in shame for the rest of his life. But he had to lie in order to make sure Zira stayed safe. As long as she was safe, nothing else mattered.

■ ■ ■

It took Zira another week to hitchhike her way north to Missoula and find the mostly-abandoned neighborhood where Tripp had taken up residence. She watched the house with the white door and blue curtains for a few hours before approaching and saw no sign of Tripp, but she supposed that was the point. She hadn't seen any sign of him when she was sent to kill the radicals in Grayridge, either. He was careful, and if she wanted to survive out here, she needed to be careful, too.

She smoothed the wrinkles in her clothes, then crossed the street and walked up to the door. She took a deep breath and gave it a quick, sharp rap. No answer. She knocked again. Nothing. She wondered if this was even the right house and checked the now-crinkled paper Seth had given her at the compound. No, this had to be it.

Zira pounded on the door again. "Open up! I know you're in there."

Moments later, it opened. Tripp leaned against the door frame, as lanky and disheveled as she remembered him. He grinned crookedly at her. "You made it, kid. Come inside. We've got a lot to talk about."

ACKNOWLEDGEMENTS

First of all, a huge thank you to my number-one critique partner, Taylor, who read and believed in this story long before it was even worth believing in. Your enthusiasm for these characters has given me some much-needed motivation over the years, and it wouldn't be where it is now without your valuable insights. Thank you for putting up with all my questions, walking me through various parts of this whole process, and being a great inspiration overall.

Thank you to Elissa, who read some of my stories before I even knew what I was doing. You've saved me and my manuscripts from several disastrous computer failures over the years, and your feedback on this story was indispensable.

Thank you to my other beta readers, Jared, Haley, Theresa, and Lindsey. Each of you offered some great suggestions and I appreciate you taking the time to read this.

I also want to thank my husband, Alex, for putting up with my crazy ideas, for picking me up on the days I feel like a failure, and for always pushing me to follow my dreams no matter what obstacles stand in my way. I don't think I ever would have had the nerve to do this without you.

And last but not least, thank *you*, the reader, for taking a chance on a new author when you opened this book. You could have chosen any book, but you picked mine, and that means more to me than you could ever know.

ABOUT THE AUTHOR

T. A. Hernandez is a science fiction and fantasy author and long-time fan of speculative fiction. She grew up with her nose habitually stuck in a book and her mind constantly wandering to make-believe worlds full of magic and adventure. She began writing after reading J. R. R. Tolkien's *The Lord of the Rings* many years ago and is now happily engaged in an exciting and lifelong quest to tell captivating stories.

She is a clinical social worker and the proud mother of two girls. She also enjoys drawing, reading, graphic design, playing video games, and making happy memories with her family and friends.

■ ■ ■

Contact T. A. Hernandez through any of the following to stay up to date on the *Secrets of PEACE* series and other works:

tahernandez.com
tahernandez@tahernandez.com
Twitter: @ta_hernandez5
Instagram: @ta_hernandez5
facebook.com/tahernandez05

Your questions and comments about the story and characters are always welcome and appreciated.

www.ingramcontent.com/pod-product-compliance
Lightning Source LLC
Chambersburg PA
CBHW070728280626
47159CB00023B/2875